Praise for Robert Asprin's MYTH series

"All the MYTH books are hysterically funny." —*Analog*

"Stuffed with rowdy fun." —*The Philadelphia Inquirer*

"Give yourself the pleasure of working through the series. But not all at once; you'll wear out your funny bone."
—*The Washington Times*

"Funny, lighthearted fantasy . . . Robert Asprin and Jody Lynn Nye are great collaborators." —*Midwest Book Review*

"Breezy, pun-filled fantasy in the vein of Piers Anthony's Xanth series . . . A hilarious bit of froth and frolic."
—*Library Journal*

"Asprin's major achievement as a writer—brisk pacing, wit, and a keen satirical eye." —*Booklist*

"An excellent, lighthearted fantasy series."
—*Epic Illustrated*

"Tension getting to you? Take an Asprin! . . . His humor is broad and grows out of the fantasy world, or dimensions, in which his characters operate." —*Fantasy Review*

"Remember the sheer joy and fun of reading the original MYTH books? For me they stand as one of the finest blends of fantasy and humor ever written." —*Baryon*

MYTH-TOLD TALES

ROBERT ASPRIN
and JODY LYNN NYE

ACE BOOKS, NEW YORK

THE BERKLEY PUBLISHING GROUP
Published by the Penguin Group
Penguin Group (USA) Inc.
375 Hudson Street, New York, New York 10014, USA
Penguin Group (Canada), 90 Eglinton Avenue East, Suite 700, Toronto, Ontario M4P 2Y3, Canada
(a division of Pearson Penguin Canada Inc.)
Penguin Books Ltd., 80 Strand, London WC2R 0RL, England
Penguin Group Ireland, 25 St. Stephen's Green, Dublin 2, Ireland (a division of Penguin Books Ltd.)
Penguin Group (Australia), 250 Camberwell Road, Camberwell, Victoria 3124, Australia
(a division of Pearson Australia Group Pty. Ltd.)
Penguin Books India Pvt. Ltd., 11 Community Centre, Panchsheel Park, New Delhi—110 017, India
Penguin Group (NZ), Cnr. Airborne and Rosedale Roads, Albany Auckland 1310, New Zealand
(a division of Pearson New Zealand Ltd.)
Penguin Books (South Africa) (Pty.) Ltd., 24 Sturdee Avenue, Rosebank, Johannesburg 2196,
South Africa

Penguin Books Ltd., Registered Offices: 80 Strand, London WC2R 0RL, England

This is a work of fiction. Names, characters, places, and incidents either are the product of the authors' imagination or are used fictitiously, and any resemblance to actual persons, living or dead, business establishments, events, or locales is entirely coincidental. The publisher does not have any control over and does not assume any responsibility for author or third-party websites or their content.

MYTH-TOLD TALES

An Ace Book / published by arrangement with Bill Fawcett & Associates

PRINTING HISTORY
Ace mass-market edition / March 2007

ISBN: 978-0-441-01486-6

ACE
Ace Books are published by The Berkley Publishing Group,
a division of Penguin Group (USA) Inc.,
375 Hudson Street, New York, New York 10014.
ACE and the "A" design are trademarks belonging to Penguin Group (USA) Inc.

PRINTED IN THE UNITED STATES OF AMERICA

10 9 8 7 6 5 4 3 2 1

Editors are the unsung heroes and heroines of publishing. If a book succeeds, then it's because the writer was great. If it falls short, it's because the editor or publisher dropped the ball. With that in mind, I dedicate this book, along with long overdue thanks, to Susan Allison, the editor who has been handling me since nearly the beginning of my career. She's edited *Myth*, *Thieves' World*, and *Phule* (she actually suggested that last one to me). In all that time, she has supported and defended me, often at the risk of her personal and professional credibility, even when I didn't deserve it.

—RLA

A toast, as well, to the memory of James Patrick Baen, former SF editor of Ace Books, and editor and publisher of Baen Books. Jim helped dozens of new writers, especially women, break into an increasingly difficult field, and nurtured them into sustained careers. He was an innovator of new ways to attract and keep readers, a delegator who trusted other people to represent the face of Baen Books, a collaborator in every facet of the publishing milieu, and he had a fabulous sense of humor. I appreciate the support he gave me as a newbie writer, and I'll miss him greatly.

—JLN

Contents

Welcome to Myth-Told Tales

In this collection you will find all the short stories yet written in the world of the Myth Adventures. A few are by Bob Asprin alone, a few by only Jody Nye, but the majority are collaborations between the two authors. Some feature Aahz and Skeeve, others feature such characters as Tananda, Chumley, Guido, and even Gleep. Three of these stories appeared in the chapbook format volume of this same title. One story, "M.Y.T.H. Inc. Instructions," is the only stand-alone story included with a Myth Adventures novel, *Something M.Y.T.H. Inc.* One other story, "Mything in Dreamland," appeared in *Fantasy Masters*, a collection of stories by top fantasy writers set in their own worlds. The rest of the stories, about half this book, are new and this is their first appearance anywhere. This is the point where an editor is supposed to say something meaningful about the literary work and its social import. Not on your life; Myth Adventures has always been about being fun to read and laughing along with the characters. So all that needs to be said is: Enjoy!

—Editor

How Robert Asprin and I Came to Be Writing New Myth Adventures

"You should work together," one of our well-meaning friends said. You're both funny. You'd be good. I remember that we eyed each other with the same suspicious expression as a couple of cats thrown together by their owners and told to play nice. "Oh, Butch will be nice to Fluffykins! See? They're making friends already," one would say as the cats growl at each other under their breath. Fluffykins is already flexing and unflexing her needle-sharp claws. Butch is baring his teeth. He has a notch out of one ear. His tail switches from side to side. Fluffykins notices this movement and suddenly arches her back. Butch's eyes widen and his ears flatten.

There is a discreet blackout.

When the scene reopens, one cat is licking the other's ear. Both are purring. You didn't see what happened in the middle, but let's just call it "staking out of territory." The owners are not looking quite as calm and complacent as they did before, but the cats have become friends, on their own terms.

I'd always been a fan of Bob's. How could I not love some-one whose best-known book was a paraphrase of one of the great comedy catch phrases of all time? And the quotes at the chapter heads made me laugh out loud. The story itself was a picaresque novel worthy of Cervantes. Here, I realized, years before I met him, was someone who'd been steeped in the same comic history I was. I loved his comic timing. I loved his characters. At that time if you'd told me I'd be working with him, that I'd work with any of the amazing people I have since I first read *Another Fine Myth*, I'd have laughed in bitter disbelief and gone back to my terrifyingly toxic day job.

I knew of Bob through another common interest, the Society for Creative Anachronism. Neither of us are active now, but he'd already retired from the field by the time I joined. Long and storied was the legend of Yang the Nauseating, founder of the Dark Horde and Loyal Opposition to the Crown. "With all due disrespect to Your Majesty," was a phrase I was told he often used in court, where the royals and nobles, who all went back to mundane jobs when they took off their silken raiment, often took themselves too seriously. Bob was the pin that punctured their self-importance.

He was a legendary figure at science fiction conventions, known for singing and playing the guitar at parties and filk sessions, drinking Irish whiskey and occupying the center of the most sought after circle in the bar, and for his prowess with the ladies. You may not know it (or you may; Bob has spread himself about a bit over the years) that he is one of the premier hand-kissers of our time. Almost everyone I knew had a "Bob story." Some were firsthand, but most were urban legends. (I have reason to know *some* of them are only urban legends.) He and some similarly inclined friends created the Dorsai Irregulars and the Klingon Diplomatic Corps, organizations to which it is considered an honor to belong.

So, steeped in the hype, I trembled when I first met him, at his home in Ann Arbor, Michigan. He and his then-wife Lynn Abbey, good and old friends of my then-fiance (now husband) Bill, did their best to put me at my ease. Both of them are truly kind and hospitable people. Bob and Lynn drew me into the conversation as best they could. I sat goggle-eyed as they talked about their other close friends as if they were just ordinary people. Those names were the stuff of legend to a newcomer like me: Gordon R. Dickson, the "Gordfather" of the Dorsai Irregulars; Wendi and Richard Pini of Elfquest; the great Poul Anderson; C. J. Cherryh; George Takei; and more. At the time they were still editing and writing in the original *Thieves' World* series, the shared-world anthology that gave shape to all the shared worlds to follow. They'd been everywhere I hoped to go. I was a literary novice, but they treated me like an equal. I adored them for it. Believe me, not everybody who's "made it" is so secure or generous.

Bob and I did have a bunch of things in common. We were the "sensitive" halves of our respective pairs. We're desperately soft touches for cats. We love the great acts of the post-vaudeville movies like the Marx brothers and Laurel and Hardy, and good funny movies in general. We both admire Damon Runyon, whose stories were the basis for the musical *Guys and Dolls*. We both liked Disney's *Sleeping Beauty*, though his favorite character was Maleficent and mine was the Fairy Godmothers. We both do needlework (really; he's very good at it). And . . . well . . . we write humor.

When the inevitable suggestion was made that we should really think about doing something together, I was willing. One of the things I admired most about his writing was that he could be funny—very funny—without being sickeningly cute or dragging a joke until it died. Though there were elements of slapstick in his stories, the characters weren't stupid. Mistakes are made out of innocence or ignorance. Comic timing evolves out of the situation. He imbued his characters with wisdom, loyalty, and warmth. You would probably like to hang out with them. I would.

Bob came up to our house one January: an act of faith, since he now lives in New Orleans and we live in the suburbs of Chicago. We talked, with Bill standing by as a referee in case things got ugly. They didn't. I gave Bob the respect he deserved for his experience and accomplishments, and he offered me acceptance as an established newcomer. Bill went back to his office to play computer games, and Bob and I started talking ideas.

Our first crack out of the box was an original book, *License Invoked* (Baen Books). We worked out our story line and characters together, then decided who would write what sections. Books change all the time while they are being written. They develop— we hope, for the better. The result was longer than a novel he would usually produce, and shorter than one of mine. The plot ran pretty much along the lines we'd laid out, though the structure and the villains changed a lot. I liked our main characters. It wouldn't bother me a bit to do something else with them—later.

By now, Myth Adventures had lain dormant for a long while. Bob had two books to run on the twelve-book contract with Donning Starblaze, the trade paperback publisher who produced the original Myth Adventures series. Because they'd gone belly-up, years had passed before the rights to books eleven and twelve could be extricated. Once they were released and resold to Meisha Merlin, interest awoke in having still more Myth after book twelve. But, Bob had other projects he wished to work on, so it was suggested that once he finished *Myth-Ion Improbable* and *Something M.Y.T.H. Inc.* he and I, proven collaborators, should put out a few new books. Because this series is Bob's special baby we decided to take a few test runs. The final three short stories in this collection were the result. They follow on from the conclusion of *Something M.Y.T.H. Inc.* and lead up to the action in our first novel, *Myth Alliances*. The others are just for fun. We hope you enjoy them.

—Jody Lynn Nye

The "Discreet Blackout"

It was interesting to read Jody's introduction. (Writer's tip: If you're doing one section of a two-part introduction, always let your partner go first. Then, all you have to do is rebut or go, "Yea. What she said.") The only trouble was, it was hard to recognize myself in it.

Okay. I know these intros are supposed to be "love and kisses and how much fun it is to write together," but there should be a limit. I'd say my application for sainthood was rejected, but I never bothered to send it in. For one thing, I assume the powers that be have better things to do with their time than read crank mail. For another, I'm used to getting paid for writing fantasy.

Just because I have good manners and write humor, people tend to assume that I'm a "nice guy." Well, okay, I am . . . but only up to a point. That point usually involves protecting me and mine. Unfortunately, "mine" includes my writing.

One thing I've discovered over the years is that the longer you write humor, the more finely tuned you become in your opinions of what is funny and what isn't. Also, the more firmly entrenched the idea becomes that you have a particular recognizable style that the readers expect from anything with your name on it.

What this all boils down to is that when it comes to collaborating, particularly on humor, I can be a real pain in the ass to work with. I like to think that I stop short of bullying my writing partners, but (even by the most generous interpretation of events) I can be "extremely stubborn" when "discussing" a particular joke or scene. When it involves two of my most popular characters, specifically Aahz and Skeeve, it borders on being nightmarish. I mention this not so much to belittle myself as to raise the awareness and appreciation of the readers to what my writing partners actually have to go through.

All that having been said, it really is a joy and a pleasure to work with Jody . . . even if our memories of certain events and conversations differ.

As an example, while I recall her visiting with Lynn and me in Ann Arbor, my memory of our first meeting was at a gaming convention. That was back in the days when I was doing two or three dozen cons a year to get my name in front of the readers, and was attending comic cons, Star Trek cons, and gaming cons as well as the science fiction–fantasy cons that were my mainstay. She was sitting behind a demonstration table in the dealers room painting lead miniatures, and I recollect getting some excellent tips on dry-brushing techniques. It was a brief meeting, so I'm not surprised that she doesn't remember it. I might have paid more attention to her, but I had learned she had a thing going with Bill Fawcett, who at that point was a friend of mine and eventually became her husband and one of my packager/publishers. (Writer's tip: If you're going to flirt with someone at a convention, try to do it with someone who isn't a girlfriend/fiancée/wife of one of your editors. It could affect your long-term book sales much more than a similar encounter with a reader.)

Another interesting overlap was when I discovered that we both had a background in theater. As an aside, I have often compared writing, particularly writing humor, with doing radio theater where you don't have the audience's feedback reactions to work off. I maintain that the most successful humor writers first honed their skills working in front of a live audience to build their sense of comic timing before attempting to create humor on paper. While my supporting role as Marcellus Washburn in a production of *The Music Man* lags far behind her leading role as Winifred the Woebegone in *Once Upon a Mattress*, I think the mutual experience contributes greatly to our ability to work together.

Anyhoo, Butch and Fluffykins are now playing together happily, and the occasional territorial growls and swats only occur when there are no witnesses to box both our ears. Jody is not only an extremely talented writer whose company is always a pleasure, she's also spirited enough to hold her own in a brawl. While, perhaps, not absolutely necessary, all three are definitely desirable in a writing partner.

—Robert Lynn Asprin

MYTH CONGENIALITY

By Robert Asprin and Jody Lynn Nye

I answered the door of the inn in my most repulsive disguise.

"Yeah?" I asked the two small children who looked up at the one-eyed, white-haired rogue with five teeth, tangled hair, bizarrely twisted features, and visible insects crawling in and out of his clothes. They didn't retreat a pace.

"Is the haunted house open?" the older one asked.

"Yeah!" the little one said, staring at me with open curiosity. "We wanna see all the monsters!"

"Monsters?" I asked, puzzled.

"Yeah! Draggins and wivverns and yuni-corns and creaky floors and stuff! We heard about it in town."

"No," I said. Out of the corner of my eye I could see my pet dragon Gleep charging for the door. He loved to answer the door. I put a foot into his chest to keep him from sticking his nose around the edge. "No monsters here." Now Buttercup wanted to know what was going on, and you can't deter a war unicorn as easily as you can a baby dragon who'd impressed upon you. "Nope. Just a law-abiding, boring old guy living quietly by himself." I could see them starting to become afraid now. I smiled wistfully. They started to back away nervously. "Just a lonely old man who'd love to have company to while away the hours. Sorry." I slammed the door shut on them just before Buttercup put his muzzle under my arm.

"Stop it, you guys," I protested, being nuzzled by a dragon on one side and snuffled by a unicorn on the other. Gleep and Buttercup looked hurt. "I keep telling you to stay out of sight. Now the townspeople have seen you. Can you believe it? A haunted house! And they *want* to come in. I wish Bunny was here."

Bunny, my former accountant, was staying here at the old inn with me, running interference and pretty much keeping house so that I could get on with my magikal studies. She'd gone off on vacation a few days before. I hadn't realized until she had been gone how lonely it was in the sprawling building by myself. Alone, as I said, except for two exuberant pets.

I let the disguise spell drop. I always had to use one when I opened the door. Nobody in Klahd would be impressed or frightened by my normal appearance. I was young, for one thing, tall but thin, with a thatch of blond hair, and I'd been told that my blue eyes reminded them of Gleep's. When I looked in a mirror I couldn't see the same innocent wide expression, but I'd been assured by Aahz that it was there.

"Come on, you guys. Let's have lunch."

I wasn't much of a cook, being used to leaning out the door of our tent at the Bazaar on Deva and being in reach of every kind of cuisine from every dimension, some delicious and toothsome, some more frightening to smell or look at than any disguise I'd ever put on. My cooking was somewhere in between, but Gleep ate everything, and Buttercup was always content with his fodder.

The kitchen, as befit one in a building constructed to serve a houseful of guests, was enormous. I kept a small fire going in one of the baking ovens instead of the huge ingle that comprised a whole wall shared with the rest of the inn. We usually ate at a small table tucked in the alcove beside it, cosy and warm. Formality was pointless, since we never had guests, and I could keep my back to the wall.

I dished up stew that had been bubbling away in a closed pot among the embers of the fire. One generous portion for me, five for Gleep. (He also caught his own meals from among the rodents in the barn, but I didn't want to know about that.) It hadn't burned, for which I was grateful, since we were short on supplies. Going into town to shop always elicited curiosity from the merchants and townsfolk as to who I was, where I came from, and what was going on in the old inn. I used to think they were just friendly, but experience made me question everybody's motives. I wasn't sure that was a good thing. I turned all the queries back on those who were asking, inquiring how they were, whether the prize cow had had her calf yet, and so on. I was thought of as a friendly guy, probably the servant of the old man at the inn, yet no one knew much about me. I was content with that, since I wasn't ready to answer those questions myself.

"Not bad," I said, tasting the squirrel-rat stew. I trapped animals for meat in the woods outside, and grew a few vegetables, skills learned long ago from my farmer father. My mother had taught me basic cooking, but I'd picked up a few hints over the years. Gleep stuffed his face into the washing bowl that served as his food dish when he ate inside. A happy "gleep" echoed out of the earthenware. I looked around for the wineskin. Still more than half full, I was pleased to note, as I poured myself a glass. So I hadn't unconsciously drunk more than I should have. My habits were getting better. I wished Aahz was there to see.

A loud POP! sounded in the center of the room. I jumped to my feet and drew my belt knife. Travel between dimensions was accomplished using incantations, spells or D-hoppers, magikal devices one dialed to reach the right destination. I had enemies as well as friends.

To my relief, it was only Bunny. I relaxed for a split second, then, at the sight of the expression on her face, scooted out around the table to meet her. Her normally immaculate clothes were disheveled, and she looked as though she'd been crying.

"What's wrong?" I asked.

I helped her to sit down and poured her a glass of wine. She downed the glass in one gulp, something I've never seen the ladylike Bunny do.

She looked at me, her large blue eyes rimmed with red. I noticed that her lids were crusted with a noxious-looking green paste, and her eyelashes had been dipped in black tar, making them stick out in spiky clusters.

"Oh, Skeeve, I need your help!"

"For what?" I frowned. "Did something happen on your vacation?"

Bunny looked abashed. "I wasn't on vacation. I asked for a few days off so I could see my uncle. Don Bruce asked me to do him a favor. He said I was the only one he could trust to do it."

Her uncle, Don Bruce, the Fairy Godfather of the Mob, had for years employed M.Y.T.H. Inc. to look after its business interests in the Bazaar at Deva. He'd sent Bunny to me in hopes that I'd marry her, to make ties between his operation and mine closer. I prefer to choose my own girlfriends, and I admit I had sold Bunny short when I first met her. Since then I'd come to appreciate her intelligence. She was our accountant and book-keeper. If Don Bruce had sent her on an errand, it was probably a tough one.

"He sent me to get a device called a Bub Tube for him from a dimension called Trofi," she continued. "I tried, Skeeve, but I just can't get it. It's too much for me." Her face contorted, and she burst into tears. "I really can't do this."

I hunted up a clean handkerchief and pushed it into her hands. "I can't believe Don Bruce would send you into a really dangerous situation without backup."

"Oh, Skeeve, I wish it *was* dangerous!"

"What?" I asked. "Why? What do you have to do?"

She lifted her face, now smudged with black and green. "Primp, parade, put on enough makeup to cover a dragon, sing, dance, wear a swimsuit in front of a panel of ogling judges, and, throughout the whole thing—smile!"

"That's demeaning," I said, shuddering. In her place I would rather have faced an active volcano.

"That's what I mean," Bunny wailed, wringing the handkerchief between her hands. She was normally so composed. I was worried. "I *hate* it."

"Couldn't I just go in, as a businessman, and meet with the owners of the Bub Tube face-to-face? I could probably negotiate for it. After working with Aahz for so many years I've gotten pretty good at it. If Don Bruce is involved, money should be no object . . ." She shook her head. I frowned. "I could steal it. My skills are pretty rusty after all this time, but now that I've been practicing magik . . ."

"It's been tried, Skeeve. Everything has been tried. There's no other way to obtain it. In this dimension there are no business meetings. Only contests. I have to win this beauty contest to get the Bub Tube. It's humiliating."

I sat back. "Well, that shouldn't be a problem," I said. "You're beautiful."

"That's not enough. Every other contestant is cheating broadside, you should excuse the expression, and I can't win. My uncle is counting on me. Will you help me? I could ask Tanda or Massha, but I'm ashamed to tell another woman what I'm going through. I'd rather trust you."

"Of course," I said. "But if I can't help negotiate, the only thing I can offer is moral support, and a little magik."

Bunny looked resigned. "That may be the only thing that will help me win."

I put together a kit of magikal items that I thought would be of some use. I put food out for Gleep and Buttercup. Bunny assured me that I could come and go between Trofi and Klahd without a problem, so I didn't have to call on any friends to look after them. I would have brought them along, but they'd have added too much to the chaos.

And chaos it was. The D-hopper delivered us into the middle of a shrieking crowd. I jumped, thinking that the shrill voices were raised because of a threat, but it turned out to be the normal voices of several hundred females, all of them with anywhere from one to a dozen attendants primping and coiffing them.

I looked around at the set faces of the contestants. There were several horned and red-skinned Deveel females clad in black and red to accent their complexions. They shot sultry glances at anyone who met their eyes. Pinky-red Imp women, stubbier and less sleek, dressed in dated fashions and too much makeup, sashayed around. A blue-skinned girl I recognized as a Gnome was holding still for four beauticians, each dabbing a different shade of makeup onto her face. She seemed fuzzy, as if she was going in and out of focus as I watched. I noticed a few Klahds, including one man dressed up, not very effectively, as a woman. Plenty of other dimensions were represented. All of the entrants looked determined and a little desperate.

"This must be one powerful magik item," I commented.

"It is," Bunny said. "It's up there." She pointed to a dais at one end of the vast chamber. High above it on a golden platform was a bulging, rectangular piece of glass with a magickal image flickering behind it. I peered at it, and found my gaze caught. Even at that distance I had to make a conscious effort to drag my eyes away from it.

"It causes people to stare helplessly at it for hours," Bunny said. "My uncle doesn't want it to fall into the wrong hands."

"Whose?" I inquired.

"Well . . . anyone's but his." But the way she hesitated made me think that there was someone specific he wanted to keep it away from. Bunny, if she knew, wasn't going to tell me.

I studied my surroundings. The room, a high-ceilinged chamber lined with mirrored doors on three sides, was a staging area. The center of the fourth wall featured a huge staircase flanked by thick black-velvet curtains leading up into a darkened area. Dozens of makeup tables were laid out in the center of the room. Each was occupied by a beautiful woman, or one of many beings who were undoubtedly considered beautiful in their own dimensions, but to my eye could scare the pith out of a reed. Not far from me sat a huge female Pervect, like Pookie, but nearly a foot taller and half as wide. Considering that Pookie was slender, this one looked unnaturally thin. When you added in the mouthful of four-inch fangs, she looked like a smiling dragon. Wearing lipstick. I gulped.

"How can I help?" I asked.

"You've probably noticed how much magik is flying around here, Skeeve. I need you to keep me from dropping too far behind in the contest."

I felt around for lines of force. Bunny was right: a hugely powerful force line ran directly underneath the building, leading toward the staircase. I wondered if the place had been constructed with it in mind. I was able to tap in without difficulty, and discovered that many fellow magicians were doing the same.

"But you know I haven't made too much progress in my lessons yet," I said. Bunny was the only one of the staff of M.Y.T.H. Inc. that I had brought with me to the isolated inn where I meant to buckle down and study. "The only thing I'm really proficient in is illusion, plus a few very minor tricks."

"That may be all I need," Bunny said. "I need to stand out in this crowd, and that won't be easy."

"But you're . . ." There was no point in denying the truth. I swallowed and plunged onward. "You're the most beautiful woman in this room. If it's really a beauty contest, you'll win it hands down."

"If it was that simple," Bunny said, "I would never

have brought you into this. I would have done it for my uncle, and no one would ever know. But I admit I'm out of my depth."

"Well, I'll do my best," I said. "Where do we begin?"

"First is the beauty parade," Bunny said. "It begins in an hour. I'll need you to cover my back."

Her back wasn't covered, nor was most of her body, during the beauty parade. She wore a brief, bright red bathing suit whose color pretty much matched my face. I was far more embarrassed than she was. Bunny disappeared into a changing room and emerged in a robe. When she shed it I thought steam would come shooting out of my ears. Her outfit started inward from her shoulders and downward from her collarbone and upward *and* downward from her navel, and left no inch of her spectacularly long, slim legs to the imagination. My hands itched to encircle her waist, which looked small enough that my fingers could meet around it. Above and below, her feminine attributes were . . . undeniable, yet very much in proportion. On her feet she wore shoes with such high, narrow heels that they made her taller than me.

Bunny's suit, if you could call three wisps and a few strings a suit, was modest compared with many of her fellow contestants assembled backstage. An Impish woman with a figure I'd once heard Aahz describe as *zaftig* had on three narrow strips of dark green cloth and an expression that if I gave in to the impulse to put my hands around *her* waist I'd shortly have no hands at all. It was no trouble at all to restrain myself. A bevy of red Deveel women glittered in silver, black, gold, and copper suits. The Pervect

wore a suggestion of golden yellow to match her eyes.
A sharklike female, clad in one strip of cloth far down by
her tail, swam by in the air. Magik, I remembered with
difficulty. That was why Bunny had called me in.

Once she'd donned her . . . er . . . suit, she had to put
on cosmetics, lots of them. The green stuff she larded
around her eyes, she assured me, was harmless, as was
the black stuff. The pale cream paint she rubbed onto her
cheeks and forehead, I thought, must be a protective layer
for the women's faces, because some of the contestants
were layering it on so heavily that there was no chance of a
hint of sun contacting skin. A huge, insectoid woman
wearing a yellow polka-dotted garment had matching goo
of bright yellow for her mandibles, with lines of black to
accent her multiple eyes. Behind her stretched a queue that
had to be hundreds long.

"There's only one prize?" I asked.

"Just one," Bunny assured me, stroking tar onto her
eyelashes and making them stick out like combs. She put
the applicator away and looked at me. Strangely enough,
under the bright lights all the cosmetics did make her
seem very attractive—at a distance. If you got close up,
you could see where all the various colors intersected,
like a mosaic.

"What happens to all the others?"

She glanced around disapprovingly, then leaned in to
whisper. "A lot of them stay around and marry. Trofi has
no business interests but contests, but they do a great deal
of matchmaking. Males from hundreds of dimensions
prize Trofi wives above all others. Sensible men don't
bother to come here. It's not worth it. Trofi wives are all
what you might call 'high-maintenance.'"

Well, I wouldn't, because I didn't know what the expression meant, and there was no time to ask for an explanation. Perhaps it had something to do with the costumes and cosmetics, both of which had to be adjusted and added to on the way to the flight of steps.

Up above, it was dark. I was aware of thousands of pairs or sets of eyes glittering in the reflected glow of spotlights swinging above the stage. There was a orchestra fanfare, then all the lights dropped but one. I peered over the edge. A lanky male Deveel, deveelishly handsome in a long-coated black suit and shiny shoes, held a short baton close to his face. He sang into the bulbous top end, and his voice was projected magickally all over the vast arena.

"There she is! / How beautiful! / Your queen of love! / How magikal! / How beautiful and magikal! / Your queen of love she is."

I found myself humming along. It was catchy. There was a hint of enchantment in the tune, causing me to crane my head to see as the Deveel stretched out his hand toward the steps. The first contestant, a serpentine woman with blue skin, ascended.

The crowd breathed an admiring sigh as the woman slithered gracefully around the stage on the arm of the Deveel host. So far, so good, I thought. The Pervect female ahead of Bunny hissed, showing her long teeth, then flicked her wrist in a meaningful gesture. She was casting a spell!

On the stage, the sighs turned to titters. I glimpsed the smooth head of the snake woman as it dipped low, far lower than I suspect she intended, then vanished entirely. The audience broke out into a laugh.

"She tripped!" Bunny whispered to me.

"Did she fall or was she pushed?" I whispered back, indicating our neighbor by a tilt of my head. Bunny's eyes widened, but she hid the expression quickly as the yellow gaze slid toward us.

The snake woman's cheeks were glowing royal blue by the time she got back to the steps. She shinnied down the railing, cursing under her breath, and was met by a wriggling mass of supporters, all exclaiming how unfortunate it was she'd suffered such an accident. The Pervect smiled smugly, a terrifying sight.

A Deveel woman glided out next. Around her head flitted tiny winged salamanders in rainbow colors, shedding gleaming lights on her face.

"Is that allowed?" a Klahd female demanded furiously, though I could tell by the aura around her that she was wearing magikal enhancements, too, to lift up and add perkiness to a wide bottom, her best feature.

"You see what I'm up against," Bunny murmured. I concurred. Trofi contests were no game for the fainthearted.

The Deveel made it almost all the way to the exit when her salamanders started belching fire. Battering at the multicolored blazes burning in her hair, the Deveel made a hasty retreat. I leaped forward to help, but as soon as she hit the stairs she put out the fire with a dampening spell.

Bunny was seventeenth in line. I kept an eye out for ill-wishes and attack spells until she was in the hands of the host. Applause broke out as she stepped gracefully around the stage, the light flashing against her long, smooth legs. The audience hooted and whistled. She smiled, and a thousand little bursts of light broke out in the darkness.

I felt disturbance brewing in the lines of force from

not one, but several points. Thankfully most of them were amateurish. I blocked many of them with a turnaround spell that I'd learned from Tananda, causing the effect to rebound upon the caster. An Imper woman three back in line jumped up and down, her shoes burning from the hot-foot she'd meant for my friend. An eight-legged arachnid girl stumbled on all eight feet, falling on her fur-covered derriere. Her mandibles clicked angrily.

A hand picked me up by my throat and turned me in mid-air.

"Gack!" I exclaimed to the Troll glaring into my face. I flailed with both hands, trying to signal that I wanted him to put me down. He paid no attention.

"Hey, youse," he said, bringing a shard-toothed mouth close. "Take girl and go home! Not go, you be sorry!"

I knew from long association with Chumley, a friendly Troll who worked under the *nom de guerre* Big Crunch, that most Trolls were more intelligent than they sounded. I kneed him in the nose and braced myself as he dropped me.

"Do you know who I am?" I hissed, glaring up at him. "I'm the Great Skeeve. Perhaps you've heard of me? Bunny there is under my protection. You leave us alone, or you'll never be able to set foot in the Bazaar on Deva again! Do you know what I mean?" I gave him a gimlet-eyed stare that I'd seen Aahz use to quail opponents.

It worked. The Troll, while not completely stupid, was no dragon–poker player. He'd heard about me, though obviously not the latest news.

"So sorry," he said, backing away. "I . . . don't hurt me, huh?"

Behind him was a Trollop, the female of the species, in a moss gray–velvet bathing suit, who gave me a glare. I kept my guard up, not wanting her to get close enough to read me. Tananda, Chumley's sister, was a powerful magician in her own right. This Trollop could probably wipe up the floor with me. I counted on my reputation, plus the fact that she was going to have to go onstage in a moment. We locked eyes, but I won. She dipped her gaze, and turned away, pretending she didn't see me.

"Awww!"

The cry from the audience told me I'd missed something. Bunny returned, her hands over her face. Her makeup had taken a direct hit from a malicious spell, and was running down her face in dark streaks. Her hair was soaking wet, and her bathing suit was beginning to shrink. Someone had cast a quick Rainshower on her while my back was turned. I threw her robe around her and hustled her out of the arena.

"I'm so sorry," I apologized, escorting her hastily past her grinning co-contestants. The next female, a granite-skinned being in a solid steel bikini, stepped up onstage, with a look that dared anyone to interfere with her. "I wasn't expecting so many attacks at once."

Bunny walked along smiling, with her head held high, as if nothing was wrong in the entire world. Night had fallen over the town. I followed the torches toward the inn where Bunny had taken rooms for us. Once we were out of sight of anyone involved with the contest, she allowed her shoulders to sag.

"I should have warned you," she said. "No one's fighting fair. If they're not using spells to puff themselves up, they're using them to knock others down."

I frowned. "What do the rules say?"

"Strictly forbidden," she told me. "No magik of any kind to enhance your talent or beauty, or to attack others.

But they're not stopping it. In fact, I think the judges are enjoying it."

"What about protective spells?" I asked.

"Not mentioned," Bunny said. "I guess they'd never believe that anyone capable of using enchantments wouldn't use everything they've got. A lot is at stake here. The Bub Tube is unique throughout the dimensions. At least now."

"Well, if they're not enforcing the rule, then we're free to use magick, too," I said. "I'll do everything I can, and leave you free to concentrate on winning."

"Touuuuu-cccchhhh meeeee, it's so eeeasy to leeeee-eeve meeeee . . ."

An Imper female in a tight evening dress belted out the climactic melody of her song, sounding like a dragon in heat. The sound went right through my head and out the other side. I gritted my teeth but applauded politely, because her entourage was watching the audience carefully, and I didn't want to draw negative attention to Bunny.

"Cats," Bunny murmured, half to herself.

"Not a chance," I whispered back. "They never sound as horrible as that."

Day Two was the talent contest. So far we'd seen contestants juggle—fire, plates, clubs, balls, and themselves—dance, in every style from slow country dancing to spastic jerking that I thought signaled mass magikal attack on the woman onstage; art; acting; declamation; twirling a shiny metal stick; bird song imitations; bird flight imitations; stand-up comedy; dragon-taming; knife-throwing; and a thinly disguised strip-tease act in which the Pervect female started a seductive dance fully clothed while a salamander crawled along the hem of her dress, burning it away in a spiraling strip. The Gnomish female did conjuring, an act that caused smug grins among the contestants until the judges determined that she wasn't using any power at all. Each of her tricks was pure prestidigitation, sleight of hand. I was really impressed. If anyone was serious competition for Bunny, it was she. Maybe, once this was over, I could find her and ask her to teach me some of those illusions—useful to impress one's opponent in situations where lines of force were scarce.

The judges were as stonefaced a group as I'd ever met on the other side of a card table, or, I ought to say, metal-faced. Trofians resembled Klahds but with shiny skin in metallic hues. A copper man, a bronze woman, a silver man, and a platinum woman flanked a slender gold-skinned female who was the chief adjudicator. When a question arose, the four all deferred to her. Ushers and assistants of every metal I'd ever seen ran back and forth to the dais with scoring sheets, beverages, and messages. A brassy young female seemed to have taken a shine to me, and winked a gleaming eyelid every time she went by our seats.

This competition wasn't free of sorcerous interference, either. Just as the Imper woman reached her high note, she developed a cough, and the orchestra had to finish the maudlin tune without her. She looked furious as she stalked off the stage. The gold judge shook her head and made a mark on her sheet. The silver man and platinum woman exchanged glances and entered their own scores. The next act went on.

Bunny clutched my hand. I held it tightly while watching the next act. The Klahd female who tripped up onstage kept on going, tripping over her feet with a wild yell and sliding face first all the way across into the opposite wings. She never reappeared. I sensed at least six spells that pushed her over. The pent-up force of so many enchantments was what drove her so far. A Deveel-ish dancer appeared next in a tiered lace dress, hard metal plates bolted to the bottom of her hooves. The tapping as she stepped rhythmically grew louder and louder until the judges themselves called a halt to her performance. She stomped deafeningly off stage, snarling at her fellow contestants.

Bad will escalated from there. The next Imper woman attempted to draw caricatures of the judges. First her paintbrushes caught fire, then the lines she produced with a charcoal pencil rearranged themselves into such scurrilously rude drawings that the judges' faces glowed with embarrassment. So did the contestant's. She burst into tears and fled off stage. She was succeeded by a multi-limbed creature with a small dummy that she set on one of her many knees and tried to throw her voice. By the look on her face, the things it said were not in the script. A tiny Salamander girl writing poetry in flames on the air was extinguished by the sudden descent from the catwalk of the fire bucket and its contents. It hissed its way off stage while the judges scribbled their notes down.

Bunny was next. She'd rehearsed her act with me in my room at the inn the night before, and if nothing went wrong she'd knock the judges off her feet. I'd never known she was so talented. She danced with a partner who was no more than a broomstick in men's clothes. The bristly end was the figure's head, gloves were attached to the end of the tunic's sleeves, and shoes were sewn onto the bottom of the hose. And as they danced, they sang a duet. Bunny did both parts, singing in her normal tone for her lines, and pitching her voice down low for her partner's.

"It was the closest to boys we had at Madam Beezel's Academy for Girls," she said apologetically. "My parents were very strict." I thought it was a terrific act, and I told her so. She squeezed my arm for good luck before the host called her name.

She swirled out onto the stage with her partner in her arms, and the music began.

"We two," Bunny sang. "We two are like one / When we're on the dance floor / Out on the town having fun / You are me and I am you / Whenever we are close I see you and me / we two, we two are like one . . ."

I enjoyed it. It reminded me a lot of what Aahz called "vawd-vil." I even saw one or two of the judges moving their heads in time with the music.

It took a little while for the others to catch on to what her act was about, but when they did, the attacks came from every direction. Gusts of wind blew her long skirt up over her head, showing tiny blue unmentionables underneath. Her feet slipped on invisible oil slicks or white patches of ice that appeared on the stage floor, then vanished without a trace. I threw defensive spell after defensive spell around her. They were bombarded by hostile magik. A few spells slipped through my protection. Bunny's "partner" grew extra arms and legs. Its face changed into a hideous mask and started to sing.

"Boo hoo, you hopeless dum-dum! / You dance with a pushbroom / we all assume you're insane / *&%$ you . . ." Bunny flagged, not knowing what to do next.

This I could help with. I tore energy from every force line I could reach, and covered the horrible face with a handsome male visage, and filled in the raucous noise with my own voice. Suddenly, instead of dancing with a broom, Bunny seemed to be in the arms of a handsome man.

"Do you mind if I cut in? / Go on with your song / you're beautiful . . ."

Over its shoulder she shot me a look of such gratitude I could feel my ears burning. I let her go on singing. Now the contestants turned their attention to me, but I was ready for them. I'd had to concentrate on doing spells while a baby dragon licked my face or while an angry Pervect yelled or while armies of heavily armed men and horses charged straight at me. What had I to fear from a thousand angry women?

Plenty, it turned out. Since I wasn't onstage, out of reach, they mobbed me, scratching, kicking, and even punching. A swipe from a felinoid female drew blood from my cheek. The Salamander burned through my boot top and singed my feet. The Perv woman cocked her arm back to throw an uppercut. I dodged her fist, and tumbled straight into the claws of the Deveel contingent, who got in a few licks of their own. Floor stewards came hurrying over to see what was the matter, but they were thrown back across the room. I hunched over in a tight ball, protecting my eyes with my arms. Whatever else happened, I couldn't let the illusion drop. Bunny's score, and her mission, depended on it.

"All right, enough!" a man's voice over my head shouted. "Ladies, back to your places or you'll be disqualified!"

The feet kicking my back withdrew, and I uncurled. A hand grabbed my arm and helped me get to my feet.

"You're not the only one who can throw your voice," Bunny said. Faces glared at me over Bunny's shoulder, but hers was the only one I cared about. She looked tired.

"How did it go?" I asked.

She held out her other arm. Her erstwhile partner lay across it. When I let the illusion drop, nothing remained but a few tatters of cloth and some ashes. They crumbled to the floor.

"Thank you for what you did," she said. "But I don't think it'll be enough to help."

I glanced over at the judges' table. The brass girl I knew was standing behind the gold judge, pouring molten liquid into a glass. She caught my eye with a sad look and shook her head. Bunny saw it, too.

"I can't win this," Bunny said. "I'm ready to give up."

"No," I insisted. "You can win it. There's still tomorrow."

"And that is what I'd do with the Bub Tube if I am so fortunate to win it," Bunny said. She put down the parchment on which her speech was written. "This is awful, Skeeve. It sounds so phony. The Bub Tube won't go to assure world peace, or harmony among the dimensions. I'm not going to be using it, my uncle is. And you know his business."

I sighed and thrust my hands into my hair. The talent contest had been a disaster. The Pervect had won, with one-fifth of a point more than the Gnome. Bunny was near the bottom of the ranking, about the same as she'd gotten from the beauty parade. This was her last chance to make good.

"This is what *you'd* do with it *if* you got it," I said, hopefully. "Or you could tell the truth. The honest answer might be such a novelty that it might surprise them into giving you the title."

"If I got it," Bunny said. "This part of the contest is worth fifty percent of the total. At best I'll come in somewhere in the middle."

I thought hard. "But you'd move up if your best competition moved down, wouldn't you? It's still possible."

"It's still possible to win," Bunny began, "but they all cheat so much. And they play dirtier than I ever dreamed." She leaned forward and touched my cheek. "Does that still hurt?"

"A little," I admitted, enjoying the play of her gentle fingers. "What if I could persuade them not to cheat?"

Bunny brightened. "Do you think you can?"

"I'll try," I said.

"Excuse me," I said, approaching a cluster of Klahdish women. They were helping one another fasten dresses and tidy their hairstyles. They straightened and eyed me warily. "Since I come from your dimension I wanted to start with you. Do you think it's fair that everyone has been using magik or technical devices during this contest?"

"Well, no," said a tall woman with red hair. "But what about it? If we don't, we'll lose for certain."

"My father is a grand wizard in Bream," said a tiny woman with black hair. "He wants the Bub Tube, and he gave me plenty of spells to make sure I'll get it."

"*I'll* get it," a buxom girl insisted, tossing her long blond tresses over her shoulder, "if I have to seduce every single judge on the panel."

"But you're all beautiful, and all intelligent," I said. "Why not play it straight and see who wins fairly and squarely?"

"Because we want to win," they chorused.

"Those Deveels all use magik," the wizard's daughter said. "If we didn't cheat, we wouldn't stand a chance."

"What if I could get them to agree to compete honestly?" I asked.

"Well . . ." the redhead appeared to consider. "But everybody would have to do it."

"All right," I said, overjoyed that my plan was going so well. All my years with Aahz, the master negotiator, were paying off. "I'll get them to agree."

But my plan hit a snag in phase two.

"Are you crazy?" the tallest Deveel women asked. "Honest! You all say that. One of you Klahds asked for a fair fight last time there was a contest on Trofi, and she cheated. We're not going to fall for that again."

"But the Klahds have given me their word they'll follow the rules," I said.

Fiery red eyes bored into mine. "You don't look that stupid. Either you believe them, or you're in on it with thcm. In any case, get lost!"

She snatched a pot of rouge off the table and threw it at me. Out of reflex I trapped it in mid-air with a tendril of power. The Deveel's eyes widened.

"Who are you?" she hissed.

"Uh, my name's Skeeve," I said. The way her face closed I knew she had heard of me. I grabbed the jar and set it gently down on the table. "Look, this is not about me. My friend Bunny . . ."

"Forget it!" she said. The others sneered down their long noses at me. "She has Skeeve the Magnificent working for her? And you want *us* to give up our advantage? You're insane. We're going to do whatever we have to to win. What are you going to do about that?"

Shoulders sagging, I went back to where Bunny was sitting, reading through her much-revised script. What would I do? What could I do?

The force line under the arena was big enough for me to use if I wanted to enforce honesty in the remaining phase of the competition, but did I have the right to impose my views on the others? If I had no stake in the contest, perhaps, but I was there as a partisan for one contestant who would benefit if everyone stopped interfering with one another.

"How did it go?" Bunny asked, then interrupted me before I could speak. "Never mind, let me tell you: they all told you to go peddle your papers. But thank you for trying. I'm proud of you for wanting to stay on the straight path. With your powers you could outstrip every one of them. That wouldn't be fair. I've decided I'm going to be honest in my essay, and face the judges on my own merits. Crom knows what they'll do to me— anything is possible, from throwing tomatoes to transformation spells."

"What's a tomato?" I asked curiously.

"A fruit that's been convinced it's a vegetable," Bunny said, mysteriously. "Look, Skeeve, I am sure to lose, but at the very least I can find out who wins the Bub Tube and let Uncle Bruce know whom he has to buy it from. I'm sure he'll be able to make her an offer she can't refuse."

"What's so important about it?" I pondered, staring up at the rectangular piece of glass on its plinth high above the judges' table. The magik that made it run drew constantly on the force line under the auditorium. Even at this distance I could clearly make out the pictures on its surface. People in brightly colored clothes performed appallingly embarrassing tasks for money. Bad singers that

I could just hear over the din in the hall wailed out their tunes, and bad dancers tripped around, all within the confines of the glass box. And over all the noise coming from the Bub Tube was the inexplicable presence of raucous laughter. I hated it, but it was as fascinating to watch as a basilisk, and just as capable of freezing its prey in place. Darkness suddenly enveloped me.

"Hey!" I protested.

"Sorry," Bunny said, pulling her cloak off my head. "You fell into its spell."

"That's dangerous," I said. "Is there a way to control it?"

"Yes, there's a guide." Bunny rose from her seat and went to the foot of the plinth. She came back with a small book featuring an amazingly lifelike illumination on the cover.

I opened it and began to read the instructions. For a magikal item it had amazingly good documentation, down to a listing of the times various images would appear on the surface. "Wild Kingdom" interested me, "being the exploits of his noble yet mad majesty King Roscoe the Disturbed, and his Knights of Chaos."

"Bunny," I said, an idea dawning on me, "if it's possible for you to win based on your essay, I'm going to see that you do. And I won't cheat at all."

The contestants were unusually subdued as they prepared for the essay portion. None of the expected sniping was going on, dropping the sound level so low I could hear the inane chatter from the Bub Tube. Every one of the women were dressed in formal costumes, even the Trol-lops, for whom formal meant fewer body parts showing than usual. Bunny emerged from her assigned cubicle in a red gown that fit her as if it had been painted on her body. A frown wrinkle was fixed between her eyebrows. I took her hand and swirled her, gracefully for me, around the corner of the room.

"You look wonderful," I said. "You're going to be a smash." Bunny blushed.

I was, unfortunately, more immediately correct than I had anticipated. As soon as Bunny made her appearance, the Deveel women appeared out of nowhere in an angry cloud like sting-wasps.

"Who do you think you are?" they demanded. One of them pushed her back against a mirror. "Red is our color! Klahds like you get blue!"

"I'm not a Klahd," Bunny said, standing her ground. "I'm half Fairy!"

"Then violet!" the chief Deveel woman said, in a tone that brooked no argument.

"No, green!" shouted another.

"Yellow! Yellow's for the Fay!"

The room stewards arrived, shouting to everyone to break it up. By the time I caught sight of her again, Bunny's dress was a rainbow of anything but red, and her face had been dyed in stripes to match. I enveloped her with a web of power and pulled her out through the crowd, which disbursed with angry looks at me. Bunny's spine was straight as a tree. If the Deveels had intended to shake her confidence, they'd failed. She was more deter-mined than ever to get through the contest honestly. I used a little power to dispel the color in her face, but a pink flush remained in her cheeks. She flatly refused to let me change her dress back.

That was the last attack, magikal or otherwise, until the essay portion began. The first woman on stage was a Klahd.

"Good evening," she said, curtsying to the judges. "If crowned the winner of this marvelous contest, I will use the Bub Tube for the benefit of all beings . . ."

Out of nowhere a red sphere came hurtling, and splatted in the contestant's face.

"*That's* a tomato," Bunny pointed out.

It was a free-for-all. The poor Klahd hopped all over the stage, avoiding hot feet, kicking at snake-spiders that suddenly appeared and tried to crawl up her legs, shouting to be heard over booing from the audience, flushing sounds and greatly amplified intestinal noises. Swarms of sting-wasps buzzed around her, zooming for her face, her hands, any exposed flesh. The judges sat at their table, calmly marking score sheets and sipping tea poured for them by their attendants. They didn't move a finger to prevent the humiliation of the first contestant. Or the second. Or the third. The fifth essayist, the Gnome, simply wasn't there when rotten fruit came flying her way, but her continual disappearing and reappearing interfered with the delivery of her speech.

". . . A benefit to all beings . . . used only for good . . . personally promise to dedicate the device . . ."

Except for the direction the missiles were coming from, stature and skin color of the victim, er, participant, the speech, the ducking, and the humiliation of each woman was nearly identical. I began to feel sorry for the contestants. It would have tried even a seasoned politician to survive a pelting like that. I glanced at Bunny. Her face was set.

An Imper woman slunk off the stage, covered with yellow paint that had sloshed down on her from a bucket that clanged to the floor after depositing its contents on her head. The Pervect woman shoved past her, speech clutched in one scaly hand. She strode to the center of the stage, showed all her teeth and stuck a clawed finger out in the direction of her fellow contestants.

"If one *single* rotten vegetable," she roared, "one bucket of *anything* or *one spell* comes my way until I have finished reading this speech, every single one of you is going to be sorry!"

My ears rang with the sound of her voice, but she'd made her point. Except for resentful muttering, it was quiet in the auditorium. She showed all of her long teeth in a feral smile. I felt her build up a spell and cast it upon herself. It didn't feel like a charm of protection, rather one to aid eloquence.

"*Now.* Good evening, honored Trofi judges. I'm proud to be allowed to tell you my plans for the Bub Tube. In the interest of universal peace and the benefit of all living beings . . ."

I gulped as the Pervect left the stage to applause by the usually stoic judges. If my plan didn't work, all the pent up resentment building through the duration of the Pervect's speech would rebound upon the very next person up, and that person was Bunny.

One of the things I'd learned in my perusal of the Bub Tube's operation manual was how the pictures it produced came into being. The original illusions flowed from the chaotic ether, or they could be superseded by ones that sprang from a magician's creative mind. Both kinds played out directly upon the front glass, known as the screen.

Following the instructions, I pointed the control wand at the glass. I focused the image that I'd had building in my mind. Bunny walked up the steps, took her place before the judges, held up the parchment containing her speech, and opened her mouth.

The first tomato came flying out of the crowd. With one hand I averted the dripping fruit from hitting Bunny. With the other, I activated the Bub Tube.

High over the judges' heads the suavely smiling face of the Deveel host greeted them. "Good evening, ladies! You all know the remaining speeches have no impact on the outcome of the contest, so I am about to announce the name of the winner of the annual Trofi beauty contest! Hold on to your wigs, ladies. First, the runners up! In 1,023rd place, from beautiful, bleak Imper—Aberdyfi! In 1,022nd place . . ."

A thousand pairs of eyes fixed on the screen, listening raptly to the voice of the host rattling off hundreds of names I'd made up, so not one of them would lose interest in what they thought would be an early peek at the results. Far below, almost unnoticed on the stage, Bunny curtsied to the judges, and began her speech.

"Honored judges, I've thought very deeply about what I'd do with the Bub Tube if I got it, but the truth is I won't be using it myself. My uncle wants it, and he sent me here in hopes of winning it. If you give it to me, it'll be in the possession of a man that I love and trust. I'm not saying that he's incapable of being harsh to his enemies, but I would like to think that a hypnotic device like the Bub Tube will help him to deal with people he wishes to teach a lesson in a non-violent manner . . ."

I listened, keeping one eye on the rest of the contestants. Her speech was well-reasoned, honest, and above all, uninterrupted. She spoke for fifteen minutes, then curtsied again, rolled up her scroll, and was off the stage again before anyone noticed.

As soon as she was safely beside me again, I cut off the transmission from the Bub Tube. The screen went blank. All the women around us blinked.

"Hey!" a Deveel woman said, lowering the raised handful of dripping stable muck she'd held poised to throw. "Where'd she go?"

The next speaker, a lizard woman in green, was pelted with vegetables and spells even before she reached the center of the stage. The other contestants had now missed attacking two women, and had plenty of dirty tricks left over they hadn't used yet.

I extended my elbow to Bunny. "Shall we go?" I asked. "The results won't be available until tomorrow. I'd like to see some more of this fine dimension."

"Let's." Beaming, Bunny tucked her hand into my arm, and we left the dressing room together.

The award ceremony was very much like the one that I'd faked for the Bub Tube. The handsome Deveel of a host stood in the middle of the stage reading from a long scroll of parchment given to him by the judges, who sat serenely in their seats on the dais. The contestants whose names had been read had all departed sobbing or shouting. The others remained in the big dressing room, clad in their finest formal gowns, hanging on every word the Deveel spoke.

"And in 887th place, right behind Shirleen, is Dev-
raila! In 886th place—nice try, dear, better luck next
year—is Elzirmona! Runner-up number 885, just a hair
too far out for the big prize, is Mumseen!"

A Deveel, a Klahd, and a rock-faced woman shoul-
dered their way out of the big crowd toward the rear. I
never saw them again. I believe I dozed off a few times
on my feet in between batches of names. I didn't hear
Bunny's spoken. Beside me she was getting more and
more excited. I didn't really hold out much hope. I had
our bags packed and waiting in her dressing cubicle along
with the D-hopper. The moment her name was read, we
were going back to Klahd.

The mass of contestants thinned more and more. After
a while I started to recognize the remaining ladies. This
was the top tier of entrants. The chief Deveel woman was
still in contention, as was the Pervect, the Gnome, two
Imper women I'd thought had been terrific in the talent
show, the shark, and one of the snake-women.

". . . In 30th place, Bindina! In 29th place, Sorg-
kandu! . . ."

Soon, only ten were left. The Deveel stopped to mop
his brow and accept a glass of wine from one of the
pages.

"Ladies," he said, turning to face our side of the stage,
"I salute you. You've all come so far, but now this is the
moment of truth! I want you all to come up on stage!
Give 'em a big hand, folks!"

To deafening applause and a horn fanfare from the orchestra, the ten remaining women hurried up the stairs and
were arranged in a line at the footlights by the beaming
host.

"Ladies and gentlemen and whatever," he said. "Here are the final runners-up. In 9th place, Amindabelia!" An Imper woman burst into tears as a page brought her a bouquet of flowers. "8th place belongs to Zmmmissa!" I saw the snake-woman's tail sag with disappointment as she, too, received an armload of flowers. She retired to the back of the stage with the Imp. Seventh, 6th, 5th and 4th were all named, and still Bunny stood at the front, beaming and waving at the audience. Had she surpassed all odds and won? I had my fingers and my toes crossed for luck.

"Third place, Moleynoo!" The host turned toward the Gnome woman with a silver loving-cup in hand, but she was nowhere in sight. Not a race to stick around when things hadn't gone their way, Moleynoo must have dimension-hopped as soon as she heard her name. Now there was a gap in the row of gracious losers. The host handed the third-place cup back to the page. "Oh, well, folks! Second place . . . this was a hard fought battle, folks . . ." Bunny, the Deveel, and the Pervect leaned toward him. The host grinned. ". . . second place belongs to Devora!"

If looks could kill, the Deveel would have dropped dead, burning like a bonfire. Devora accepted her second-place award and stepped back. Now there were only two contestants. Bunny's shoulders were so tight above the band of her strapless gown my dragon could have alit upon them without making her bend. The Pervect leaned forward avidly.

"Now, before I name our first place winner," the host said. "I want to give our compensation award. This goes to the contestant who scored the lowest overall, but has still been a beam of sunshine and brightened our days

here on Trofi. The award for Miss Congeniality goes
to . . . Bunny!"

Bunny's hands rose, trembling, then covered her face
as she burst into tears. The Pervect strode to the center of
the stage, clasping both hands over her head for victory.

The host trailed her, talking into his padded stick.
"Yes, that means the winner of this year's beauty pageant
is . . . Oshleen! Congratulations, dear lady!"

Oshleen was surrounded by pages. One draped a huge
blue ribbon banner from the Pervect's skinny shoulder to
the opposite hip. One threw a white fur cloak over her
shoulders, another tied the ribbons in front. Yet another
trio came toward her with a huge bouquet of red thorn-
roses, a scepter with a gleaming jewel in it, and a glittering tiara that Oshleen had to duck down slightly to have
placed upon her scaly green head. The pages led her out
on the catwalk to take a victory lap out into the audience,
who continued to applaud loudly.

"Yes, there she is, your queen of love! Oshleen!"

The Pervect returned to the center of the stage, and the
Deveel took her hand and Bunny's.

Well, that was that.

"Now, we have a special presentation to make. You all
know about our grand prize. The great and powerful Bub
Tube!" He pointed to the plinth above the judges' table.
"Now, there are always a few irregularities in a contest of
this size. There are many rules, and many of them are
broken by accident, but in other cases, they are openly
defied to gain an unfair advantage. To be blunt, contestants cheat. We know that you, the audience, would feel
it was wrong to give our grand prize to someone who
skirted the regulations under which our contest was run.
The judges have been keeping a running tally of tricks

and subterfuge, magikal and otherwise, and subtracted
these totals from the overall scores. They have come up
with a winner. They are unanimous on this decision. It is
not Oshleen."

"What?" the Pervect bellowed, trying unsuccessfully
to free her hand. The Deveel must have had a pure heart
because his strength was as the strength of ten. She
stayed where she was, as if bound there.

"Yes, indeed," the Deveel continued, smoothly. "And
so, for cheating less than any of the other contestants, the
citizens of Trofi are pleased to award the Bub Tube to
Bunny! Take a bow, Bunny!"

Startled, Bunny lurched forward a pace, and offered
a deep curtsy to the audience, then another one to the
judges. By the time she stood fully upright the truth had
dawned on her at last. She began beaming.

The pillar sank into the floor until the Bub Tube was
within arm's reach of the stage. The Pervect stretched out
a hand to take it, but the Deveel beat her to it. He snatched
it off the plinth and, with a deep bow, handed it to Bunny.
"Congratulations, you lovely lady! Would you like to say
a few words?"

The truth had also dawned upon her fellow contestants. The last-place loser was getting the prize! Out-
rageous! In a mass, they started to move in on Bunny.

No one was paying attention to me. I dashed back to
her dressing room, snatched up the D-hopper, and shoved
my way through the crowd. I would never make it before
they would be on her in a mob.

"Bunny!" I shouted, hoping to be heard. "Catch!"

She looked up at the sound of my voice, and held up a
hand just in time to catch the short baton. Then I was
knocked off my feet by the rush of furious women. I'd

never make it to her. Dropping to my hands and knees, I crawled back through the sea of threshing legs to her dressing room and locked the door behind me. The cubicle was too small to lie down, but I huddled against the wall to nurse my bruises.

Unperturbed by the chaos going on around him, the Deveel host put his arm around Oshleen and began to sing. "There she is! / How beautiful! / Your queen of love! / How magikal! / How beautiful and magickal! / Your queen of love she is."

I scrabbled backward as a body appeared in the middle of the small space. It was Bunny, clutching both the D-hopper and the Bub Tube.

"Hurry," she said. "They're tearing the place apart."

"You don't have to tell me twice," I said, springing to my feet and putting my hand on her arm so the spell would carry both of us out of Trofi for good. In a moment I felt the wrenching sensation that accompanied any trip by D-hopper.

"Whew!" I said, as I looked around at familiar surroundings. We were back at the inn, with my string of laundry drying across an open window, dirty dishes on the table, Gleep and Buttercup bearing down on us as if we were the last sausages at a picnic. I staved off my dragon's slimy tongue, but I was smiling. "This is the most beautiful thing I've seen in three days—present company excepted, of course."

"Thank you for helping me," Bunny said, giving me a big kiss on the cheek. "Uncle Bruce is going to be so pleased to get the Bub Tube. You saved my life."

"Well, you saved mine just now," I pointed out, enjoying the sensation. "A favor for a favor. Let's call it even. What are friends for?"

"You haven't gotten off scot-free," she said, with a coy smile. "You'll have to listen to my acceptance speech."

"Sure," I agreed, stretching gratefully in a chair front of the fireplace in the old inn's kitchen, and pouring myself one—just one—well deserved cup of wine. "Just one thing: what's a scot?"

M.Y.T.H. INC.
INSTRUCTIONS

By Robert Asprin and Jody Lynn Nye

First down the long white aisle came the flower girls, ten of them dressed in green organza tossing handfuls of petals into the air. I got a faceful of their perfume and sneezed. That expression caused me to bare my teeth involuntarily, causing an equally involuntary back step by the six people standing nearest to me in the great hall of Possiltum Palace. I never expect Klahds to really appreciate Pervect teeth like mine.

I tugged at the tight collar of the formal tunic I'd let Massha talk me into wearing. If she hadn't become such a valued associate of mine and Skeeve's, I would tactfully have arranged to be elsewhere on this, her special day of days. But if you are smart you will never say "no" to a woman about to get married, unless you're planning on finishing the sentence with "of *course* I don't mind you dressing me up like an organ grinder's monkey." Which, naturally, leads your former apprentice and present partner to ask what an organ grinder is. When I explained he said it sounds like a devious torture device that, now that I come to think of it, isn't all that far from being accurate, if you consider your inner ear an organ.

The horde of little girls was succeeded by a host of little boys dressed up like pages. Every one of them looked like I felt. I know Massha has a somewhat garish color sense, but I'd have done a little better for these kids than coral-and-pink striped satin breeches and caps, and bright aqua tunics. All around me I could see optic nerves shorting out, and the bridal attendants hadn't started down the aisle yet.

Before I'd finished the thought, here they came in a bevy. A lot of the bridesmaids were of Massha's globular body type, though none of them matched her in sheer magnificence (this is her wedding day—it behooves me to be more than my usual tactful self). Her confidence and warmth brought out the best in fellow large ladies of the Possiltum court, who sought her out as a friend and role model, helping them to like themselves as they were. She had plenty of friends there. Even Queen Hemlock, whom I would have voted "Girl Least Likely to Have Friends of Her Own Species," had gotten on to cordial, even warm terms with her.

In an unusual display of insecurity Massha had run color choices for the ladies' gowns past Bunny, who has a good eye for fashion. Instead of a wallow of wild hues, which is what I would have expected, the bridesmaids were all dressed in pale pink silk. In spite of the vast differences in complexions and sizes, the pink served to flatter rather than draw attention. Bunny herself looked glorious and demure in her gown. The pink even looked good

against the green of Tananda's hair. She resembled some
species of orchid, shapely and exotic. I'd never before seen
bridesmaids' dresses that didn't look like bedspreads or
horror costumes. Mentally, I awarded points to Bunny for
skill, and Massha for knowing when to ask for help. It just
showed what kind of trust the team inspired.

Subtlety ended with the arrival of an entire marching
band. Two women in pink and aqua skirts, shorter than
anything Tanda had ever worn on a job, catapulted into the
room and began to turn flips down the white carpet. Behind them, a drum major in bright orange and blue came
to a halt at the door and blew a sharp blast on a whistle. He
hoisted his baton on high and marched forward, leading
the Possiltum army's music corps in full dress uniform,
playing Honywagen's "Wedding March." This was a dis-
cordant dirge that had become traditional for weddings
across the dimensions, to the everlasting regret of real music lovers. Since the band was a little heavy on bagpipes
and horns, the effect was as hard on the ears as their outfits
were on the eyes. Since we Pervects have more sensitive
ears than Klahds, I was ready to kill someone by the time
they finished mauling Honywagen and struck up "A Pretty
Girl is Like a Melody."

A full color guard strode in time to the tune. The eight
soldiers took positions at intervals along the white carpet,
holding the Possiltum flag high. Ten more soldiers, Klahds
in the peak of physical perfection, such as it is, marched in
past the flag bearers, sabers drawn and held erect in front
of their noses. At a cue, they formed an arch with their
swords. The band halted in the middle of its song, and
struck up the Possiltum marching song. Enter Big Julie, in
his best armor, clanking with weapons.

There'd been a lot of discussion about who would be

the General's best man, but the former strongman turned out to be the perfect choice. After all, the traditional role of best man was to hold the door and keep unwanted visitors from intruding on the ceremony. Except for me, Guido, Chumley, and a few of Don Bruce's enforcers who were present as invited guests, Big Julie was the only person who was big enough and mean enough to prevent any potential interruptions. As soon as he reached the front of the room Hugh Badaxe appeared at the door.

If there was ever a groom who wasn't nervous at his wedding I never met him. The big man had beads of sweat on his forehead under the crest of his helmet. He ought to be nervous; he was getting a terrific wife who had a lot of dangerous friends who'd still be looking out for her well-being even after she married him. The people around me backed farther away. I realized I was smiling again. Still, he bore himself with military pride. Pretty good under the circumstances.

Badaxe wasn't a young man, but neither was Massha a spring chicken. I hated wallowing in sentimentality, but it was kind of nice that they'd found each other at a comfortable time of life. I admired him for his honesty. He ran a good army. She was a terrific woman, and a decent magician, even if her power did come from gizmos. It was a good match.

As if he suddenly remembered where he was and what he was supposed to be doing, Badaxe lurched forward, then regained his composure. He walked forward with his head high, smiling at faces he recognized in the audience. I caught his eye, and he nodded to me. I nodded back, warrior to warrior, businessman to businessman. Once at the front of the room, he removed his helmet and handed it off to Big Julie.

A team of acrobats came hurtling into the room, followed by jugglers and fire-eaters. Dancers, accompanied by musicians playing zithers, harps, and flutes, undulated down the white strip, flirting with guests and flicking colored scarves around like filmy rainbows. In their midst, eight pink- and purple-dyed ponies drew a flatbed cart down the aisle. On it sat a tall, slender, bearded man in black leather pants and a silver tunic playing arpeggios on a tall, slender silver harp.

"Quite some thing, eh?" Chumley whispered. Behind me, he was leaning against a pillar so he wouldn't block anyone else's view. I nodded. Neither one of us wanted or needed to be part of the ceremony. It was busy enough without us.

There wasn't a hint of magik anywhere. Massha wanted things to go well, but she wasn't going to force them that way artificially. I thought it was pretty brave of her.

The dancers and jugglers surrounded the altar at the front of the room where a green-robed priestess was waiting with the bridesmaids and the groom.

The harp struck up the Honywagen fanfare, and all eyes turned to the door.

In my wildest dreams I could never have pictured Massha looking lovely. Radiant, perhaps, but something about the look of joy on her face transformed her from plain to fancy. The unspoken rule that crossed dimensions held good here: all brides are beautiful.

The bodice of the white silk gown could have gone around Tananda or Bunny five or six times. It was sewn with crystals, pearls, and, if my eye was still good, genuine gemstones. Massha probably had a bundle left over from her income at M.Y.T.H. Inc., and here was where she'd chosen to spend it. The skirt, which extended behind her into a train five yards long, was picked out in crystals that flashed on and off as she walked, and embroidered with little scenes in white silk thread. I'd have to get a close look at them later and find out what she thought was important enough to memorialize on her wedding dress. Never one to wear shoes just for looks, she'd broken her own rule and splashed out on crystal sandals with five-inch spike heels. Her orange hair was gathered into a loose knot underneath a wreath of pink and orange lilies and a white veil that flowed down around her shoulders. I wondered about the symbolism of all the white and thought it was quite possible she was entitled to it. Even if the color was purely for the ceremony, it looked great on her. She was like a glistening pearl as she entered on Skeeve's arm.

My partner, who often looked like a kid in spite of his years, looked grave and thoughtful, which went well with his full magician's robes. I thought it was a nice touch: since Badaxe was wearing his uniform, Skeeve, who was giving away the bride, wore his. I knew Massha and the seamstresses had been working on the outfit while Skeeve was away. The plum velvet was picked out in silver and gold constellations, magik sigils, and mystic symbols, which, on closer scrutiny proved to be phrases in languages from other dimensions. I particularly liked the one in Deveel near his knee that read, "This space for rent." Massha squeezed his arm and he smiled up at her.

I watched them go up the aisle, master and apprentice together. It was hard to know which one was which sometimes. Skeeve seemed to be everybody's apprentice, as well as mine. He learned from everybody he met, including Massha, but sometimes, like now, he was an adult guiding someone who trusted him. He was the only person who was surprised when Massha asked him to give her away. I felt my eyes burn suspiciously.

"I'm not crying," I muttered, my teeth gritted. "This doesn't move me at all." I heard Chumley sniffle audibly behind me.

The general stepped into the aisle. Skeeve met him, shook hands, and transferred Massha's hand from his arm to the groom's. Massha kissed him. Skeeve blushed as he sat down beside the Queen with the other honored guests in the front row. Gazing at one another, the bride and groom went to stand before the altar.

"Dearly beloved," the priestess began, smiling. "We are all here to stand witness to the love of this man and this woman, who wish to become husband and wife. Marriage is a wonderful institution, but should not be entered into lightly let those who understand it stay quiet and let this couple learn it for themselves yet let us allow one or both of them to unburden his or her heart to you but always remembering that it's usually the husband who doesn't understand what the wife is saying and the wife who claims the husband isn't listening to her anyhow and though you may wish to side with one or the other of them you shouldn't do that because they are both blessed under Heaven and nobody's perfect let the chips fall where they may and they will form a more perfect union in tolerance so they'll both live to a happy old age together and love is rare enough in this world that you should give them the benefit of the doubt and should this union be blessed with children their names will live on into infinity as honored ancestors and anyhow it's much more fun to spoil grandchildren than children your mileage may vary you can remind them of this day on anniversaries for years to come even if they don't remember which present you gave them. Do you Hugh Badaxe take this woman to be your wife? You do? Repeat after me: 'With this ring I thee wed.' Do you, Massha, take this man to be your husband? You do? Repeat after me: 'With this ring I thee wed.' By the power vested in me by the great gods all around us and the government of Possiltum, I now pronounce this couple to be husband and wife for ever and ever under Heaven onward into joyful eternity and beyond. Letanyonewhohasanyobjectionslethimspeaknoworforeverholdhispeace amen!"

"I need a drink," I told Chumley as soon as the wedding party marched out. "Several."

"Unless I'm greatly mistaken," the Troll said, "there's Poconos punch in the courtyard."

"Good. If there's any left the guests can have some." I strode through the crowd, which parted like a curtain before me. The Klahds were used to our outworldly appearance by now, but it didn't mean they wanted to be close to us. That suited me just fine.

The first gulp of Poconos exploded behind my sinuses and burned down my throat like lava. I drank down two more cups of the fire-red liquid before sensation returned. I emitted a healthy belch, spitting a stream of fire three feet long.

"That's more like it," I said.

"I say!" Chumley exclaimed, his eyes watering. "I suspect Little Sister had something to do with the mixing of this."

"Tanda always could mix a good drink," I said.

There must have been three hundred people in the palace courtyard. Dancing had already started near one wall. I could tell where the jugglers were by the gouts of fire shooting up into the sky. Deveels and other transdimensional travelers were doing small spells to the astonishment and delight of the Klahds (and no doubt to their own profit). Music and laughter rose over the din of people shouting happily at one another. I took my cup and went to stand in the reception line.

Massha and Badaxe accepted congratulations, handshakes, and hugs from everybody.

"Dear, I expecially loved the birds singing while you recited your vows."

"The jugglers made me remember my wedding day."

"Hey, what legs! What style! And you looked pretty, too, babe."

Massha showed off the gaudy ring on her left hand, and Badaxe beamed with pleasure. Don Bruce and his enforcers were just ahead of me in line. The Fairy Godfather, dressed in a formal lilac tux that went well with his usual violet fedora, fluttered high enough to kiss Massha on the cheek.

"You take care of her," he warned Badaxe. "Oh. I brought a little something for you." He snapped his fingers. Two of his largest henchmen staggered toward him with a giftwrapped box the size of a young dragon. "You should enjoy it. If it doesn't fit, tell Skeeve. He'll let me know." He turned to introduce the others in his retinue: a slim, sharp-eyed man with bushy black eyebrows, and a stocky, short man with no neck and short, wide hands suitable for making a point without using a weapon. "These are new associates of mine, Don Don deDondon and Don Surleone."

"A pleasure," Don Don said, bowing over Massha's hand. Don Surleone's huge hands folded around Badaxe's. I noticed the general's face contort at the pressure. The burly man must be incredibly strong.

The dancing and singing continued long into the night. I kept an eye on things to make sure nobody got out of line. I maintained eye contact with Big Julie, who was across the courtyard from me. He had the same idea, especially as so many people from the Bazaar kept turning up to give the happy couple their good wishes. So long as they stuck to that intention, I didn't mind.

"Hey, short, green, and scaly, how about cutting a rug?" The cuddly presence that draped itself across my chest could only be Tananda. The pink dress was cut low enough on her shapely decolletage to cause traffic jams. I'd seen a few already.

"I appreciate the invitation, but I'm watching," I said.

"Who'd dare to cause trouble here and now?" she asked, but she was a professional. She understood my concerns. Enough of our old clientele and our present neighbors were around to spread the word across the Bazaar if something blew up and we couldn't handle it. We'd be going back there in a day or two. Fresh rumors would make it tougher than it had to be. "I'll get Chumley to watch things, too."

Noticing our tête-à-tête Guido and Nunzio stopped by for a chat, and got my take on the situation. Skeeve was hanging out by himself. None of us wanted to bother him. He'd had enough stresses the last couple of weeks, between the near-fatal accident to Gleep and acting as best man. Keeping an eye on his back was only what one partner would do for another. He needed some time to himself.

"Aahz, can I talk to you?"

I turned. The bride was there in neon and white. Her

face looked worried in the torchlight. "Massha! How come you and Hugh aren't dancing?"

"I've got a little problem," she said, edging close and putting her hand through my arm. Any time someone looked at us she beamed at them, but not convincingly. "We started opening the wedding presents, and one of them kind of blew up on us."

"What?" I bellowed. The whole crowd turned to look. I grabbed Massha and planted a kiss on her cheek. "Congratulations! You'll make a great court magician." Skeeve had let me know about Queen Hemlock's decision. I concurred that it was the best solution for both of them. That way she and Badaxe would have equal status at court. I knew I was trumping Hemlock's own announcement, but it was the most legitimate way I could think of to cover my outburst.

"Thanks, Aahz," Massha said, beaming from the teeth out. The crowd lost interest and went back to their drinks and conversation. She looked like she might burst into tears.

"Which gift?" I murmured.

"Don Bruce's."

My eyes must have started glowing, because she grabbed my arm. "Hold on, hot stuff. It's not his fault. If anything, it's ours. When we peeled off the paper there was this big box with a red button on one side. No instructions. My detector," she showed me the gaudy bracelet studded with orange stones on one arm, "didn't show any harmful magik inside, so we went ahead and pushed the button."

I sighed. "What happened? What was it?"

She giggled, torn between worry and amusement. "A house. A cottage, really. It's lovely. The carpets are deep enough to hide your feet, the walls are draped with silk hangings embroidered with all of Hugh's victories, and the windows are sixteen colors of leaded glass. The trouble is it's in the middle of the throne room."

It was. An otherwise good-looking, split-level cottage with a two-stall stable and a white picket fence had appeared practically on the steps of Queen Hemlock's throne. The room had been designated as the repository for wedding gifts, since security there was always tight, and no one was likely to wander in without an invitation, no matter how curious they were about Massha's china pattern. Tananda and Chumley were on guard in the room. Tanda had taken off her elaborate headpiece. Chumley, a bow tie now undone under his furry chin, sat with his back against the doorpost. Nunzio and Guido, dapper yet businesslike in tuxedos, had arrived. They'd donned their fedoras in a sign to anyone who knew the trade that they were working. Massha's bridesmaids were clustered around a table full of presents. One of them was making a bouquet out of the ribbons. Another had a big bag full of discarded wrappings. Another had a quill and a bottle of ink, writing down who had given what.

"Has anyone told Skeeve yet?" I asked, taking the members of M.Y.T.H. Inc. to one side.

"No," said Massha.

"Don't," I said flatly.

"The Boss has a right to know," Guido said automatically, then looked guilty. "You got it. Mum."

"Have you tried to get it back in the box?"

"Of course," Massha said. "But the button has disappeared. So has the box."

I peered at the house. Fairy-tale honeymoon cottages didn't come cheap. This couldn't be construed as an insult from Don Bruce. Besides as far as I knew, based upon updates from Tanda and Bunny, that we were in good books with the Fairy Godfather. He was a careful man. He would have furnished instructions. So where were they?

"Has anyone else been in here that shouldn't have been?" I asked.

"No one," the bridesmaid with the quill said. Her name was Fulsa. She had round hazel eyes in a round, pink face. "A few people peeked in. Oh! There was a blue dragon in here for a while. I think he belongs to the Court Magician."

Gleep? I glanced at Massha.

"He just came in to sniff around the presents," she explained. "I think he felt left out, but I didn't really think he was well enough to be in the ceremony." She studied my face. "Any reason I should be worried about him?"

"I don't know," I said. But the two of us went out to the stable to make sure.

I'd never been thrilled that Skeeve had acquired a baby dragon. They live for hundreds of years, so their infancy and youth is correspondingly long. Gleep was still considered to be a very young dragon. He had a playful streak that sometimes wreaked havoc on our habitations. Skeeve believed he was a lot smarter than I did. But other times, I was reconciled to his presence, even grateful. He was still recovering from having stopped an arrow. The foot-wide trail through the straw on the way to his stall showed that something long and heavy had passed through there at least once.

A scaly blue mass in the corner began to snore as I entered. I went to stand by its head.

"Come on, Gleep," I said. "I know you're only pretending to be asleep. If you're as intelligent as Skeeve thinks, I'm sure you understand me."

The long neck uncoiled, and the head levered up until it was eye to eye with me. "Gleep!" the dragon said brightly. I jumped back, gagging. That reptile's breath could peel paint off a wall.

"Did you take a piece of parchment from the throne room?" I asked.

Gleep cocked his head. "Gleep?"

Massha came to nestle close to the dragon. "I know you were there," she crooned, running a finger around Gleep's jowls. The dragon almost purred, enjoying the chin rub. "Did you take something you shouldn't?"

The dragon shook his head. "Gleep!"

"Are you sure?"

"Gleep!" He nodded energetically.

Massha turned to me and shrugged. At that moment I spotted the corner of a parchment hidden under a pile of straw. I lunged for it. Gleep got in between me and it. I dodged to one side. He swung his long neck to intercept me.

"All right, lizard-breath, you asked for it. Partner's pet or no partner." I grabbed him around the neck just underneath his chin and held on. He writhed and struggled to get loose. I let go when Massha retrieved the paper. It was torn at one corner, where it had obviously been ripped away from a tack. Gleep tried to grab it back, but I stiff-armed him. He retired to the corner of his stall.

"It's the instructions," she said, scanning the page. " 'Choose the location you wish to site your Handy Dandy Forever After Honeymoon Cottage, then push the button.' Then below is an incantation." Massha's worried eyes met mine. "We didn't chant this! What if something terrible happens because we missed out on the verbal part of the spell? It might fall down!" She hurried out of the stable. Gleep let out a honk of alarm and scooted out after her.

"Come back here!" I said, setting off in pursuit. I was not going to let that goofy dragon upset the festivities. It was bad enough one of Massha's wedding presents had misfired.

Gleep was quicker than both of us. To the alarm of the bridesmaids, Gleep blocked the doorway of the throne room and was whipping back and forth, preventing Massha from entering. Guido and Nunzio ran over, their right hands automatically reaching into their coats.

"Grab him," I said.

"Be careful," Nunzio warned. "He's still healing. What's upset him?"

"He doesn't want Massha to read the spell that came with Don Bruce's present," I said. I stopped for a moment to think. That was how the situation appeared, now that I considered it. But that was ridiculous. "He can't read. How could he know something like that?"

Nunzio came up to lay a gentle hand on Gleep's neck. "Maybe he smelled a bad scent on the parchment," he said. "Dragons have a remarkable sense of smell."

Massha held out the paper in alarm. "Do you think it's booby-trapped?"

"I don't know," I said, grabbing it from her. I started to read. My eyebrows rose until I thought they'd fly off the top of my head. "I see. Good boy, Gleep!"

"Gleep!" the dragon said, relaxing. He stuck his head under my hand and fluttered hopeful eyelids at me. I scratched behind his ears.

"What is it, Hot Stuff?"

I snorted. "I don't know how that dumb dragon knew, but his instincts were good. This isn't a barn-raising spell, it's a barn-*razing* spell. If you'd recited it, it would have blown up the building and everyone inside!"

Massha's eyes went wide. "But why would Don Bruce want to do that?"

I scanned the page again. "I don't think he did. Look, the spell is printed in a different hand than the instructions." The swirling handwriting above was Don Bruce's. The message below, though also in lavender ink, was written by a stranger.

"How do we find out who did it?"

"With a little subterfuge," I said. "And a little dragon."

The boom that shook the castle was barely audible above the noise of the crowd and the musicians. I staggered out, supporting Massha. Her dress was torn and patched with black burns, and her hair was askew. Guido threaded his way ahead of us, making sure that Skeeve was nowhere in sight. We all agreed he shouldn't be bothered. I was pretty certain we could handle this by ourselves. He spotted Don Bruce and his two associates, boozing it up at one of the tables near the harpist. Don Bruce set down his goblet and kissed his fingers at the musician.

"Beautiful! That boy plays beautifully." Then he turned, and spotted us. "Aahz! Massha! What has happened to you?"

"The house," Massha said, playing her part. She let go of me and threw her meaty arms around the Fairy Godfather. "My husband! Oh, I can't say."

"What happened?" the don demanded.

Massha sobbed into a handkerchief. "We only just got married!"

"Are you saying that my present killed your husband?" Don Bruce demanded, drawing himself up four feet into the air.

"If the Prada pump fits," I growled, "wear it. The news will be all over the Bazaar in an hour: Don Bruce ices associates at a wedding!"

But I wasn't watching Don Bruce. I had my eye on his two associates. Surleone's heavy brows drew down over his stubby nose, but he looked concerned. Don Don de-Dondon couldn't keep the glee off his weaselly face.

"I'm good with casualties," he said, starting to rise from the bench. "I'd better go and see if I can help." Suddenly, a blue, scaly face was nose to nose with his. Gleep hissed. "Help?"

The dragon bared his teeth and flicked his tail from side to side. It was all the proof I needed that Don de-Dondon had his hands on the parchment I'd had Gleep sniff, but I thrust it in front of his skinny nose.

"This your handwriting?" I asked.

"Gimme dat," said Don Surleone. He looked over the page. "Yeah, dat's his."

DeDondon threw up his hands. "No! I have nothing to do with any explosion! Call off your dragon!"

I did, but Guido and Nunzio were there flanking him, hand crossbows drawn but held low against the don's sides so they wouldn't disturb the other wedding guests. "You can clean up again, Massha. We have a confession."

"Confession?" Don Bruce demanded, fluttering madly, as Massha's bruises faded and her dress and coiffure regained their gaudy glory. "What's the deal?"

"I don't know the whole story," I said, sitting down and grabbing the pitcher of ale from the center of the table. I took a swig. Subterfuge was thirsty work. "But I can guess. New people in any organization tend to be ambitious. They want to get ahead right away. Either they find a niche to fill, or they move on. When you introduced these dons to Massha and Badaxe their names didn't ring any bells with me. At first. Then you said they were new.

"The present you gave Massha was princely, but it also provided a heck of an opportunity to take you down, and at least a few of us with you. The box containing the house had a sheet of instructions attached to it. How easy would it be to add a booby trap that Massha would innocently set off when she went to open your present? We trust you; she'd follow the instructions as they were written. Your reputation for doing business in an honorable fashion would be ruined. But your enemy didn't take into account you have a host of intelligent beings working for you from a number of species."

"Gleep!" the dragon interjected. He'd withdrawn to a safe distance, with his head against Nunzio's knee.

"Something with so easy a trigger mechanism wouldn't need extra incantations to operate. The additional verbiage aroused our suspicions, enabling us to figure the puzzle out in time to stave off disaster."

"Then why the costume drama?" Don Bruce asked, snatching the pitcher out of my hand and pouring himself a drink.

I grinned. "To draw out the culprit," I said. "If you and your associates were innocent you'd be concerned about the loss of life. And Don deDondon here knew about an explosion even though Massha never used the word. He was thinking about it, because he'd rigged one to go off."

"But it did!" the scrawny don protested. "I felt it."

"A little subsonic vibration, courtesy of Massha's magik," I said, with a bow to her. "Nothing too difficult for a member of M.Y.T.H. Inc., which is why Don Bruce employs us to watch out for his interests in the Bazaar at Deva."

The Fairy Godfather turned as purple as his suit. He spun in the air to face the cowering don. "You wanted me to lose face in front of my valued associates? Surleone, Guido, Nunzio, please escort our former employee back to the Bazaar. I'll be along shortly." The meaty mafioso took deDondon by the arm and flicked a D-hopper out of his pocket. In a twinkling, they were gone.

Don Bruce hovered over to take Massha's hand. "I offer my sincere apologies if anything that I or my people have done to mar your wedding day in even the slightest way. I'll send someone with the counterspell to pack the house up again. I hope you and your husband have a long and happy life together. You made a beautiful bride." In a flutter of violet wings, he was gone, too.

"I'm glad that's over," I said, draining the rest of the ale. "Take that silly dragon back to the stables, and let's keep the party rolling."

Gleep's ears drooped.

"Now, Aahz," Massha said, "you owe him an apology. If it wasn't for Gleep, the palace would have been blown sky high."

The dragon rolled huge blue eyes at me. I fought with my inner self, but at last I had to admit she was right.

"I'm sorry, Gleep," I told him. "You were a hero."

"Gleep!" the dragon exclaimed happily. His long tongue darted out and slimed my face. I jumped back, swearing.

"And no one tells Skeeve what happened here to-night!" I insisted. "None of it! Not a word!"

"Who, me?" Massha asked, innocently, as Badaxe wandered in out of the shadows, in search of his wife. She sauntered over and attached herself to his arm with a fluid langour that would have been a credit to Tanda. "In a few minutes I'll be on my honeymoon. Nighty-night, Aahz."

MYTH-ADVENTURERS

By Robert Asprin

"I'm sorry, Pookie. I just don't get it. Maybe I'm slow."

"Don't apologize, dear," her companion said. "It doesn't go with being a lady. And as far as being slow . . . well, little sister, trust me. You needn't have any worries on that score."

Even a casual observer would realize in an instant that the two women weren't really sisters. One was a human female, a Klahd, actually, with a short unruly head of hair framing her fierce expression. The female on the opposite side of the table had obviously emerged from an entirely different gene pool. Instead of pink skin, she was covered with the green scales, offset by pointed ears and yellow eyes, that marked her to any experienced dimension traveler as a Pervert . . . or Pervect if they knew what was good for them. Still, they both had that lithe, athletic, graceful look that put one in mind of a pair of lionesses discussing a kill. Different genotypes or not, it was clear they had more in common with each other than with many of their own species.

If their builds and manner weren't enough of a give-away, their outfits completed the picture. The Pervect, Pookie, was wearing one of her favorite action leather jumpsuits with multiple zippers, which both insured a skin-tight fit and held the tools of her trade. The Klahd, Spyder, was still working on her look, but today had set-tled for calf-high boots with fishnet stockings, a dark plaid mini-skirt, and a sleeveless black leather halter top, which left considerable portions of her midriff bare. All in all, she looked like a parochial schoolgirl gone Goth gone biker slut. What united their outfits were the acces-sories, which was to say, the weapons. Throwing stars and knife hilts jutted from their sleeves and belts, along with various mysterious instruments a viewer hoped they would never see close enough to examine carefully.

The fact that this mismatched duo and their weaponry went practically unnoticed was an indication of the nor-mal atmosphere and clientele of the tavern they were en-sconced in.

"If I'm *not* slow, then why is it taking me so long to fig-ure out this whole adventurer thing?" Spyder countered.

"Well, not to make too big a thing of it," Pookie said, "for one thing you're still young. I've been at this game for a couple centuries . . . we'll not dwell on exactly how many . . . and you've only been at it for a few months. It takes awhile to get the hang of anything new. Just be pa-tient and listen to your big sister."

"I guess it's just not what I was expecting is all," Spy-der said, almost to herself.

"Really?" her green companion said. "Maybe we've

been going at this backward. This time, why don't you explain to me what it was you thought adventuring involved."

"I don't know. I was thinking we'd be doing bodyguard work or something."

Pookie heaved a sigh. "We've gone over this before, Little Sister. First of all, we don't have the manpower to do real bodyguard work. To do the job right, it takes at least a six-person team to guard someone around the clock. You keep forgetting that we'd have to sleep sometime."

"But Guido and Nunzio guard Skeeve as a two-man team," Spyder insisted stubbornly.

"From what I understand, they were assigned to Skeeve by Don Bruce primarily as an honor guard," Pookie said. "Besides, there are a lot more people on the team watching over Skeeve than just Guido and Nunzio."

"But . . ."

"And even if we were to hire on as a token-show force, believe me, you wouldn't like it,." Pookie continued. "Remember, we're female, and like it or not that influences the people who hire us. Believe me, the kind of swell-headed, self-centered celebrity types who hire female body guards are primarily looking for arm candy. The pay might look good, but they're not really people you want to hang around for any length of time. Usually, by the end of the job, you're ready to kill them yourself."

"So what is it exactly that adventurers do?" Spyder said.

Her green companion took a long swallow from her flagon. "If you scrape away the bardic lyrics and all the escapist literature romantics, what it all boils down to is that basically adventurers are either thieves or killers . . . or both."

Spyder leaned back and blinked. "How's that again?"

"Look at it close." Pookie shrugged. "If you're going after a treasure or artifact, it means you're taking it away from someone who thinks it's theirs . . . even if they stole it themselves originally. That's stealing. Even if you're unearthing or rediscovering a long-lost item, by law it belongs to whoever's property it is that you're on at the time. If you don't hand it over and maybe settle for a reward, if you try to smuggle it out without admitting you've found anything, that's still stealing.

"On the other hand, there's the 'slay the monster/bandit who is terrorizing the neighborhood,' or the traditional 'rescue the princess/damsel from the evil whoever.' Both of those, bluntly, involve killing."

"Um . . . Pookie?" Spyder said slowly. "If those are really the choices, I think I'd rather do thieving assignments if we can manage it. I mean, I try to be tough and put on a good front, but I really don't think of myself as a killer."

"If you say so." Pookie shrugged. "I'll keep it in mind. Personally, I lean toward the killing side, myself. There's usually less risk involved."

"Now, I'm not saying you're wrong," Spyder said, "but Skeeve and his M.Y.T.H. Inc. crew don't seem to fit with what you're saying."

"Don't forget that crew is pretty much top-of-the-heap right now," Pookie said. "As near as I can tell, it's taken them over ten years to work their way up into the position they're in, where people come to them with work. I'll bet you, though, if you look closely at some of their early work, it involved things that wouldn't stand up to close scrutiny. For example, I know for a fact that Tananda was primarily an assassin before she hooked up with Skeeve. And as for Aahz . . . I probably shouldn't speak ill of my own cousin, but he's always been one of the family's black sheep. If anything, I was surprised to find out he was involved in something that was even vaguely legitimate."

"I guess you're right," Spyder said, sighing. "Even Skeeve had to start somewhere. Of course, he had a Pervect for a trainer."

"Don't forget, Little Sister," Pookie said, winking, "so do you. I'm not one to brag, but if I can't teach you as well or better than Aahz taught Skeeve, I'll hang it up. If nothing else, I think I've got better material to work with from the get go."

"Thanks, Pookie." Spyder smiled. "That means a lot to me."

"Don't mention it," Pookie said, holding up her flagon for her companion to clink with. "If nothing else, it beats the military gig you just got clear of."

"No question there." Spyder nodded. She took a long pull of her own drink, then set it on the table with a decisive thump. "So, how do we go about looking for work?"

Pookie cocked her head in surprise. "Why, exactly what we're doing now. What did you think we were doing?"

"The same thing we've been doing for the last month." Spyder shrugged. "Sitting around a tavern and drinking. Frankly I've been wondering when we were going to get started adventuring."

Pookie held her hand over her eyes for a few long moments before responding. "Look, dear," she said finally, "remember what I was saying about us being pretty much criminals? Well, the old adage that 'Crime does not pay' is actually a shortened form of 'Crime does not pay *well*.' Well, in our line of work, that means that either you do a lot of little jobs . . . which ups the odds of something going wrong . . . or a few big jobs and live on the proceeds between."

"So what does that have to do with us sitting around a tavern?" Spyder frowned.

"I'm coming to that. Now there's primarily two ways of finding work. Either we roam around and try to pick up a rumor or situation that takes our fancy, or we sit in one place and let the information come to us. Taverns in general are goldmines of information, and ones like this that caters to dimension travelers of all types are prime places to hear about a specific caper."

She glanced toward the door. "Speaking of which, here comes a likely prospect now. Let me take the lead here, Little Sister."

Spyder turned to follow Pookie's gaze. Just inside the door, steadying himself on the back of a chair, was a warrior. His chainmail, helmet, and sword marked him as such, even though the body that was wearing it was rotund and hairy, topped with a head that sported a pig snout and tusks. Also noticeable was the fact that his left arm was in a sling, and he moved with a noticeable limp.

"Care to join us, friend?" Pookie said, raising her voice. "You look like you could use a drink and some sympathetic company."

The newcomer studied them for a moment, then shrugged and lurched his way over to their table.

"Thanks for the invite," he said, dropping heavily into a seat. "It's more than I expected. Whoever said 'No one likes a loser' sure knew what they were talking about."

"First things first," Pookie said and waved the barmaid over.

After another round had been ordered and delivered, including a large flagon of ale for the guest, the three settled into conversation. "Thanks again," the warrior said, taking a long draught from his flagon.

"Truth to tell, I was trying to decide between having a drink or getting a room. The war chest is about tapped out after paying the healers. By the way, the name's Trog."

"Pookie and Spyder here," Pookie said, indicating who was who with a wave of her hand. "Looks like you're coming off a rough job."

"Darn near got my head handed to me," Trog said, taking another drink. "Sounded easy going in, but they all do until you're up against it."

"What was the job, anyway?" Pookie asked. "You look to me like someone who could handle most anything and anybody."

"It was one of those 'Kill or scare off the beast that's terrorizing the countryside' deals," Trog explained. "This time around, it was a Hefalump. Never tangled with one before, but, like you say, I can handle most things without much problem."

"Don't tell me, let me guess," Pookie said. "No money up front. Just a reward if you're successful. Right?"

"Got it in one," the warrior confirmed. "That's where the 'It always looks easy going in' part caught up with me."

"Where was this anyway? Around here or another dimension?"

Trog leaned back in his seat and studied them with narrowed eyes.

"Not to sound ungrateful," he said carefully, "but you're asking a lot of questions. More than one might expect from casual curiosity. What's your interest in all this?"

"It's no big secret." Pookie shrugged. "We're in the same line of work as you and looking for a job. Since it sounds like your last find is still open and from the looks of things you won't be up to trying it again for a while, we might just look into it ourselves if the pay's right."

Trog set his flagon down with a loud think. "And what makes you think two females could pull it off when I couldn't?" he demanded.

"For one thing, as you pointed out, there are two of us." Pookie smiled. "And don't downcheck us because we're female. We've been around for a while and are still here. A lot who went up against us aren't."

Trog started to say something, then stopped and cocked his head. "Wait a minute," he said. "A Klahd and a Pervect working together? Are you two Aahz and Skeeve?"

Spyder choked on her drink.

"Right lineage, wrong gender," Pookie said. "Like I said, we're Spyder and Pookie. We know Aahz and Skeeve, though."

"You do?" Trog said, visibly impressed.

"Yeah. We worked with them on our last job," Spyder put in, wiping her chin.

"Let me handle this, Little Sister," Pookie said with a warning glance. "Since you seem to have heard of them, Trog, you should know that if we can hold our own free-lancing with the M.Y.T.H. Inc. crew, we might stand a chance with your Hefalump."

"Got to agree with you there," Trog said. "That gang has be tough rep."

"So where is the job you were talking about?"

"It's on a backwater dimension. Rinky-dink."

"That bad, huh?"

"No. That's the name of the dimension. Rinky-dink. I'll give you directions if you'll spot me another round."

"Really, Spyder, dear," Pookie said. "You have to be more careful about what you say and who you say it to."

"But I didn't say anything!" Spyder protested. "I did what you told me. I kept my mouth shut and let you take the lead."

"Except when you mentioned that we had done our last job with Aahz and Skeeve."

"What's wrong with that?" Spyder said. "He seemed really impressed. Besides, you were the one who mentioned that we knew them."

"That we knew them. Not that we had just worked with them," Pookie pointed out. "Think about it. The reason he was impressed is that Skeeve's crew has a rep for drawing the high-end, high-pay jobs."

"So?"

"So if we just worked with them, then it's not too big of a logic step to figure that we've got more than a bit of money on us. Not exactly the wisest thing to mention in front of an adventurer who just botched a job and is admittedly short of cash."

Spyder stopped short. "You mean he might have tried to take it away from us?"

"There's always that chance," Pookie said with a shrug. "I believe I mentioned that most adventurers are some form of thief. Not to worry, though. I kept an eye behind us when we left the tavern. He doesn't seem to be following us."

Spyder threw a quick glance behind them. Obviously, the possibility of their being followed hadn't occurred to her until just now. Pookie pretended not to notice.

"Well, we probably could have taken him if he tried anything," Spyder said with firm confidence.

"Probably," Pookie agreed. "Still, there's no need to stir up trouble unnecessarily. Remember we're professionals, dear. We're not supposed to fight for free. Ah! This should be the place just ahead."

Spyder hung back, slowing her pace. "Explain to me again, Pookie. Why is it we're going to talk to the sheriff?"

"Since we're pretty much legit this time around, it doesn't hurt to check in with the local law," her partner said.

"Never did like talking to the law." Spyder scowled. "It doesn't ever seem to work out to my advantage. In fact, I usually end up in trouble."

"That might be because you were usually in trouble before you talked to them," Pookie said, sweetly. "Look at it this way, Little Sister. From what we've heard, this job is going to involve us working the countryside. That's never been my favorite setting, since it's invariably full of things that go squish when you step on them and bite you when you're trying to sleep. If at all possible, I'd like to know what or who else will be out there with us. All we need is a bunch of trigger-happy bounty hunters that let fly at anything that moves. The sheriff here should be able to supply us with that information if we ask him nice. So smile pretty, and let me take the lead again."

The office they entered was small and cluttered, with empty wineskins and half-eaten plates of food scattered here and there. It was dominated, though, by the sheriff. He was stocky with a noticeable bulge around his waist-line, and outfitted in a wrinkled ranger uniform that

looked like he slept in it. That suspicion was easily confirmed by the fact that he was currently sitting behind his
desk with his head down on his arms, snoring nasally.
Spyder looked at Pookie with her eyebrows raised. Her
partner responded with a shrug and a roll of her eyes before clearing her throat.

"Um . . . Excuse me. Sheriff? Are you the sheriff?"

The man lurched upright, blinking dazedly. He did a
slight doubletake when he realized the nature of his company, and wiped a grubby hand over his face and beard,
forcing a smile.

"Sorry," he mumbled. "Long night and a slow day.
So . . . What can I do to help you . . . ladies?"

"We've heard that you've been having some problems
with a Hefalump," Pookie said. "Thought we might give a
shot at going after it . . . if the price is right."

"You have to take that up with the Duc." The sheriff
yawned. "He's the one putting up the reward. I can tell
you the money's good, though. Enough to draw a small
troop of sell-swords trying to collect it."

"The Duc?"

"He's the one who runs the territory around here. Actually, his name is Duke Rybred, but most folks call him the
Duc on account of the way he's built. He pretty much
stays on his estate just north of the town and leaves the tax
collecting and keeping of order to me and my deputies."

"If you don't mind my asking," Pookie said carefully,
"why isn't he having you and your deputies take care of
this Hefalump instead of advertising for outside help?"

"What, me? Go traipsing around the woods chasing
some huge critter that's only bothering the farmers?" The
sheriff seemed actually surprised at the thought. "That
wasn't what we were hired for. I'm more than happy to

leave it to the youngbloods who are out to make a name for themselves."

"Anyone out there ahead of us right now?"

"Naw," the sheriff said, scratching his beard. "Last one came back and left a couple days ago. There were a fair number parading through here for a while, but it's kind of petered out lately. Guess the word has gotten out that the Hefalump is tougher than anyone thought and doesn't take kindly to anyone trying to shoo it away."

Pookie looked at Spyder who shrugged in return. "Well, I guess we'll go talk to the Duc . . . Duke, now," the Pervect said. "Any tips you can give us on handling the Hefalump?"

The sheriff thought for a moment. "Take extra bandages," he said finally. "And be sure your insurance is paid up."

If the sheriff was unimpressive, the Duke of Rybred was positively underwhelming. Whereas the sheriff had been stocky with a bit of a pot belly, the Duc was short and pudgy. He also walked with a rolling waddle that made him look . . . well, like a duck. Though he dressed well, he had a habit of rubbing his hands together and licking his lips like a miser with an unexpected tax refund. It left one with a feeling one should count one's fingers after shaking hands . . . if one cared to shake hands at all.

"Well, well, well," he said, licking his lips and rubbing his hands together. "If nothing else, you two are the most attractive adventurers to try our little quest. Tell you what. Instead of going after the Hefalump and maybe getting your sweet selves dinged up or killed, what would you say to hiring on as my personal bodyguards? It would only be for public appearances . . . though I'm sure we would work out some kind of a bonus program for overtime."

"I think we'll take our chances with the Hefalump," Pookie said. "That was for five hundred in gold. Right?"

"That's right," the Duc said, apparently unaffected by the rejection. "Five hundred once the beast is killed or scared off. Now you two girls be careful when you go after it."

"You have no idea how careful we can be." Pookie smiled. "For example, how do we know we'll get out money after we've killed the critter?"

The Duc's smile wavered a little. "Why, because I've told you I'll pay you. Surely you don't doubt my word?"

"Not yours specifically," Pookie said. "Still, it isn't entirely unheard of that an adventurer has taken on some dangerous assignment only to find that when it was over, whoever hired him had a sudden memory lapse as to the exact amount promised. Some have even forgotten that payment was promised at all. On the off chance that something like that happened to us, we don't have much recourse. I mean, what can we do? Sue you? As I understand it you're the one who sits in judgment around here. We couldn't forcibly take it from you without having to face your household guards who, of course, would be on the alert at that time. Even if we got mad and just killed you, that still wouldn't get us our money. See what I mean?"

"Yes. I can see where that would be a problem," the Duc said, avoiding their eyes.

"Now, we don't mind risking our necks for money," Pookie said. "That's our business. It's just that we'd like

some kind of assurance that we'll actually get our money
at the end of it."

"What do you suggest?"

"Put it in escrow," Pookie said with a shrug. "Send the
money to . . . say, the sheriff to hold until the job's over.
We check with him, make sure the money's there and
waiting for us, then we go after your Hefalump."

"That's fine by me," the Duc said, licking his lips. "I'll
be glad when this situation is handled, believe me. As far
as I'm concerned, the beast could go on doing its thing. It
didn't bother anybody until they expanded their fields
into its territory. If the farmers hadn't threatened to withhold their taxes until I did something about it, I would
have just ignored the whole thing."

"Part of the price of ruling, I guess," Pookie said. "So, if
we're in agreement, we'll drop by the sheriff's . . . say, tomorrow to check on the reward. Then we'll be on our way."

". . . 496 . . . 497 . . . 498 . . . 499 . . . 500! It's all here."

Pookie waved at her junior partner as she poured yet
another flagon of wine for the sheriff.

"I gotta hand it to you two," the sheriff said, raising
the flagon in a mock toast. "I always thought the Duc was
clever, but you've got him beat. 'Put the money in escrow.' I tell you with all the sell-swords and adventurers
that have come through here, no one else has come up
with that move."

"We've just had a little more experience with money
grubbers than most." Pookie smiled, sipping at her own
drink.

"Umm . . . can I ask a question?" Spyder said.

"You not only can, you may," her companion said.

"Huh?"

"Never mind." Pookie waved. "What's the question?"

"Well, you keep talking about how clever the Duc is," Spyder said with a frown. "I wasn't all that impressed with him."

"Bit of a scum bag, isn't he," Pookie said with a grimace. "Do you see what I mean about the offers female bodyguards get?"

"So what makes him so clever?"

"You have to learn to listen closer, dear," Pookie said. "The Duc had no intention of paying us . . . or anyone else regardless of the failure or success."

"He didn't?"

"Add up the pieces," Pookie said, counting off the points on her fingers. "First, the farmers try to expand their holdings and run into a local critter, the Hefalump, that takes offense at their trespassing. Second, by his own admission, the Duc would have ignored it, but the farmers threatened to withhold their tax monies unless he did something. His response was to offer a reward to anyone who would kill or scare off the beast."

Spyder frowned thoughtfully, then shook her head. "So what's wrong with that?"

"Nothing's wrong with it," Pookie said. "It's actually very clever. He had to do something, so what he did was make an offer. A move that cost him no money or effort. Simply by making the offer, he kept the farmers paying taxes."

"And if anyone were actually successful going up against the Hefalump, he could renege on the payment and it still cost him nothing," Spyder finished. "That is kind of clever. But we outfoxed him with this escrow thing, huh."

"Not really." Pookie shrugged. "Remember the sheriff here answers to the Duc. That's why the Duc agreed so readily. Tell me, Sheriff, were your instructions to send the money back as soon as we went after the Hefalump, or were you supposed to wait until tomorrow?"

Silence answered her.

"Hey! He's asleep!" Spyder said.

"Yes," Pookie said without looking. "And with what I put in his drink, he should be out until well after midnight."

She rose to her feet and stretched. "So, Little Sister, gather up that lovely gold and we'll be on our way."

"What?" Spyder exclaimed. "You mean we're just going to take the gold without going after the Hefalump at all? But that's . . ."

"Stealing," Pookie said. "If you want to pretty it up, the Duc was ready to swindle adventurers by taking advantage of their short-sightedness. We're just returning the favor. Remember I told you that adventurers are thieves or killers . . . and you specifically said that, if possible, you'd rather be a thief?"

She paused and considered the sleeping sheriff. "Of course, if you've changed your mind, we could slit his throat on the way out."

"But won't they come after us?"

"And admit that they've been flimflammed? By a couple females?" Pookie smiled. "I doubt it. Even if they do, they don't even have our names when it comes to tracking us down. Looking for a Klahd and a Pervect, they'd be lucky if they didn't run smack into Aahz and Skeeve."

MYTH-CALCULATIONS

By Robert Asprin and Jody Lynn Nye

I eyed Guido as he slid into the booth opposite me. We were at the very back of the inn in the Bazaar, a favorite spot of ours to relax, but also to do business. It was one of the few places where a Troll such as I fit behind the tables as readily as Deveels, Klahds, and Imps, probably a tribute to their high-fat cuisine. I signed to the innkeeper to bring us the specialty of the house.

"Three strawberry milkshakes," I said. "Will that suit you, Tananda?" My little sister nodded, still keeping her attention on Guido. The Mob enforcer, as dapper as ever in his big-shouldered sharkskin suit, seemed uncomfortable, shifting on the slick bench. I caught the bartender just before he turned away. "Oh, and if anyone's looking for us, we're not here."

"Whatever you say, Chumley," the proprietor said, with a cheery wave.

"Thanks, Chumley," Guido said, keeping his fedora in front of his face.

"Well," I said, keeping my voice low, since Guido had asked for confidentiality. "To what do we owe this meeting? We always welcome a chance to chat with friends."

Guido worked a finger under his collar as if to loosen it. "Dis is by way of bein' business," he admitted. "Don Bruce has gotta problem."

Tananda's eyebrows went up, and I know mine were the mirror of hers. Though my face was masculine, enormous, and covered by fur, with tusks at the corners of my mouth, and hers was female, elfin, and beautiful, those people who knew our family could easily see the resemblance. "What kind of problem would he have that he can't handle by himself?" I asked.

"It's kind of embarrassin'," Guido said, hesitating again. "It's a financial problem. He's still flush, for now, but if word gets around he might start havin' to reach further down in his pockets, and dat he does not like to do."

I was cognizant of that. The Don was generous to his friends and those of his relatives on whom he doted, but he disliked having to "shell out," as he would say. "Word of what?"

"Well, it's somethin' goin' on here in the Bazaar, which is why I come to youse." Guido shot a quick glance around to make certain we were not overheard. Several Deveel merchants had noticed the three of us for, though we were in a private booth at the rear of the establishment, my size did not lend itself to subtle concealment. When I turned toward them and bared my teeth, they quickly not-looked at something else. Guido continued.

"You know how the Don's interests stand here on Deva. He takes a . . . personal interest in the well-bein' of the businesspeople here. For this service he expects a small weekly kickba—I mean, honorarium. That's just for goodwill. It ain't supposed to put no one out of business, and it ain't supposed to make anyone hurt. That comes if somethin' goes wrong. In exchange, we are, like, on call in case there's trouble. No one leans on one of our clients without us comin' in and makin' 'em stop."

"I understand all that, but where does the problem arise?"

Guido's face darkened. "There's someone else hornin' in on our deal here, you should excuse the expression. The deveel's in the details. The Don suspects dese same individuals have been runnin' small loans for the little guy. Now, you know how it's hard for anyone to operate in the Bazaar. Once in a while you need a little extra cash. Normally they go to one of the usual establishments, or they come to us. Everything's fine if you pay back on time. Anyone who tries to skip out gets leaned on. Now between the loans and the protection . . . I mean, insurance payments, all the action is with dis new group, and we're not gettin' our cut. The way they do it is not so different on the way youse guys were helpin' run the Don's operation, but when defaulters get the treatment from these new people, they ain't the same anymore. Geddit?"

"I believe so," I said. "Would you mind elucidating further?"

"I don't do no elucidatin'," Guido said, "but I'll tell ya some more. This action has been cuttin' into the profits the Mob has come to expect. I've tried talkin' to 'em myself, but they're not answerin'. And they're not trottin' back into the fold, like the Don wants. He sent me here, but I'm out of my depth. I need an enforcer to bring 'em all back into line."

"Why ask us?" I inquired. "Why not someone like Aahz?"

"Well," Guido admitted, "he ain't felt what you would call motivated lately, since the Boss left."

"He's the logical person, being, well . . . formidable."

"Yeah," Guido said, glumly. "I got him to go and lean on one of the, uh, clients, but they was too scared to comply."

"They wouldn't comply? With a Pervert?" Tananda asked, astonished.

"Per*vect*." I quelled my little sister with a look. Aahz was an old friend, and shouldn't be referred to by a derogatory title, especially one he personally eschewed. "What could possibly cause such a breakdown in authority?"

"More to the point," Tananda asked, interrupting me, "*who* is it? A rival gang?"

"I dunno," Guido said. "The, er, clients *can't* talk about it. We used . . . a li'l magikal persuasion, but I gotta tell ya, the results was not what you would call pretty. A guy explodes rather than give with the information like we asked him. And I know me and Nunzio didn't use nothin' that would have caused that kind of effect. It was self-inflicted." Guido toyed uneasily with his empty mug. "I'm askin', like, as a pal, to see if youse can't get these accounts back into the tidy line like Don Bruce prefers to see."

Thoughtfully, I ordered another round of milkshakes. The bartender, usually a loquacious soul, delivered our beverages, then departed hastily. I am accustomed to the looks of strangers, the horrified expressions when they gaze at me, a full-grown, and, if I may say it (as it is my stock-in-trade), a ferocious-looking Troll, but this Deveel was an old acquaintance of ours. Nor did any of the males in the immediate environ deliver the generally lascivious, speculative leers I have observed when they behold my sister the Trollop.

I might add that many have made the foolish assumption that because of my size and demeanor that I am the more formidable opponent of the two. It is not the case. Tananda is the fiercer sibling. I am proud of my little sister. For anyone who believes that I am at all jealous of her prowess, I remind them of *my* above-mentioned characteristics and invite them to take up the matter with me, personally, some time when I feel like enjoying a spot of freelance exercise or, as our friend Aahz calls it, a free sample reminder. No one has ever asked for two.

Guido was clearly hoping it would take only a visit from one or both of us to redirect the flow of funds toward Don Bruce's coffers from whatever inappropriate stream into which it was currently running. We were willing to give it a go, for old time's sake.

"Whoever it is must be packing some serious magikal hardware," Little Sister mused. "Guido, do you have a list of the merchants who are, uh, not complying?"

The enforcer pulled a hand-stitched leather document case from the inside breast pocket of his immaculately pressed suit. He extracted therefrom a small scroll and gave it to Tananda. She held it up to the light, frowned, then pointed a long-nailed finger at it. There was a POP! and a puff of green smoke.

"Not my color," Tananda said, wrinkling her nose at the acrid smell. "Don Bruce isn't taking chances on anyone reading this, is he?"

"That is the middle crux of the issue," Guido agreed.

"What was sealing the scroll?" I asked curiously. Magik is not an entirely closed book to me, but I may say that my expertise runs in the direction of physical exertion, not elder lore.

"Nasty Assassin's trick, Big Brother. You really wouldn't want to know the details. You'd call the results insalubrious or some other two-gold-piece word."

As I said, I am proud of my little sister. To detect and disarm such a trap in two economical motions is the hallmark of the consummate professional, sometimes defined as one that is still alive after more than one mission.

Tananda unrolled the document and spread it out. "Hmm. Cartablanca, the manuscript merchant, Vineezer the herbalist, Bochro, who deals in exotic toys—plenty of mixed technology in that shop . . ."

"What about Scotios?" I inquired.

Guido shook his head. "He's behavin' himself."

There were several more names on the list. Tananda and I read it several more times. She met my eyes with a puzzled glance. "What do all these people have in common?"

"I couldn't say," I admitted. "They're all Deveels, but that is the only trait I can detect."

"Most of 'em work alone," Guido said. "That'd make them vulnerable to a shakedown . . . I mean, an insurance proposal. That is why the Don takes so much interest in protectin' them."

"Not Melicronda," I pointed out. The wine merchant was in a tent not far from M.Y.T.H. Inc.'s own. "She employs three of her sons full time."

"What about the quality of their merchandise?" Tananda suggested. "All of them sell fragile or ephemeral goods."

Guido shifted in his seat, suddenly sweeping a glance at the other patrons of the inn. Inadvertantly, all of them retreated a half-step. "So does Palaka the rug dealer, but she's not on the list. And some of these are what you might call service providers. Though not the kind of service providers Don Bruce likes to keep under his protection."

"I see," I said.

"It's no good," Tananda said, rolling up the scroll and re-bespelling it before tucking it into her cleavage. "We'll have to visit each of them and find out for ourselves."

"No comment," said Vineezer, edging past me with a bubbling retort in his hands. The old Deveel put it onto a stone slab and reached for a big open jar and a minute spoon. The small shop smelled very pleasant with its heady aromas of drying herbs hanging in bunches all around the ceiling. A bit too heady, I thought, as I fought to contain a titanic sneeze.

"Atishoo!"

Plant matter went flying in every direction. The old Deveel was rendered momentarily green with powdered snakewort. A wreath of laurel hung drunkenly from one of his horns.

"I am so sorry," I said, attempting to brush him off. "Quite by accident, I assure you."

In the close confines of the tent I succeeded only in knocking him over. Guido grabbed his arm and heaved him up to a standing position.

"Why's he talking like a book?" Vineezer asked, eying me uneasily.

"Eloquence curse," Tananda said, leaning against the center tent pole with her arms crossed. "Plays merry hell with his strength. But that will be back soon. Maybe *very* soon, if I can't persuade you to tell me what I want to hear."

"I . . . I can't," Vineezer said, retreating from the fierce look in her eye. His normal red complexion paled to an almost Imp-pink. "They'll put their mark on this place—they did it once already."

The three of us looked around.

"I don't see no mark," Guido growled, his hand moving toward the inner pocket where I know he stowed his miniature crossbow.

"They did!" Vineezer protested desperately. "Look at this place! Look at that!"

We all did. "Place okay," I said, remembering to use my Big Crunch voice. "Place clean."

"That's just part of it," the merchant wailed. "A herbalist's shop isn't supposed to be *clean*. The dust floating in the air is full of magik. I use it to tweak potions too delicate for enhancement spells. A millionth part of dragon scale—I can't afford a balance sensitive enough to weigh that out. When this place is properly dusty I can snatch a fragment out of the air. I haven't made a decent scrying potion in a week!"

"They cleaned out your shop?" Tananda mused.

"Yes, and that's not all they'd do . . . if I talked. So, please go away. I can't tell you any more."

Guido muscled up to the trembling Deveel. "You don't really want me to go back to Don Bruce and tell him you was unwillin' to fulfill the part of the bargain that he was so obligin' to make with you, do you? He might have to ask me to interfere wit' you personally."

Vineezer's face flushed burgundy red, and he shoved us back toward the tent flap and out into the street.

"It's better than being *alphabetized*," he hissed. The tent flap swished down between us and clicked locked with an audible snap. I set my shoulder, prepared to charge back inside so Tananda could ask him again, but she laid a hand on my arm.

"Never mind, Big Brother," she said. "Maybe some of the others will be more communicative."

Her assumption proved to be incorrect. If anything, our further researches were less fruitful than our first attempt. Yet we did not return to the tent empty-handed. We gleaned certain points concerning our unknown quarry.

"They're very neat," Tananda said, glancing around at our tent and appearing to compare our housekeeping unfavorably to that of our foes'.

"They are more cautious in the way they phrase their verbal contracts," Guido said, sitting down and putting his fedora on his knee. "Not one word concerning their appearance can be gleaned from our converse with our clients. It appears to be a condition of the protection racket—I mean, arrangement."

"And they aren't very greedy," I added. "With no disrespect to Don Bruce, their demands are relatively modest."

"But they go by a flat fee," Guido protested. "Don Bruce prefers a percentage. When times is good, he prospers alongside his clients. When times is hard, well, they all get a break. This way, they all give the same even if business is bad. And you saw how scared the clients were not to miss a payment."

"It strikes me that this means they're not in this for the long haul," Tananda concluded. "If they did they would take market fluctuation into account the way the Mob does."

"But who knows how long this short haul will run?" Guido asked. "Don Bruce ain't gonna wait for them to get out. He wants 'em gone *now*."

"Right," I said. "That will take decisive action on our

part. We need to catch them in the act of collection and dissuade them from doing any further business in the Bazaar."

"Right!" Guido agreed, smacking one big fist into the other palm. "We'll teach 'em they just can't march in an' take over somebody else's territory."

The easiest place to observe was Bochro's Toy Shop. His tent stood next to Melicronda's wine shop, nearly opposite the M.Y.T.H. Inc's establishment on the same thoroughfare. Since none of our associates were presently in residence, we three took the vigil in turns.

Naturally it was our business to know something of the comings and goings throughout the Bazaar, but I had never before made a close study of the traffic that came and went over the course of a day. The streets were as empty as they ever were: the perfect time for someone to pass unnoticed. I peered through the gathering gloom. It was no use looking for strangers. The nature of the Bazaar as a nexus in between so many dimensions meant that only one in twenty passersby was familiar, and only one in two hundred was a friend. I knew that there was little that could not be had for a bargain, but even I was not prepared to see some of the goings-on. It was just after twilight, when most of the merchants had folded up their tents for the day, but before the night life of the Bazaar really got under way.

Directly in front of our tent two tough babies, clad in black leather diapers, toddled up and kicked the legs out from underneath a plump, insectoid shopper, and stole its bags. Since officially we were not supposed to be at home

I had to restrain myself from leaping out there to assist. In any case my help was not needed. The insectoid extended its carapace to reveal a long, sinuous body and a dozen more legs. The babies hadn't made it past three store fronts before their victim stretched overhead, retrieved its possessions, and delivered a sound spanking to each one of them. They sat down on the ground to cry until another likely victim came their way.

As night fell, the character of the transactions became more personal. Beings of the evening made offers to passersby for various services of the usual and unusual kind. A token or two would change hands, and a pair or trio or group would wander off to a handy tent.

Almost all the traffic was outbound from the merchants' establishments. The rare ingress was what I was interested in. If Guido was correct, this was the day on which payments were normally due to the Don. Though they were now diverted to person or persons unknown, they were being picked up on the same schedule.

I saw someone I knew weaving in and out of the crowd of tourists looking for a likely (and safe) place to have dinner: a fellow Troll named Percy—his real name. His nom de guerre, as mine was Big Crunch, was Mangler.

His was not a casual visit to our street. His movements were as furtive as a Troll's could be, attempting not to step on the party of Imps who had stopped to look over a street map in the middle of the thoroughfare, as he "not-looked" at the tents opposite our own. When he was nearly in front of our doorway, he quickly looked both ways, then pushed into Bochro's.

Quietly I tiptoed into Tananda's room and whispered from the doorway, "We have a bite."

Before I'd quite finished the sentence she'd sprung off

her bed and bounded to my side. "I'll get Guido," she said. "Can you handle him alone?"

"I think so," I said, albeit a trifle uncertainly. Mangler was a good foot wider than I was. I'd known him in school, where he was all-varsity wrestling champion our final year, though in hand-to-hand martial arts I held higher ranking.

Hoping he had not come and gone while my back was turned, I left our tent and turned into the flow of traffic. At the end of the row, still keeping an occasional eye on my destination, I pretended to have forgotten something, clapped a hand to my head, and plowed deliberately into a group of Deveel merchants holding a quick negotiation in the open area of the intersection.

"Damned clumsy Troll," one of them snarled.

I showed my teeth and snarled back. They blanched pink, and scattered, their deal forgotten. I turned back. Mangler was emerging from the tent, still furtive in his actions. He made for Melicronda's. I opened my stride and caught him just before he went inside.

"What ho, Percy, old thing," I said, draping an arm across his shoulders.

"Chumley!" he said, surprised. "Me mean, Crunch! Me punch!"

"You Mangler, me strangler," I said, raising a fist. I lowered my voice. "What say we nip around the corner for a quick drink, old friend?"

"Chumley, I can't be seen talking to you, old chap," Percy said, looking worried. "It's more than my job's worth. Or my hide."

We'd gathered an audience by that time: Klahds, who were looking for free entertainment; Imps, who would bet on anything; and Deveels, who were willing to indulge them. Percy shook his head almost imperceptibly. I understood. I advanced on him with a roar, my arms above my head. He countered by growling back, and swiping at my chest with an open, clawed hand. Swiftly, I knocked it aside and closed with him, wrapping my arms around his body.

Any other Troll in the audience would quickly have recognized Scenario Number 15 of the *Trollia Handbook for Dealing with Other Species*. In order for a pair of Trolls to have a private conversation in public, when all other means failed, this particular brawl would ensure that we had frequent close contact, while making very certain all others stayed out of the way of our wild-looking, but carefully choreographed, swings. Even a dragon would have hesitated to wander into the fray between two full-grown Trolls.

"What is it, old man? Deveels?" I asked. I twisted around, grabbed his wrist, wrenched upward, and Percy flipped into the air, landing on his back. The fall wouldn't hurt him. It didn't even knock the breath out of him. He scissored out his powerful, furry legs and caught me about the waist. I dropped back, and he sprang up and knelt on my chest, hands going for my throat. I roared aloud to cover his furtive whisper.

"No, worse!" I grabbed his throat with one hand, and he let out a loud squeak, which covered my next question.

"What could be worse than Deveels?" I asked. A further grunt covered another query as he shook his head. "Do you owe money to the Gnomes?" We rolled over and over together in the dust. An open path cleared ahead as our audience pursued behind. I bellowed.

"Worse!" Percy whispered, his face desperate. "I can't tell you! The old one will get me if I talk!"

I almost forgot to wait for his covering roar. "Who?"

"Don't ask any more, old man," Percy said, sitting on my back as he twisted my foot around. I shouted in pain. He was so nervous he was actually hurting me. "Please. I'm asking you as an old friend. I can't say any more; we might be overheard. Hmm, this is your turf. I know M.Y.T.H. Inc. well. I'd best let you win this round."

It was good of him to realize that. I assessed my position, face down in the dust. The only winning move I could make would render me utterly filthy, but that, as Aahz might observe, was show biz. I gathered my three free limbs underneath me, grabbed the earth and turned myself until I was aligned with my twisted limb. In doing so I mashed a great deal of the street into the front of my fur, but it was worth it for the denouement: I rose to all threes, Percy still riding my back, and, pushing myself upright on my one leg, deposited him to the ground. He fell, as though stunned. I jumped on him, grabbed him by shoulder and crotch, heaved him into the air, and threw him into the crowd.

"Thanks, old man," he said, just before I let go. Deveels, Imps, Ssslissi, Klahds, and others went down as a full-grown Troll landed on them.

Brushing myself off, I stumped up the street. Tananda was standing in between two tents cleaning her nails with a dagger, where she had a perfect view of the whole brawl. She grinned up at me. Guido hulked in the shadows behind her.

"Messy but effective, Big Brother."

"What'd he tell you?" Guido asked.

I glanced around. Night had fallen sufficiently to conceal our return to our tent. "Let's go inside."

"The old one?" Tananda asked, sitting at our conference table after I brought them up to date on my tête-à-tête with Percy. "Old what? A dragon? What's big enough to intimidate a Troll?"

"Well, we aint' gonna get no data out of the victims, or outta their collectors," Guido reasoned. "What's next?"

"Next," I said, tenting my fingers together on the table rather like logs at the corner of a rustic cabin, "we must lure our perpetrators out of hiding."

"How do we do that?" Guido asked, skeptically.

"They target small enterprises, do they not?" I asked. The other two nodded. "Then we establish our own."

"And wait to be approached," Little Sister said, approvingly. "Good idea, Big Brother. Now, all we need to do is figure out what would attract their interest."

"Somethin' that earns a lot of money," Guido said. "Alla the businesses have a much higher income than overhead."

"It's too much trouble to do market research on growing trends and get in merchandise from another dimension," Tananda said thoughtfully, "so, a service business of some kind. I think I know just what will do the job."

I didn't like the mischievious gleam in my sister's green eyes. "What do you have in mind?"

"Hairdressers?" Guido said, disbelievingly, surveying the contents of our hastily rented tent.

"Beauticians," Tananda corrected him, spreading out her hands in satisfaction. "It's perfect. We don't need any merchandise, apart from a few bottles of commercial tonic and cologne. And believe me, every being alive has a streak of vanity that could use a little buffing up. We will simply cater to that streak."

"But we know nothing about beauty culture," I protested. "We might disfigure someone, or hurt them."

"That's the beauty of it, if you will excuse the joke," Tananda said. "You don't have to know anything. You make it up as you go along. You can do whatever you want to the customers, and they will love it. They'll come back for more and they will bring their friends! Trust me."

And so it proved. The very next day dawned upon the opening of A Tough, A Troll and A Trollop, Beauty Specialists. The flaps of our tent were flipped coyly open to reveal the furnishings that we had obtained overnight from a few merchants who knew us well enough to open at midnight and ask no questions as to why we suddenly required three reclining pedestal chairs, diverse mirrors, basins, curlers, irons, combs and brushes, lacquers for hair, and nail files, unguents, lotions, shampoos, dyes, and spangles. Tananda appeared trim and professional in a green smock that matched her hair. Guido and I felt awkward in identical green coats. They fit, but that was all that a charitable mind might admit.

"We look like morons," Guido said, echoing my very thoughts.

"You look fine," Tananda assured us. "Smile! Here comes our first customer."

I seized the comb and scissors that I had chosen to be my tools. Guido picked a hot towel out of the salamander-powered steam box. Into the tent peered an Imp matron. We braced ourselves.

"Are you . . . open?" she asked.

"Yes, we are!" Tananda beamed, putting her arm about

the Imp's shoulders. "Come in!" She winked at me over the pink female's horned head. "What can we do for you?"

I held the scissors in my fist like a weapon, the points just sticking out beyond the percussion edge of my palm. Was she the "old one" Percy feared? To me she appeared to be only of middle age. Her reply, delivered shyly, easily assuaged my concern.

"Well, I need . . . I'd like to look better."

"You look wonderful," Tananda assured her, maneuvering her deftly into the center chair. "All we do here is to enchance your natural beauty. Don't we, boys?"

"Yeah," Guido said, all but throttling the towel in his hands.

"Yeh," I grunted. As advertised, a Troll and a Tough. The Trollop already had the matter in hand.

"You see? We just want you to feel confident in your own charm."

"Oh!" The matron pinked up, looking pleased. "Then . . . I'd like the works!"

Tananda clapped her hands.

We did not emulate a well-oiled machine, but swing into action we did. The Imp found herself the vortex of a whirlwind of tasteful scarves and draperies that covered her dress's loud print (Imps have notoriously tacky clothes sense), leaving her head and face thrown into stark relief. For an Imp she was not unpleasant to behold once her garments ceased clashing with her cerise complexion.

"Scalp massage," Tananda ordered. Nervously, I moved in, oiled fingertips at the ready. A Troll's fingers are strong enough to punch holes in the skulls of most of my fellow dimensional beings. I hesitated to touch her until Tananda

delivered a sharp slap to my upper back. I plunged ahead,
grasping the Imp's scalp between my hands, and began
to rub.

"Oooh!" the Imp cried. "Oh! Aaaggh!" I halted at
once, concerned that I'd hurt her. "Oooh aaah!" the Imp
moaned, tilting her face to look up into my eyes. "That
feels so good! Don't stop, please!"

So I didn't. I massaged away, accompanied by an aria
of moans and cries of pleasure. Guido, seeming as awkward as I'd felt, applied a hot towel to her face, eliciting a
shrill scream, also of pleasure. Tananda moved in and attacked the Imp's long nails with file and a pointed stick.

Guido tossed aside the towel and moved in with the
box of paints. My hands were too large, and Tananda was
occupied with a more delicate job, so it had fallen to Guido
to become the cosmetician. He was not happy about it, but
Little Sister had explained that no beauty salon was complete without a purveyor of color and texture, so he was
elected by default. His first essay with a brushful of black
paint was not salubrious; the Imp jerked her head back
just as he applied it to her brow, causing the horizontal
line to extend vertically up her forehead. Seeing that it
was impossible to salvage his original design, he made the
other side the same. Then, bright orange cream in hand, he
daubed at one eyelid. By the time his brush arrived at her
face, however, the Imp had moved again, and the dot hit
her somewhere over the ear.

"Hell with it," Guido breathed. Attacking his palette
like a virtuoso attacks his instrument, Guido drew and
dotted, limned and lined, until the Imp's horned head was
a work of art, if one cared for the oeuvre of a modern ab-
stractionist. At that, it was not unpleasant to behold.

The female continued to shriek and cry out, but by the time we released her from the chair and placed a hand mirror before her she was smiling broadly. We'd also attracted an audience. As the Imp opened her belt pouch and poured a handful of coins into Tananda's palm, there was a rush toward the chairs. A bevy of females, Deveel and others, got into a scratching, kicking fistfight over who would occupy the third seat. Tananda shot me a quick but meaningful look. I stomped over to the crowd, every step making the floor shake, selected one female at random, lifted her by the scruff and plumped her decisively into the disputed chair. With my brows drawn down nearly to my eyes, I aimed a look at the others that quelled their grumbling. They crowded outward against the tent's inner perimeter to watch.

The Imp staggered out, and we turned our attention to our new customers.

Many hours later, Guido folded down the tent flaps and tied them in a double knot.

"I don't want no one else comin' in here today," he said firmly. "I am so tired I could fall asleep over the salamander box. Broads! You were right, Tanda! You can do any fool thing to 'em, and they love it! I spilled face cream down one woman's cleavage, then they was all clamorin' for the same thing. And then when that Deveel showed up with a cart full of scarves, I thought they'd tear him to pieces. They all wanted to try his stuff on at once."

"I told you," Tananda said, smugly, counting through the day's receipts. She piled the coins in stacks. There were several, one of them of gold. "Very, very nice. And our cut of the Deveel's profits make a nice addition to our income. We've already nearly paid for our furnishings. This business is very profitable! Once our job is over we might keep the salon going."

"Speak for yourself, Little Sister," I said, pouring the last basin of iced water over my head and sinking to the carpet that was covered with clippings of hair, shed scales, and feathers, and dozens of dirty towels. "I would rather go back to my nice, peaceful life as an unfashionable intimidator."

"There's just one thing more left to do," Tananda said. "Birkli! Did you get all of them?"

A small creature popped out from behind a tent panel. His body was about the length of my hand, with a hard, blue-black carapace that glittered in the twinkling light of our oil lamps. He was a Shutterbug, from Mount Olimpis in the dimension of Nikkonia. In their natural habitat the males used their ability to reproduce beautiful sights they'd seen on the iridescent scales of their compound wings to impress prospective mates, so they were both artistic and well-traveled. Tanda had had no trouble persuading one to come to Deva to assist us, promising him unique views that he could use to wow the ladies back home.

"All right on the roll," Birkli chirped, extending a thin black leg. Wrapped around it was a narrow coil of a translucent substance. Tananda unrolled it and looked at it with the aid of a magic lantern behind. The lantern expanded the images so they were visible to larger creatures than the diminutive Shutterbug. "I put them together so you could see them easier. What do you think? What do you think? Do you like them?"

As was the case with all males of his species, he was eager for Tananda's approval. Guido gave me a grin. He and I might as well have been absent. Tananda patted the Shutterbug on the shell and he glowed.

"They're perfect," she said. From the collection on the table under the mirror she handed him a small but brightly polished silver coin. "There, a Gnomish groat. And the same every day, as we agreed?"

"Perfect, perfect, perfect!" the little creature carolled happily, stowing the coin away under his hard shell. I believe he was happier to receive praise than money. We have had less amenable allies.

"Good," Guido grunted, as the Shutterbug climbed up into the canvas roof to sleep. "Let's go see if your buddy can recognize any of these dames."

"Gentlemen, gentlemen, take it outside, please!" pleaded the bartender at the Shoppers' Repose, an inn at some miles remove from our establishment. Percy agreed to meet me there for a prescheduled brawl. Roaring, I threw a table at the innkeeper. Percy snagged it neatly out of the air before it came anywhere near the Deveel, and broke it over his knee. "I'm begging you, go aw—watch out!"

Percy threw a lamp at me. I crushed the glass chimney, but kept the lit torch in my hand as he charged me, thrusting me out into the street.

"I want you to study these images and tell me if you recognize any of them," I whispered, as we grappled for the torch. We were festooned with strands of horse brasses, banners that had lately decorated the ceiling of the bar, and hanks of one another's fur. No one who was not looking for it would see a strip of microscopic portraits. It draped across his eyes.

"I've told you I can't do it," Percy howled. I pushed against his throat with my forearm. With a resigned sigh that sounded to the uninitiated like a moan of pain, scanned it while I bore him to the ground, still with the flaming brand over his head to light up the beetle-wing cells. "No! No one!"

He put a foot into my belly and flipped me over him. I landed on a party of Imps coming in the door. I scrambled to my feet, hoisted them up and dusted them off. With a final look of seeming disgust toward Percy, I uttered a loud "Huh!" and stumbled out into the street.

Tananda and Guido fell into step alongside me as I left the tavern. "Even I saw his reaction," she said. "Relief, more than anything. None of these is our pigeon."

"Well, he certainly ain't no pigeon himself," Guido admitted. "Back to the hairspray, huh?"

"Every day until we get it right," Tananda said. "Cheer up! Maybe you'll start to like it."

"I was hired by Don Bruce to rub out trouble," the enforcer said grimly. "Not massage it."

After four days more of primping, polishing, and grooming I was beginning to get the hang of the higher beauty culture. As far as I could see it was as easy as Tananda had said: all one had to do was look confident and improvise, and the customers would be pleased. Ladies who had always retreated to the other side of the thoroughfare when I stomped toward them in the Bazaar were stopping me to coo and offer praise.

"I'll never go back to Mr. Fernando after you!" one Deveel maiden said, clinging to my arm, her face still a symphony of fluorescent colors from Guido's brush. "I told him, 'you give a good scalp rub, but nothing as wonderful as I get at A Tough, A Troll and A Trollop!' And your Mr. Guido's sense with cosmetics! Inspired! I feel so beautiful when I leave.' "

I grunted some sort of acknowledgment as I stumped toward the beauty shop. Mr. Fernando was probably not best pleased to have his clientele deserting him.

"We had better solve this problem soon," I told my two partners, as I reached our rented tent, "or every other personal care specialist is going to be out for our blood."

Guido reached into his coat and patted the miniature crossbow that I knew reposed there. "That kinda fight I'd welcome," he said. "Not this fancy-dancy stuff with a dozen perfumes and green drapes."

"And who cuts your hair?" Tananda asked, teasingly.

"Mr. Chapparal," Guido said, with an indignant look. "He's a cousin of Don Bruce. Does a real good job. His shop's all violet with stained-glass mirrors."

"I understand the problem we're creating," Tananda said with a sigh. "But we can't force our quarry out of the woodwork. They have to emerge by themselves."

"I wish they'd hurry," I admitted. "Percy grows more nervous with every nighttime encounter we have. He may flee the next one."

We had not much longer to wait. As I assisted one ravished Gnome lady from a chair late one afternoon, I became aware that two figures were standing in the doorway. The two Pervect women, one an elderly female in a flowered frock and straw hat leaning on a cane, the other much younger and more fashionable in a split, knee-length leather skirt and a very tight bustier, looked as though they might be potential customers, but their all-over mien did not speak of devotees in search of a superior pedicure.

The Pervects' aspect also attracted the attention of the other customers in the tent. One by one they found excuses to slip out of the door or melt unobtrusively through gaps between the canvas panels of the walls. Before too long we three were alone with the Pervects and one hapless Imp matron who lay in a chair with her feet up, unable to leave because she was being ministered to with a foot massage by Guido. As soon as the chair tilted down, she sprang from it, pressed a large silver coin on Guido, and waddled hastily out of the tent.

"You've forgotten your hat," Tananda shouted after her, waving a straw round-crowned chapeau pierced twice in the crown to allow the Imp's horns to protrude through. The Imp did not turn back, but undulated faster up the way, becoming lost in the crowd. Tananda, annoyed, spun and bent an annoyed eye upon the two remaining visitors. "Thanks. You've just lost us our profit for the afternoon. A few days like this and you'll put us out of business."

"Oh, we would never do a thing like that on purpose," the elderly Pervect said, grinning so that her yellow teeth looked like a chestful of knives. "They must all have misunderstood. We want you to stay in business. Don't we, Charilor?"

The other Pervect, shorter and stockier, resembling a female Aahz, smiled, her own dentition gleaming like sheet lightning. "But of course, Vergetta. That way everyone makes a profit."

"That's what I like to hear," Tananda said.

"Including us," Vergetta added, with emphasis.

"I beg your pardon?" my little sister asked, putting steel into her voice.

"Not at all, darling," the elder Pervect said, taking her hand in a grip that caused Tananda to wince. I moved forward, but the shorter Charilor moved in between me and them. "You're setting out on a difficult enterprise, you little dears, and that involves risks. Now, you may not be aware of how many risks, but an old lady like me, I've seen a lot in my life. I want you to stop worrying about outside pressures and succeed. To do that, you have to minimize disruptions."

"Like this visit of yours," Tananda said, pointedly.

"Exactly. Now," said Vergetta as she settled heavily into one of our chairs and put her feet up on the foot rest, "you wouldn't believe how far I've walked today, darlings. Would you have a glass of tea somewhere? No? You will next time."

"What makes you think there's gonna be a next time?" Guido asked. He didn't pat his breast pocket for emphasis; one only did that to underline a threat, and we were meant to look harmless. Besides, to indicate to a stronger enemy such as Charilor where his weapon was located was only to provide an extra one for her.

"Oh, of course there's going to be a next time, you *muzhik*. Here's the proposition." Vergetta slapped her scaly knees. "We keep disruptions out of your way. You do business. You're grateful, so you give us a present . . ."

"Like . . . a cut of our profits?" Tananda finished. "No way, grandma. We just barely made enough in the last few days to pay rent on our equipment."

"This trash? You may also need our friends in the moving . . . I mean, furniture trade. Not a cut of the profits; a flat fee is what we have in mind. A fixed expense, like rent. Five gold coins. So you always know how much you have to clear every week, because that's when we'll be back."

"Week? Five coins a lot! Bad week, no money," I interposed. "What if no money?"

"What if you have a bad week?" Vergetta asked, looking up at me. "Oh, my darling, you don't want to find out what happens."

"We're only getting started," Tananda said, looking alarmed. "If you take our profits this week, there won't be a next week."

"All right," Vergetta said, getting to her feet. She patted Tananda's cheek. "So maybe we give you a freebie this time. But we will be back. We are watching you."

"And don't get cute," Charilor grunted. "The Bazaar is big, but if you fold up tent here and start up somewhere else, we will find you."

"They *are* new in town," Tananda said, once we'd sealed the tent and put a spy-eye on it to make sure no one was listening in magickally. "Birkli!"

"Ye-es!" The Shutterbug flitted down from his concealed perch. "Scary green ladies! But I managed to get all the others before they ran away. I'm good! I'm the best!" He landed on Tananda's shoulder and handed her a coil of underwing cells.

"Of course you are," Tananda said indulgently as she unreeled the Shutterbug's images and held them up to the magik lantern. "Subtlety is dead, gentlemen. I thought we'd have to uncover their identities from a crowd of subjects, but they just marched in here and made their proposition on the first visit."

"Dat means," Guido said, raising his eyebrows, "dat dey're in a hurry."

"Yes," I added thoughtfully. "I wonder why."

"We'll have to learn more about them," my little sister said.

"Should I take the images to Percy?" I asked.

"No. No sense in frightening him. We're sure who they

are. We'll just have to play along for a week or two, and hope they don't hop before we figure out their angle and close it up for good. I'd hate to have them think they can just march in and use the Bazaar for an ATM." She looked around. "I miss Skeeve. He'd have asked what that is."

I'd have been hard pressed to put my finger on the difference between the days before the two Pervects made their visit and the time after, but I sensed an uneasiness in our clientele that had not been there before. Not that I ever anticipated that Deveels, Imps, and the like would ever have become comfortable, nay, eager, to have a Troll anywhere near them with an eyelash curler, but palpable fear began to percolate through the tent. I didn't like it. During the subsequent days I found myself growling quietly while mixing cosmetics, provoked by I know not what unknown pressures. Guido kept casting his eyes around suspiciously, his hand never far away from the weapon concealed underneath his green smock. Tananda also was more highly strung than usual, pushing back cuticles with heartless precision, only snapping out of her trance when a customer yelped in pain.

"I don't like this," she whispered, when she stopped near my chair to toss a basin of water out the tent flap. "I sense depressing magik surrounding us like a cone. I've felt all over the place, but I can't find the source—no live magician within range, not even a handy line of force."

"It may be purely technological," I remarked. "A remote installation that makes use of a stored source of power. Perv is known to be comfortable with both technology and magik."

"Well, so are we," Tananda said. "We had better do something, or by the end of the week we won't have a single client."

That night we took the place apart, quite literally. I wrenched up the chairs one at a time so that Guido and Tanda could look underneath them. We unstitched the tent panels, tested every jar, vase, bottle, and container that might conceal a device. We checked the lamps and rugs for disgruntled Djinni or Efreets, both known to inhabit such items. Little Sister even employed Assassin techniques to find footprints or airprints of every being that had been anywhere near us since the Pervects' visit.

"Anyone who's been here has come in on foot except Birkli," Tananda said, after our searches proved fruitless. "See the wing prints?" Guido and I looked at the feathery traces on the air that her magik had brought out.

"Wait a minute," Guido said, pointing at two different lines of flutter marks. "Dese ain't the same as dose. I've tracked a lotta fly-by-nights, and I know my wing prints."

"By heavens, you're right," I declared, after a quick inspection. "What can that mean?"

"I don't know, but I know who can tell us," Tananda said, tapping her foot impatiently. "Birkli!"

"Coming right this minute, lovely lady! Ready when you are!" The gaudy Shutterbug dropped out of the ceiling. "Here are today's ladies, one and all! Are they perfect? Are they beautiful?"

Tananda held out a hand and he lit upon it. She drew him close to her face, her voice purring. "But you're leaving one out, aren't you, Birkli?"

"Not one, not one, fair green girl!" Birkli protested, his antenna drawing down over his multiple-lensed eyes. But he seemed a bit put out.

"Who is she?" Tananda asked.

"Who?" I interrupted.

"The flitter who made those other wing prints," she said, without breaking eye contact with the Bug. "You were supposed to take an exposure of every being who came into this tent except us. Why didn't you take one of her?"

"How'd you know it's a she?" Guido asked.

"How do I know?" Tananda repeated. "Look at him!"

The Shutterbug did seem to be in the deepest throes of embarrassment. "Forgive one who loves too well but not wisely," he wailed. "Such a beauty was this Lady Bug, to fall in beside me as I flew out among the fabulous sights of the Bazaar. Her spots, so black; her shell so red! She praised my wings, my legs, my scales! I thought it would do no harm to bring her here, where it was private. I showed her my images, and she was impressed, most impressed!"

"If that isn't the oldest line there is, bringing a girl back to look at his etchings," Tananda fumed. "And I suppose she left you a keepsake of some kind?"

Birkli flew back into the folded cloth that served as his temporary quarters and returned with a small glowing sphere the size of his head. "Only this, fair lady. Forgive an ardent male too easily blinded by the beauties of female-hood!"

Tananda held it up between her thumb and forefinger. "As we surmised, Big Brother. A bug, as only a Bug Lady can make it. Compact, powerful and easily concealed." She tossed it to me, and I crushed it in my fist. Birkli backed away uneasily as I let the powdered remains fall from my hand to the floor.

"We're not gonna dust you," Guido said, going eye to eye with the Shutterbug. "Not if you cooperate. Now, let's see the pic of the moll."

Hastily Birkli produced a strip of wing-cells and handed them over. The denizens of Trollia were ardent lovers themselves, but even I felt abashed as Tananda held them in front of the magik lantern. "Hot stuff, what?" I said, awkwardly.

"We're not trying to pry into your private life," Tananda assured Birkli, "but we've got to be careful. I thought we told you that."

We accepted Birkli's apologies. Tananda paid him off and sent him back to Nikkonia. "We don't really need him any longer," she explained. "We know who our enemies are now, and we know they're quick-thinking and willing to exploit any weakness they perceive."

"I agree," Guido said. "We were buggin' ourselves, under the circumstances. How do we know he didn't sell 'em images of us?"

"Didn't need 'em," Tananda said shortly. "They knew we were here. Two days' observation would tell them that if we weren't the beauticians we claimed to be, we were putting in enough work to prove we wanted to be taken for beauticians. To a blackmailer, that's enough to exploit."

"So, what is our next attack?" I asked.

"We pay them," Tananda said simply.

"What?" Don Bruce's enforcer burst out. "Not a bent nickel."

"Yes, a bent nickel," Tananda corrected him, with a wide grin on her face. "And whatever else they ask for. *This* week. I have a plan."

With a wave around our heads to create a silence spell to

shut out any potential eavesdroppers, my little sister drew us close. In a moment, we were smiling as widely as she.

Tananda allowed us to look as sour as possible when Charilor came by the next afternoon to collect their fee. "There, I told you," the Pervect said, watching Little Sister count coins grudgingly into a sack. "Five gold coins wasn't so hard to raise!"

"It would have been a lot easier if you hadn't put a gloom spell on the place for two days," Guido said resentfully.

"That was Vergetta's idea," the chunky Pervect said, with a twist of her lips, as she glanced back toward the elder female waiting by the entrance to the tent. Did I sense disapproval of her senior's methods? "But you still managed to raise the dough. We should've asked for more."

"We couldn't have raised more," Tananda said, eyes wide, managing to sound a little desperate. "This is all we made this week. I mean, everything! We've even had to put off some of our expenses, and our creditors are not happy. You're not going to raise your . . . fee . . . are you?"

Charilor swept the leather purse into her belt pouch and stood up. "No. You have our word: our demands will never go up."

Vergetta shook a finger at us from the doorway. "You'd still better have the same waiting for us next week."

"We will have your payment here waiting for you," Tananda promised. The Pervects stalked out. Warily, shyly, our regular customers started slinking in.

Guido chafed visibly over the course of the next week. He objected to the delay during which Don Bruce would lose

yet another round of "insurance" payments. I also knew
he was worried lest anyone from the Mob would come in
and see him performing beauty rituals instead of his
usual, somewhat more insalubrious tasks. Yet, when he
wasn't thinking about public humiliation, he handled his
duties with aplomb. Now comfortable with the balms and
unguents, he massaged, polished, and clipped with a flourish. He'd completely lost his fear of the body paints, and
where he'd created cranial graffiti before, he was now
performing abstract art, each piece unique for the lady
who bore it, smiling, out of our salon. The customers
adored him. He was gathering quite a little coterie. Some
of his regulars had begun to bring him small gifts, treats,
and gratuities. Those attentions embarrassed him as much
as would the appearance at the door of one of his Mob fellows.

I myself found it difficult to keep from humming a little tune as I awaited the arrival of our extortionists. Action, that was what was called for. Tananda's plan had
risks, to be sure, but in her estimation it had at least a
forty percent chance of success. Those were not odds I
would normally have celebrated, but since no one else
had succeeded in resisting or exposing these blackmail-
ing females, it was worth a try.

At the lunch hour on the appointed day, we supped
alone in the tent. We had deliberately made few bookings
to coincide with the time we expected Vergetta and Charilor to appear. Our midday repast was simple, consisting
of food that we had prepared ourselves from ingredients
we had not allowed out of our sight since we had brought
them from another dimension early that morning. The
chances that the Pervects had observed and followed us to
our sources of supply were nil: while on a provisioning

run we never returned to a dimension twice, and we took all precautions upon our return. That suggestion had been made by Guido, who had, during his military career, accrued lengthy experience in existing in hostile territory. For all the years that we had lived in the Bazaar, I had never before had cause to feel it hostile, but for survival's sake, and the sake of our mission, I must think so now.

Darkness interrupted the blaze of sunshine from the doorway. I glanced up from my now empty trencher. It was the Pervects. Guido, beside me, clenched his fists on his knees underneath our humble tabletop.

"Good afternoon, darlings," Vergetta said, sailing into the salon as though she owned it. But she did not. Yet.

"Hello," Tananda said cautiously.

"So, are you ready for us?" The elderly Pervect sat down on the bench and nudged Tananda until she moved over to make room.

"I suppose so," Tananda said. She produced the box that contained our receipts for the week. Vergetta rubbed her hands together vigorously, then dumped the load of coins out onto the table. Her fingers began to sort through the coins as though they were indeed greatly practiced at the skill. With a stern expression Charilor loomed over my shoulder, if such a term could be used to describe the actions of a being considerably shorter than the one being loomed over.

"Hold on here," Vergetta said, piling the last coin in a neat stack. She peered at Tananda, her yellow eyes narrowed to horizontal slits. "There's only four and three-quarters gold coins' worth here."

"That's all we've got," Tananda said. "It's been a slow week."

"I don't believe you."

"Well, that's all there is. Take it or leave it."

Charilor leaned across the table and took my little sister by the throat of her smock. "Just who do you think you're talking to, babycakes?"

Tananda looked up at her without fear. "Blackmailers, that's who. Scaly ones, at that."

"Why, you pipsqueak!" Charilor heaved her up over her head and flung her at the mirror, cracking it across. Two silver coins' replacement value! Tananda dropped to the floor.

"Oh, I say!" was surprised out of me. Charilor turned her attention on me, grabbing the fur of my upper arm in a perfectly manicured claw. With the amazing strength that was one of the Pervish people's advantages, she heaved me over the table, and began to pummel my back and head. I twisted, wrenching my arm loose. She merely swung a leg up and planted it on my back, continuing to pound. Her blows hurt!

"Chumley!" Guido stood up to come to my aid. Vergetta, feeble as she seemed, was still a Pervect. As he rose, she swept her cane out and around in front of him, snagging an ankle. He tripped. She hauled him up into her lap like a toddler and held him helpless around the shoulders and body, while shouting encouragement at Charilor.

"*&^% you!" Guido snarled. "Lemme go!"

"Such language!" Vergetta snapped, shocked. She opened up her befanged mouth and roared. "Nobody uses that kind of language around me!" Guido's hair blew over his ear from the blast.

In the meanwhile, at the cost of a hank of my fur I worked free and sprang up out of reach. Charilor charged after me. Tananda leaped to her feet and launched herself at the back of the Pervect.

"You leave my big brother alone!" she yelled. She landed on Charilor's back as the Pervect reached for my throat. I knocked her arms apart and made to put my hands around her neck and face, closing off her airways. Against the combined might of an Assassin-trained Trollop and a Troll trained in the martial arts, the contest should have been over at that moment.

It was not. Charilor used the last minim of space remaining between her mighty jaws to draw in a pinch of the palm covering her mouth, and chomped down.

"Ow!" I bellowed. I am ashamed to say that I lost my grip. Blood dripped from my hand. My wits regained, I threw my shoulder at her body. Tananda applied her arms in a nerve-blocking hold that ought to have disabled Charilor.

It only seemed to make her angry. She went into a whirlwind frenzy, striking out with arms and legs. For a time I could see nothing but a green blur, then the maelstrom drew us in. The room revolved around and around us. I recall punching, kicking, even biting, but when the scene resolved itself, Tananda was draped over a chair, panting, and Charilor was literally wiping up the mess on the floor using yours very truly as a mop. Guido, sporting an eye in several colors that would have done credit to his palette, was lying face down yelping across Vergetta's lap. She spanked the mob enforcer's backside again and again, punctuating each blow with a syllable.

"You must *ne*-ver use that kind of *lang*-uage in front of a *la*-dy!"

If I had not been resolved already to discredit and drive these females from my purview, I was now. How dared she humiliate my friend! Charilor let go of my chest fur and let me stagger uneasily to my feet. I went to my little sister's aid, raising her from the chair across which she was draped.

"I'm okay," she croaked, though her face was as color-ful as Guido's. I imagine that if one were to part my fur I would be as battered as she. She clung to me for a while, then tottered away. "Look at this place!"

I surveyed the ruin of our erstwhile establishment, then looked back at her. "Place mess," I said.

Vergetta looked up from the punishment she was deal-ing Guido. "Why, you're right. Charilor, this will never do!" She sprang up, spryly for her appearance. "We must clean up this tent at once."

"You bet," the younger Pervect said. As readily as they had set about destroying it, they began to tidy it. With a wave of her hand the elder Pervect reunited the shards of our shattered mirror, heaving it back into place on the hook on the wall. Charilor picked up all the scattered bot-tles and jars, and sorted them into various shelves and boxes.

"No, they don't go there," Tananda said, running after her. "Put that over there. No, the cosmetics go on *that* shelf! Please! Don't mix the scale colorants with the nail varnishes! We won't be able to find *anything* when you're done!"

Charilor paid no attention, though Tananda pounded on her back with all her strength. I went to take her by the shoulders. They were shaking with fury. Her eyes blazed up at me.

"No wonder Vineezer didn't want them in his shop anymore!"

"Take it easy, Little Sister," I whispered. "Calm. Keep control. We're nearly there."

Stifling her anger, she watched as the two females transformed the ruin they had created into a perfectly neat and incomprehensible whole.

"There!" Vergetta said, dusting her hands together. "All better. Now, there's just the little matter of the last quarter gold coin that you owe us for this week."

This was it. I held myself tense as Tananda went humbly forward, her hands working together.

"I told you, we just don't have it. You've got all the money we took in. We're even talking about food money."

"Now, now, chicken, it's not so bad," Vergetta said, picking up Tananda's chin with a cocked finger. "You'll eat tomorrow. What about bookings?"

Tananda showed her the appointment ledger. "We didn't make any more for today. We didn't know when you were coming, and frankly, you scare the other customers."

"So?" Vergetta asked, raising a scaly eyebrow. "How do you plan to pay off the rest of your debt?"

"Service?" Tananda asked, hopefully. Only I saw the glint in her eye. "If you'll let us give you the works . . . I mean, our best beauty treatment, everything, exfoliation, styling, manicure, makeup, I *promise* you'll get your money's worth. It'll be more than a quarter gold coin's value."

The two Pervects conferred for a moment. "It's not so standard, but why not?" the elder said. "Just this once, maybe."

"Yeah," Charilor agreed. "You do a pretty good job on the others. Okay." She swung into the nearest, most recently repaired chair and settled back. The works. Careful, though. I'm ticklish."

I moved in on her, fingers outstretched, to begin the scalp massage. I hoped neither of them could see the tremble in my hands.

It took longer than we expected, since none of us could find a thing in the rearranged shelves. Tananda kept up a pleasant line of meaningless chatter as she filed the tips off the Pervects' claws and varnished each one a shimmering hue.

"The gold goes with your eyes," she assured them. "All my Pervect customers like yellow, but *this* is a special shade I save for the best clients."

Like every being who had sat, crouched, or hovered in those chairs during the last few weeks, Vergetta and Charilor preened and bridled when they beheld their gradual transformation in the glass.

"And now," Tananda said, winding cotton batting in between their fingers so the top coat of the polish wouldn't smear, "our cosmetician, Mr. Guido, will put the crowning touches on your beauty treatment."

We both held our breath. Guido didn't look at all tense. He knew the job he had to do.

"Okay, ladies," he said, loading a brush with pigment. "Tell me if it tickles."

In all his days as a reluctant beauty consultant he never had a finer hour. His strokes were ones of genius, drawing subtle tones of red, ochre, and more gold up to the tips of the Pervects' large, pointed ears, down to the sides of their cheeks and over their brows. Curlicues of jewel hues decorated their eyelids and around their cheekbones. An orange-red that did not shock against the green of their scales was applied to their lips. As they admired their reflections, Guido took up his fluorescent palette and added very subtle enhancements here and there, decorating the backs of their heads in a Baroque and complicated design. When at last he put down his brushes, Vergetta rose and picked him up in an enveloping hug.

"Honey, you're a genius. And this is all original art?"

"I'll never do another one like it," the enforcer promised, a grin coming unbidden to his lips.

"Okay," Charilor said to Tananda. "You're right. This is worth more than a quarter coin. Good job."

"I think so," my little sister gushed, trying not to laugh in front of them. "Thank you. Now, enjoy your day. I think you'll find it feels so different when you've been worked over . . . I mean, given the full treatment . . . I mean, been *enhanced* by A Tough, A Troll and A Trollop."

Vergetta pinched her cheek. "You're so cute. See you next week, then, darling."

And the two Pervects sauntered out into the sunlight. We watched them until they were out of earshot.

"How long do we have until the paint starts to react?" Tananda asked.

"About fifteen minutes," Guido replied.

"We had better depart from here, then," I said. "When does Murgatroyd's team come to retrieve the equipment?"

Tananda squinted at the sun. "In about an hour. I paid the damage deposit."

"We won't get it back," I said, cheerfully. "Coming, Guido?"

"Just one more thing," the enforcer said. He carefully put his slab of paints down on the floor, then smashed his foot through it. Wiping his foot on the bare ground, he grinned up at us. "I've been wanting to do that for over a week."

"You've earned it," I assured him. "Don Bruce will be very pleased with you that everything is going to be back as he prefers it."

"As long as he don't hear about how I did it." He felt an eye with gingerly fingers. "Including the part about lettin' myself get beaten up so they'd fall for the ploy."

"He won't hear it from us," I promised. "It would bode ill for our reputations, as well."

"In about five minutes, those two are going to come boiling back here," Tananda said, digging out our D-hopper from its concealed space under the rug. "We'd better hop out of this dimension for a while. I would also like to put some ice on this eye, and maybe a little concealer."

"Don't do a thing," I told her, taking her arm and escorting her out into the sun. "You look beautiful just the way you are."

"Twice now those three T's have gotten away with paying short," Charilor complained, as she and Vergetta marched down the street toward their next stop.

"Don't worry so much," Vergetta said, waving a hand. "This time did they tell us to go away? No, they found a way to pay in kind. That shows they're intimidated. They'll behave themselves."

"Good," Charilor said "I'd hate a good cleaning to go unappreciated."

"Oh, how I hate it when they grouse," Vergetta agreed, tapping the ground with her cane. "But we do look gorgeous. Admit it."

"Ex . . ." a Deveel said, peering curiously as he overtook them.

Vergetta nodded her head regally.

"What does 'ex' mean?" Charilor asked.

"Who knows? Might be the latest slang for 'pretty hot mama.'"

Two Imp maidens carrying embroidered straw marketing bags passed them, then giggled loudly. Charilor spun, glaring. The girls hurried away. A male voice behind them spoke slowly, as if uncertain what he was saying.

"Extor . . . ?"

Vergetta rounded upon a Gnome, whose eyes widened as she glared at him. He disappeared in a puff of smoke.

"Extoringist," said a little voice near their feet. "Mama, what does 'extoringist' mean?"

"Hush!" a Deveel matron said, hustling her toddler away from the furious Pervects.

"Extortionist!"

"Extortionist!"

"Extortionist!" More voices took up the cry.

"Where?" Vergetta demanded. "Where? Who's saying that?"

"It's right there," a Klahdish male said, grinning right in their faces. "Says so, right on the back of your heads. Yeah, both of you!"

"Why, you . . . !" Charilor started for him, manicured nails out and ready to tear his face.

"That's right," a mournful voice broke over the sound of the crowd. It was the herbalist Vineezer, standing in the door of his dusty shop, his eyes glowing with unrequited revenge. "Those horrible women have been taking money away from poor old honest merchants like me for *weeks*, now."

Vergetta shouted at him. "You! Did you do this to us?"

He only grinned, as the crowd continued to chant. "Extortionist, extortionist, extortionist!"

"They've robbed me, too!" yelled Melicronda, as her three strapping sons flanked their mother at the door of the wine shop. "Taking bread out of our mouths!"

Gradually, ominously, the faces of the shoppers in the crowd turned from idle interest to open anger. Instead of being frightened as Charilor and Vergetta lunged at their erstwhile victims, they moved toward them, seizing whatever they could find to use as weapons.

"We'd better get out of here," Vergetta said, turning and fleeing up the street with the mob in pursuit.

"What about the plan?" Charilor wailed, as a thrown stone zinged past her ear. "We still need more money!"

Vergetta ducked a few stones as she felt in her purse for their D-hopper. "To the pits with the plan! The plan won't go anywhere if we're not alive to help! It's those damned beauticians! They marked us! Labeled us! Now everyone knows who we are!"

"Grr!" Charilor growled. "I knew that 'free makeover' was too good to be true!"

Vergetta spun the wheels on the little device and grabbed for Charilor's hand. She pushed the button as they dashed around a corner in between two shops. Her voice echoed on the air as they vanished. "As soon as the coast's clear again, I'm going to go back into that tent and tear all three of them into pieces they can stuff in their own little cosmetic bottles!"

But no one was left to confront. Within an hour, five or six heavy, multi-legged creatures, supervised by a Deveel with a clipboard, arrived and cleared out everything, including a broken cosmetic palette on the floor. Shortly, there was nothing remaining of A Tough, A Troll and A Trollop but the sign hanging by one hook over the door.

An Imp matron passing by peered forlornly into the empty tent.

"Mr. Guido?" she called.

MYTH-TER RIGHT

By Robert Asprin and Jody Lynn Nye

I sauntered into the Palace of Possiltum like I owned the place, pretty much my normal way of entering a building. Massha's summons had sounded urgent, but I wasn't going to look as though I was in a hurry, in case the problem she was having was with someone here. I had been taking some time alone for myself, but I didn't like it when my friends were in trouble.

"Hey, Kaufuman," I called to one of the uniformed guards at the portcullis. "How's it hanging?"

For a moment the pink-faced guy goggled. There was only one short, green-scaled guy with handsomely pointed ears, mysterious yellow eyes, and dagger-pointed four-inch fangs in the kingdom, to my knowledge. Kaufuman recognized me immediately.

"Lord Aahz, sir!" Immediately he straightened up and held his halberd higher. I threw him a salute as I went by, sighing over the inadequacy of sharp pointy sticks as deterrents to invasion. I had never been able to convince Hugh Badaxe to go more high-tech in the castle armament. He claimed that they could get it if they wanted it, but in the meantime it just meant more accidents. Couldn't argue there. For what Queen Hemlock paid her soldiers, she was lucky to get men who could hold the weapons the right way up, let alone ones who were as dedicated to her defense as the guys who served her and Rodrick.

I ran into the current Minister of Agriculture on the stairs leading to Skeeve's—I mean, the quarters of the Court Magician. Even after a few months I was still not used to the status quo. "Hey, Beadle, Massha upstairs?"

"Oh, hello, Lord Aahz," the square-built Klahd said, peering up from his scrolls of paperwork. The guy really needed a good secretary. "No, I believe the Lady Magician is in the Residence. The cottage. Out in the gardens." He waved a vague hand.

"I know the way."

Since she'd married General Hugh Badaxe and taken over Skeeve's job as Court Magician, Massha had really blossomed. She'd gained confidence, starting to rely upon her own magikal skills as much as the wealth of gizmos that hung jingling about her more than generous figure.

When I got to the cottage, a wedding present from Don Bruce, Massha was hanging in the air like an orange balloon in the cathedral-ceilinged living room, supervising a couple of guys on a ladder who were replacing the chandelier.

"Careful, you cuties! There are sixty crystal drops on

this one, and I want sixty to get the floor all at the same time. Get it?"

"Yes, Lady Massha," they chorused as if they'd heard it before. But one of them accidentally knocked a hanging prism loose, and it fell.

"There, what did I tell you?" she exclaimed, tilting into a nosedive to save the crystal, but I got to it before she did.

"Did you lose something?" I asked, holding it up to her.

"Aahz, sweetie!" she cried, throwing her arms around me. Between her strength and her levitation bracelet, she lifted me right off the ground. "You came! Thank you."

"So," I said, when I got my breath back, "what's the problem?"

"Come this way," Massha said, leading me through the archway into the kitchen-dining area. "We can get some privacy in here. I love this house to pieces, but it's cozy— read 'small' in real estate terms." She gestured to a large carved wooden chair with a cushion on the seat and a few small pillows to stuff in between sore lumbar muscles and the tall curved back. "That's Hugh's favorite chair. It's low slung so he can stick his legs out in front of him. He hates footstools."

"Too easy to knock out from under you in a confrontation," I agreed. Badaxe and I had been on opposite sides at one time, but never on the subject of strategy. "Glad to hear he's not going soft even though he went in for wedded bliss."

"It's great," Massha said, firmly. "When you find the right person, it's heaven. You should try it, Aahz."

"Been there, done that, bought the T-shirt," I said, settling into the chair with pleasure. It really was comfortable.

She drew me a mug of beer from a cask in a cradle on the counter. All the comforts of home. "So, what's so urgent? You've evaded the question twice. I know there's a favor involved, but we're old friends. The answer's yes on almost anything, exceptions being on things like getting married again."

Massha let her antigravs bring her down to earth, and she perched on the front of a handsome upholstered chair made to her measure. I could have curled up in it sideways.

"I just feel awkward knowing I have to call in a favor," Massha said with a sigh. "Do you do much formal hunting?"

"No. If I'm hungry I know a thousand restaurants a D-hop away. If I'm really stuck out in the boonies I'll kill and eat whatever looks edible, no ceremony involved. The formal stuff's like the guy said, 'the unspeakable in pursuit of the uneatable.'" I glanced at her. She was plucking at the edge of her orange harem pants with uneasy fingers. "Why don't you take riding lessons from Hugh?"

Massha dropped the filmy cloth and gave me an exasperated expression. "Aahz, honey, look at me. You've known me for years. Can you see me on a horse?"

"Well, no," I admitted. Massha had no illusions about her figure, and I cared enough about her as a friend not to pretend I didn't understand. "But you don't expect me to do the riding, do you? I scare the hell out of horses."

"Not these," she assured me hastily. "They'll handle a Pervect. They're trained to hunt beside dragons."

Some memory stirred. "Massha," I asked warily. "How'd you get involved with the Wylde Hunt?"

"Princess Gloriannamarjolie is an old pal," Massha

said. "I was her babysitter for a while on Brakespear. She was a real brat when she was six or seven. No one had ever said 'no' to her before I did. There were some pretty fierce tantrums before she learned her limits. She liked it when I did magik for her, and I thought there was a great girl inside all that spoiled nonsense. We achieved a mutual respect, and we've been corresponding off and on for years. Now she's old enough to lead the hunt, and she asked for my help."

"She's the quarry? It's a suicide mission!" Unlike the Klahds, who rode horses and followed a pack of dogs after fox-wolves over fields and through forests, a brutal enough sport, Brakespear had a pack of dragons that pursued a wily princess across the landscape. The hunt began at dawn. If the princess kept away from the hunters until sunset she was free. If the dragons caught up with her, well, there usually wasn't much left. The mask or ears was awarded to the winning hunter. I was appalled that this was still going on.

Massha read the look on my face. "Those days are gone. It's only scent-hunting now. Glory's got to keep away from the hounds until sunset. The hunters are judged on style, fair play, riding, control of their dragons, and, if they're lucky, catching up with the princess. She's been training all her life for this. She's ready."

"But for this we'll need a dragon for the pack. We haven't got one."

"Yes, we have," Massha said, with a little coy smile that should have sent me racing out the door as soon as I saw it. "I borrowed one." She opened the back door of the cottage. A sinuous blue form twisted around in its own length at the noise, recognized me, and came streaking toward

me. It knocked me over and started licking my face with a
long pink tongue and breath that smelled like a volcano's
dung heap.

"Gleep!" it carolled joyfully, in between slurps.

"Dammit, get off me!" I roared. Massha put a hand in
Gleep's collar and hauled him back. I sat up, wiping the
slime off with my sleeve. "You say you *borrowed* Gleep?
Skeeve's not here?"

"No," Massha admitted.

"Then who's gonna handle this fool lizard?" I asked.
Gleep rolled his large blue eyes at me, wanting to get
loose and greet me again.

"I've agreed to undertake the task," said Nunzio, coming in the same door as the dragon, but at a easier pace.
"We get along pretty well, don't we, boy?"

"Gleep!" Gleep agreed, trotting over to lave the Mob
man with the Tongue of Doom.

"So why do you need me?" I asked Massha. *Slurp.*
Gleep trotted back and soaked me again. I wiped the disgusting wetness off with the back of my hand. ". . . Me,
the overgrown newt and Nunzio?" Gleep gave me a look
of adoration mingled with reproach, or maybe I was reading too much into his expression. He was still a baby, for
all that he was twice as big as any of us except Chumley.

"There's still a prize," Massha said. "For the hunter
who bags the princess, or, if she's better than they are,
earns the highest points, the finest treasure the king has to
offer. And I've got to tell you, Aahz, Brakespear has some
terrifically hot stuff in the treasury. As crown princess,
Glory had the keys to the playground. We used to go
down there and try things on. It was enough to give a girl
dreams."

I liked the sound of the treasure, but I was too old a

hand to believe in a free lunch for the guy who could stay on his horse the longest. "What's the catch?" I asked.

"Glory has been out looking over the course every day for the last three months. She's been seeing . . . well, shadows or shapes. She's certain someone's following her over the landscape, getting a look at where she's planning to go. She's afraid that whoever it is is out to interfere with the hunt. Every once in a while they get protesters who picket the hunt, calling it brutal and outdated. Glory's dad has guards posted around, and they know the signs of an incipient demonstration. Whoever's been out there is more subtle than that. And the king has recently acquired a few terrific goodies for the treasury, a couple of them genuinely magikal. The prize is likely to be one of those. Glory wants her hunt to be fair and square. It's dangerous, you know, hot stuff. People can still get killed, even though it's for fun. If anyone's messing with it, I want it stopped."

"All right," I said. "You've convinced me. Your Princess Glory sounds like she's reading all the signs right."

Massha leaped up and hugged me again. "So you'll do it?"

"I'll do it," I gasped out. Joyfully, Gleep sprang over and licked me again. "Dammit, don't *do* that!"

The following week found me wearing ridiculous breeches and a jacket that only needed the too-tight sleeves to tie behind my back to make it fit for lunatics. I refused outright to put on the helmetlike hat a bunch of the participants were wearing, preferring to depend upon the toughness of my Pervect skull and save my reputation as a snappy dresser from total ruin. The boots were the only things I liked: shiny black leather with just enough heel to catch the stirrups but wouldn't make me trip while back down on terra firma.

It was the day before the hunt. My borrowed mount, a hiphippohippus named Fireball, came from Glorianna-marjolie's own stables, a buckskin mount like a cross be-tween a horse and a rhinoceros. Its big barrel-like body had one deep, diagonal ridge running from midpoint down to a leg's length beneath the withers. It had delicate legs for its build, with bunched muscles in the shoulders and haunches that would make it a good jumper. The beast's spoon-shaped ears swiveled back and forth as I climbed aboard to try it out for size. The natural saddle ridge was suprisingly comfortable. A harness buckled about his barrel in front of the rider provided reins and stirrups. The grooms on both sides shortened the stirrups considerably until my feet fit into them. Not one adult Brakespearan I saw was my height. All of them were at least a head taller, usually more. When the princess had taken us on a welcome tour of the palace guard I felt like I was walking through a forest.

Gloriannamarjolie herself was a strapping girl; not in Massha's class, of course, but tall and big boned, with a healthy, pink-cheeked outdoorsy complexion, long blond hair, and green eyes similar to the fox-wolves that hunters in other dimensions pursued. Brakespearans resembled Klahds fairly closely, except that their ears were pointed at the top instead of round, and their hands were almost pawlike with short fingers, the fifth digit a cross between a thumb and a dewclaw, and a sixth digit just like it on the opposite side of the palm. Plenty of good manipulative talent, and, by the cording in the sturdy arm attached, the strength to back it up. The carvings that decorated both wooden and stone surfaces would have been considered art anywhere.

"All set?" the princess asked. She sat towering over me on a white beast with a set of wicked little pointed horns in between its ears. It lifted its lip in a sneer at me. I bared my teeth and growled back. The 'hippus danced out of reach, and I wheeled Fireball around.

"Ready," I said.

"Then let's move out!"

Massha and Nunzio, the latter holding an eager Gleep on a leash, stepped back. She looped the reins between the dewclaws on either side of her right hand, set her left hand on her hip, and kicked her mount in the sides. "Come on, Suzicue." Fireball and I followed.

"Don't fall off, Hot Stuff!" Massha called. Setting my teeth, I clenched my knees around Fireball's sides. We thundered away.

The hunting course was off limits, but Glory led us out on a path in a stretch of woods that ran beside the river that fed the castle moat. A stiff wind beat the water up into mini-whitecaps. I could feel the tips of my ears starting to chill.

"A bracing breeze!" Glory shouted over the gale. "Open him up and see what he can do!"

My mount was already galloping hard, jarring my rear like a jackhammer. I dug in my heels, and was nearly bowled over the beast's tail as Fireball threw it into over-drive. If I hadn't seen dragons move I would never have believed a creature that big could move so fast. The trees around me blurred into a brown picket fence. Another white blur passed me as Glory, on Suzicue, hurtled ahead. I heard the princess's hearty laugh.

"Ha hah! Exhilarating, isn't it? Tally ho! Yoicks!"

The thundering gait turned into a speedy lollop, easier on my spine than the canter, but now we were running into the forest. Low-lying branches swept over me, threatening to scoop me off. Grimly I clenched the reins and leaned down over Fireball's neck. As I told Massha, I'm not built for the saddle. I found myself digging my toe talons into the mount's side. He didn't seem to notice, probably because of the boots. He was too busy tossing his head to clear twigs out of his eyes. I put my head down next to his neck as I tried to keep Suzicue in sight. It'd take me forever to find my way back in these thick woods. If I'd had my magik, I'd have popped back to the castle and told Massha I resigned.

Over hill and down dale we galloped, pounding through the undergrowth. We were following a trail, but it was thickly overgrown. No surprise, if no one used it but Glory and her family. Birds fluttered upward, calling. Showers of leaves and seeds rained down on me. I tightened my grasp on Fireball.

A thin branch hit me in the forehead like a hot wire. I let out a bellow of pain.

Through the trees I saw mottled shapes scatter and flee: animals running from the sound of my voice. As Fireball crested the hill in Suzicue's wake I spotted another shape, one moving *toward* me. It stood upright on two legs, not on all fours or all sixes like the rest of Brakespear's wildlife. I squinted, trying to see details. Twigs lashed my face. I spat out leaves. Just as suddenly as I had spotted it, the mysterious shape vanished. Whatever it was had gotten close enough to get a look at us, then disappeared on the spot. That spoke of intelligence and probably advanced magik or technology. I caught up with Glory, and rode back to the castle in thoughtful silence.

"You were right to call us in," I told her and the others, once we were closeted in her personal study and Massha's privacy bracelet had drawn a cone of silence around us. "There is someone out there, scoping out the woods."

"I have a thousand forest rangers," Glory argued. "It could have been one of them." I could see she didn't believe what she was saying.

"So what do we do?" Massha asked.

I sighed down to my bruised end. "We go with Plan A, but we'd better have Plans B and C as backups. We join the hunt tomorrow."

"Gleep!" announced the dragon. He was the only one who seemed happy about it.

"Stirrup cup, good sir?" asked a strapping Brakespearan appearing next to my mount. He presented me with a brimming silver goblet shaped like a skull.

"Heady liquor, is it?" I asked.

"Sire?"

"Never mind." I took the cup and drained it. "Tally ho and yoicks." I tossed the empty back to him. He withdrew, bowing. I took a good look around.

The misty morning air was full of the smell of brimstone and rotting meat as the Master of Hounds, as he was still called, organized five dozen assorted dragons by size with the help of a dozen handlers. Gleep, one of the smallest, was at the front with a couple of wyverns and a half-grown wurm. Nunzio, holding up a meaty bone, made him sit up and beg. Even though Gleep had been a royal pain in the posterior since the day Skeeve, er, acquired him, he was kind of cute. At a distance.

Fireball started at something invisible, dancing under me. I tightened my knees, and my muscles reminded me that they'd had a hard time the day before.

"How are you doing, Aahz?" Massha floated over to me from the royal reviewing stand. She was dressed in brown and green, the royal colors of Brakespear, to match Gloriannamarjolie.

"I'm remembering why I don't do this for fun," I gritted.

"Attention, all of you!" We turned to face the stand. King Henryarthurjon smiled down on us. He was a big, muscular Brakespearan with fox-red hair going white at the temples and green eyes like his daughter's. He held out his hands for silence, spreading out all four thumbs in a gesture of welcome. "We are gratified to see so many puissant hunters assembled here to participate in our daughter's Royal Hunt!" Rousing cheers interrupted him, and he smiled paternally at Glory. Glory held her hands up over her head in a gesture of victory. Her outfit was classic camouflage: A long-sleeved dress of light-absorbing brown and green mottled fabric covered her from shoulders to knees; no velcro or zippers. Tall, soft boots that would absorb the sound of stepped-on leaves or twigs were cross-gartered on her long legs, and slung across from one shoulder to the opposite hip was a split-leather bag that appeared to be driving the dragons into a greater frenzy than they'd usually be in. I assumed it contained the bait she would use to draw her trail. A pair of gloves were tucked into her belt. "She will give you a good run, my friends. The rules are three in number: the hunt shall commence at my signal. It will continue until sunset or until a hunter captures the princess—alive, naturally. Points will be given for style, courtesy, riding, coursing, handling of one's hound, and, of course, success. The hunter who bags the princess wins the grand prize, the finest treasure in the kingdom." He snapped his fingers, and two pages in army-surplus tabards staggered up onto the dais carrying a solid gold box. "This is a most remarkable treasure chest, my friends and guests. Once an item has been entrusted to its depths, it will always be safe, even when it is taken out again. If a treasure is stolen, one can always retrieve it by reaching into the chest. As far as I know this coffer is unique throughout the dimensions. I think you will agree it is a worthy prize, what ho?"

The assembled hunters let out a collective " 'Oooooh." I raised an eyebrow. I was impressed. That was definitely a goodie worth having.

The king raised a finger. "*However*, if she manages to elude all of you, the prize will go to my daughter. A con-solation award goes to the hunter who has garnered the most points. These are our five judges, and their decision is final."

The king gestured behind him with an arm toward the others on the stand. Massha was among the five. We'd agreed that the best way for her to keep an eye on things was a bird's-eye view, floating above with the help of her flying ring. As an official judge she could call for help from the others or from the army of forest rangers who'd be accompanying the hunt.

I looked around me at the other riders, trying to spot which one might have been the shadowy figure in the woods. Massha and I had scanned the area looking for footprints or any other identifying spoor and come up empty. Like me, the hunters were already in the saddle—ridge, so it was hard to guess which could be the right height. In riding hats, helmets, little red riding hoods, and crowns, none of the heads matched the silhouette I had

half-seen. I couldn't exactly go up to the Samiram of
Porzimm and tell him to take off his turban. This snake-
skinned nobleman had an entourage bigger than Elvis's.
Next to him, on a dancing charger the size of a rhinoceros,
was a good-looking Whelf seven feet tall named Prince
Bosheer. The magnificent pointed ears sticking out of his
mop of wavy black hair weren't as handsome as my own,
since they were tan like the rest of his skin. Something
about Bosheer made me look at him twice, but I couldn't
put my finger on what made me uneasy. I was definitely
concerned about The Niraba, a dark-furred female with a
whip-thin body whose personal attributes far outweighed
the rest of her. She looked us all up and down with a spec-
ulatively sensual expression on her face. Reminded me of
a former girlfriend of mine. I always made sure I was heavily armed when we went anywhere, because fights tended
to break out about whom she was going home with. I recognized a Deveel called Alf—short, I now learned, for Al-
fibiades (you can't sue your parents for that kind of abuse;
it's a way they get even with you in advance for the time
you wreck the family chariot). He looked uneasy on his
'hippus, a beast even smaller than mine. His eyes absolutely glittered when he saw the treasure chest. Right
there I knew I had my number-one suspect. Deveels were
just exactly the type to tilt the playing field in their direction by scoping out the field in advance. I wished I could
analyze some of the mud on his hooves.

Nunzio showed up at my side. He put a small studded
wand into my hand. "It's a controller. Gleep has never
needed one to behave, but it's a way for you to keep in
touch with him over distance. If you push this button," he
indicated a baby-blue stud, "he'll stop. The red one will

make him sit down, and the green one will make him run back to you wherever you are. That will help if you get lost."

"I don't get lost," I growled, mentally crossing my fingers that I wouldn't have to eat those words.

Nunzio nodded. He knew me. "Right. The other thing you're gonna need is this." He gave me a red, football-shaped mass the size of my hand. "In case one of the dragons gets out of hand. Toss it into its mouth or into its flame. The smoke will paralyze it. Good luck."

I tucked away my aces in the hole and clenched my reins. Mass assassination by dragon was by no means out of the question as a way to win this contest. If none of the hunters was out to cut the others' throats, we all ought to be perfectly safe, but better to consider the worst possible scenario in advance than later while they're trying to identify your remains to return to your family.

The Master of the Hunt blew a fanfare on his horn. "My lords and ladies, the hunt will now commence! Forth the quarry!"

Gloriannamarjolie grinned at the assembly, then leaped off the dais. Before our eyes, she seemed to vanish. I heard rustling in the undergrowth.

The Master of the Hunt held up a wrist sundial and waited until the shadow shifted slightly. He raised a finger, giving her a long count of a hundred, then brought it down. "Forth the hounds!"

The dragonmaster blew a sour blatt on a duck whistle. In unison, the sixty dragons raised their noses to the sky and howled, some of them belching gouts of flame into the air. The sight was enough to send half the non-hunters scurrying for the safety of the castle. I stood my ground.

I wasn't too worried about my own safety: I had the D-hopper, Nunzio's gadgets, and a few little tricks of my own, but I kept thinking about the princess's well-being. She had a tough job ahead, staying far enough ahead of an army of killer dragons to finish the course.

"Forth the hunters!"

Hearing the cry, Fireball leaped forward. Cursing, I held on with both hands and both legs to keep from being bucked off as the rotund beast thundered after the pack of bigger 'hippuses.

In the sparse forest outside the courtyard the riders spread out behind the dragons. The firebreathers were sniffing the ground for the princess's scent. I'd never seen control like it. Normally, adult dragons would be straining against the controllers, fighting to get loose to kill and loot. These behaved like a troop of experienced bloodhounds. Then I gave myself a mental slap on the forehead: they *were* experienced bloodhounds. These dragons and their owners rode on hunts all year round. Only those in the hands of strangers like Alf who were here only for the prize had to hang on tight and keep their dragons on the job. Gleep, swift-footed and smaller than the others, kept dashing underneath the feet of the big ones, smelling a patch of ground here, nibbling a leaf there. I swear at one point he looked up and gave me a wink.

Naw. Couldn't be. Must have been dust in his eye.

I didn't have much of a chance to concentrate on the dragons. Just staying on my mount took all my attention. The trees that weren't hammered down by the stampede of dragons whipped at us with blade-sharp twigs. I spat out leaves and hunkered grimly over Fireball's neck. Not a hundred yards out of the courtyard I saw riders dropping out of sight and heard their yells—the first fence and ditch had claimed its victims. I calculated from my approach vector my 'hippus was going to have to gather himself and leap up six feet and forward twenty. As if he could read my thoughts, he danced sideways and cast an eye over the fence into the pit, where a dozen of his fellows and their riders were crawling out of the mud.

"Come on, Fireball."

It peered back at me, and distinctly shook its head. That tore it for me. I grabbed a handful of its mane, shoved its face into the fence rail.

"Come on, you mangy barrel of shark bait!" I shouted, giving it my full lung power. "Jump that fence or I'll throw you over!" My voice echoed in the forest, momentarily drowning out the dragons. Fireball's head swayed, as though its ears were ringing. With an expression of new respect, it backed up slowly, then broke into a steadily increasing gallop. I braced myself, and we sailed over the rails and the ditch, landing a dozen feet clear. My spine jarred heavily. I saw a couple of my fellow hunters grin at me, as they stood up in their stirrups to absorb the impact with their knees. Jerks.

Fireball didn't miss a step, going straight from that balletic leap into a full canter.

The landscape cleared almost at once from thick forest to open scrubland. Miles ahead of me the dragons had already fanned out with their noses to the ground. In the midst of the red, green, gold, or black giants was a little blue form, scooting back and forth like a mouse under elephants' feet. An ouroboros, its tail still tucked in its mouth, lay on the ground twitching, probably trampled by one of its big cousins as it tried to roll among them. Pages from the palace ran out with a stretcher and a medical kit. I felt a momentary qualm. If Gleep got squished

Skeeve'd be upset. I'd better look out for the little guy.

In the meantime I had to keep an eye on the rest of the hunters. The head count before we'd ridden out was twenty. I could still see the other nineteen. Unless one of them had left behind an illusionary twin, that was. I peered at each one, trying to see if any had fuzzy edges or were repeating the same actions over and over. Nothing so far.

I'd have hated to see this landscape during spring floods; it would be so soggy you could grow cranberries. As it was, the going was messy. Fireball's big hooves caked with mud that went *suck-pop*! whenever he picked up a foot. Prince Bosheer halted to take a look around, and his 'hippus sank up to its belly, and we all learned an important lesson about this field: if you stopped you got mired. I kept my heels ready to kick if Fireball looked like he was slowing down.

"Bad luck," I called, as I suck-popped past him.

"No problem," he said, cheerfully, freeing a field shovel from his saddle pack. He climbed off and started digging. Quite a guy. I had to have respect for somebody who could be philosophical about a situation that could put him out of the running so early in the contest.

The dragons collided as they charged toward a gap that led out of the meadow into the hills. Two of the fire-breathers who wanted to go through at the same time started to fight. One of them hauled back his head and let out a jet of flame that incinerated a stand of trees. On the way it hit the other dragon square in the face, and annoyed him. It tore up cart-size clawfuls of earth and heaved it at its opponent, following up with a huge blast of lightning from its own throat. The first one let out a roar that shook the ground. The Master of the Hounds charged directly at the two dragons and started shouting commands. The rest of the dragons and hunters milled around in the muck waiting until the owners came forward with control wands to pull the combatants apart. That traffic jam wasn't going to clear for a while. I looked around. There were several other gaps to try. I could take one and hope that the paths met up again after a while. It would be easier than waiting here.

The judges seemed to have the same idea. I saw five shapes go overhead. One of them was Massha's familiar roundness. She gave me a thumb's-up as she veered to the right. I turned to the left and lost sight of her.

Beyond the lip of the valley hills closed in on the path until I was threading a round-topped maze. Hoofprints told me at least one of the others had come this way, too. It had been a brilliant idea, but I didn't flatter myself that it was unique. I kicked Fireball into a trot. We rode along the bed of a foot-wide stream, kicking pebbles. I didn't care if Glory heard me; I wasn't in the running for the prize, nice as it would be to have. I was there to see that there wasn't any funny stuff. So far I had not lost track of any of the hunters. I took a small device that Massha had given me out of my belt pouch (you can't get into pants pockets in the saddle) and flipped it open.

The flat screen was as neat as any tracker you could buy in a hunting and fishing shop on Perv: the tiny blips superimposed over a map of the landscape indicated the contestants, the dragons, the observers and the palace staff. We'd purposely unblipped Glory so that if the device fell into someone else's hands they couldn't use it to find her. I traced the trails. Yes, sooner or later they all met up ahead. I'd just go and wait up there for the confusion to clear up. Nothing was in my way. Except one blip, almost directly ahead of me. I looked up.

"You! What are you doing out here?"

"Hello, Aahz."

"Massha, look to your left! Fine that rider five points. He's cheating!" Carisweather ordered. The big fluffy guy pointed. I looked down. The fancy-pants dude in the turban had slipped a gizmo out and was twisting a dial on the face of it. You couldn't call me big know-all when it came to hunting contests, but if I'm an expert in anything, it's magikal gadgets. I knew a variable-output controller when I saw it. The silky snake was breaking in on the spells being used by hunters trying to control their dragons and, by the smirk on his scaly face, he was enjoying the resultant chaos. With a flick of my flight ring I dropped down next to him and picked it out of his hand.

"Naughty, naughty," I said, waggling my finger at him. In fury, his forked tongue flicked in and out of his mouth. "Promises, promises," I sighed, and flew up to join my fellow judges. Three of the four had big grins on their faces, but Carisweather shook his head.

"We're only observers, Mistress Massha," he said, disapprovingly.

"You can say that if you want, big chief," I told him, "but one of those dragons could kill somebody."

"That, alas, is one of the pitfalls of the contest," Carisweather said, mournfully. "These are blood sports, and, once in a while, blood runs."

"That should be when it's unavoidable, Hot Pants," I said, in a huff. I can't stand it when people give me that "accidents of war" garbage. "This is avoidable. Short of searching everybody, we can't find these tricks until they try to use one, but that doesn't mean they get to keep it once we see it." I tossed the disk in the air and caught it again. "He can have it back at the end of the race."

Carisweather sighed. I looked around again for Glory. She had shot away on foot from the starting position so fast I hadn't seen which way she went. Once we hit the skies I saw her prints on the soft ground. She had always been a good runner when she was a little thing, able to outdistance elk-deer and wrestle them down with her bare hands. She told me she'd been training hard for more than a year to make this the best contest Brakespear had ever seen. I wanted it all to work out for her.

With only suspicions on her part and Aahz's spotting of that mystery figure in the woods it was tough to figure out who to keep a eye on. None of them had a good-conduct prize coming that I could see. Besides Snake-dude trying to mess up the dragons, we'd already spotted the scrawny-butt black-furred nymph scattering slow-weed for the other 'hippuses to eat, making sure they'd all be too groggy to run after Glory in the backstretch I knew was up ahead, and both Deveels had tried to make alliances with other riders to let them win.

The noon sun beat down on my back like a hot towel. I wanted to show the colors for Glory, but I'd have been happier in my usual lightweight clothes. A girl my size doesn't need the extra insulation; we generate a fair bit of heat on our own. How she kept moving the way she was amazed me.

If I levitated high above the forest I could see her in the distance, sure-footed as a unicorn. Not the only thing she had in common with that fabled beast, if you get my drift. Once in a while when she crested a ridge the others could see her, too. That Prince Bosheer practically bounded out of his saddle-ridge every time he spotted her. That boy had it bad for her. He must have been bitten by the love-bug the second he set eyes on her. I wondered if Glory knew it.

Silly me. She must have known it even before he did. I knew when Hugh fell for me; Crom knows I waited long enough for Mr. Right that I was certain I recognized that look on a man's face when it finally happened. I was seeing it in front of me at this very moment. I started rooting for him to win.

It wasn't going to be easy. The Cosus of Elova had easily the fastest steed, bought directly out of Glory's dad's stables not two weeks ago. The big white 'hippus knew the terrain and didn't have to be magikally adapted to the local atmosphere and gravity as some of the others did. He was in the lead, spurring Sugarpie every time Glory's blond head became visible amid the sparse trees. The others fought for distance, galloping heavily behind him.

The occasional peeks were for the benefit of the riders, she'd told me. The dragons were following her own scent plus the spoor she laid down from the brimstone pellets in her belt pouch. One of the big reds suddenly got frustrated with having to thread its way through the trees and let out a blast of fire. With an expression on his big chops I can only call smug, he slithered forward on his belly over the smouldering ashes. The rest of the dragons followed his lead, and the king had a head start on this year's controlled burn. I had a coughing fit as the wind carried clouds of hot cinders up into the sky, so I missed Belizara, a Weeka from Sowen, zoom down on her broom to break up a disagreement between a pair of contestants as to who got precedence to cross a bridge.

Riding alongside but not with the group was the king. He rode a handsome black stallion. Behind him, a litter slung between two beasts carried the prize. No one accompanied him; I mean, who was going to bother the king? Nobody would, especially not a king as well prepared for an attack: Hank was in full armor, carrying a sword, sixteen spears including the famous Broken Spear, a dagger in his belt and each boot, bandoliers of throwing stars, a shield, a mace, and a morning star. So far, everything was running well. With Aahz keeping an eye on the action down below, and me up here, nothing should go wrong.

"You!" I demanded, as Nunzio slunk out of the shadows. "What are you doing here? You ought to be back there keeping an eye on Gleep."

"He doesn't need me, Aahz," the Mob enforcer said. "I had to talk to you in private."

I eyed him. "What's going on that you couldn't ask me back there? Who don't you want to hear you?"

"Massha," Nunzio sighed, sitting down on a stone and fanning himself with his broad-brimmed hat. "She's queering the whole deal."

"What deal?" I glanced over his head. No sign of the dragon pack yet, but they couldn't be too far behind me. "Talk fast."

"The safe, the first prize, isn't supposed to be in circulation. It was going to be stopped, but there's been a mix-up."

"What kind of mix-up?" I asked. "Who doesn't want it out there?"

"The Council of Wizards."

"Uh-huh," I nodded, thinking hard. The COW was a transdimensional advisory board that had a representative for every gateway to a dimension that used magik. They did a pretty good job of helping keeping items out of a place that wasn't ready for 'em, but there were occasional slip-ups.

"Yes. The safe was a prototype, designed to protect irreplaceable artifacts, but once the scientists let the critics get a look at it, they figured out it was just too easily used for ill-gotten gains," Nunzio said. "Think of what would happen if you put loot from a . . . business transaction into it. Law enforcement could retrieve the merchandise, but all a perpetrator would have to do to get it back again was to reach into the safe . . ."

"I get it," I said. I let out a long whistle. "Pretty smooth. Another case of technology running too far ahead of the law. So of course they've got to get it out of circulation again. You'd think something like this would have a major APB out. I never heard anything about it."

"You might not have, perhaps because you've been a little out of the loop lately." Nunzio looked abashed, thinking he'd hurt my feelings. I felt a twinge, but he was right: I had had a lot of other things on my mind.

"So the transaction's going to take place where no one can see it. Who's out there?"

"Someone from COW," said Nunzio. I shrugged again. Who was I to disagree with COW? "They're going to stick up the king."

"What?!!?" My voice echoed down the narrow valley.

"Let it happen," Nunzio said, quietly. "He's the one

who called COW in the first place and told them he had it. He's an honest man. A crook would never have let it go."

I peered closely at Nunzio. "So he never intended to give it away at this race?"

"The race is good cover," the enforcer said. "So's a robbery. Otherwise there might have been too many questions asked, the king just giving up a choice piece of merchandise like that. It's a shame that Princess Glory caught some mention of it. She called Massha, Massha called you, and here we are, where none of us ought to have been in the first place."

"Uh-huh." I nodded, as all the pieces fell into place. "So that'd explain the figure in the woods." Another truth dawned on me. "So I'm getting saddle sores for *nothing*?" I bellowed. Fireball danced under me, responding to my outburst. Nunzio looked really embarrassed. "All right. All right! I'll look the other way. Crom save me from future eavesdropping princesses."

Nunzio nodded once. He was a man of relatively few words; once he knew he'd convinced me he didn't waste any more of them. He slid into a crevice, vanishing among the shadows. Pretty good disappearing act for someone with no magik. I gave Fireball a kick to get him started again. He didn't need it. Just as Nunzio disappeared, the knot of dragons caught up with me. Fireball whinnied and took off, me clinging to his neck. We bounded down the canyon with the yelps of thirty couples of drakes, wyverns, wurms, firebreathers, and Gleep behind us.

While Fireball ran I had time to think. I needed to figure out a way to distract Massha and the other judges at the time of the stickup. I glanced up as the airborne quintet zoomed overhead. I owed it to her to tell her the truth, but there wasn't any time. The day was rushing by.

I had to get out of the way of the dragons. With the help of the tracker I located the next handy pocket canyon, and yanked Fireball aside as we reached it. The horde thundered past me with the hunters in their wake. Now that I knew none of the others were involved I could stop babysitting them. As he rode by, Prince Bosheer tipped me a merry wave and a salute. I grimaced back. Whelves wrote the book on cheerfulness. I could only take them in small doses.

Now, to locate the king.

I quivered with joy as we flew along above the hunters. We were in the ride to the finish. Over the top of the trees the castle came back into sight. Glory was going to make it!

Down below I saw Aahz rejoin the pack. He gestured furiously at the Samiram, and made a throat-cutting gesture with his finger. That must be our man. I *thought* he was too scaly to live. I was going to keep an eye on *him*. Mr. Wrong was never going to have a chance to blow the contest. I tipped a thumbs-up to Aahz, but he was already zipping back into the woods.

Glory was on her way. She was in the zone now, running hard, her cheeks bright pink. She stumbled, and the dragons let out a howl of delight as they gained a few steps on their prey. With the castle so close she couldn't afford to make any detours, or the hunters would cut her off. She was still on top of her game, with lots of energy left. I was so proud of her.

Little Gleep turned out to be amazingly fast for his size. He zoomed out ahead of the pack until he was running side by side with Glory. She reached out and patted him on the head, earning a wide-eyed look of adoration. That dragon was just a love sponge. The big green dragon in the lead, shoving out into the open field, took a few steps and launched himself into the air, gaining on Glory. He set down within a few paces of her. Gleep wheeled on his little blue tail and hissed. The big dragon was so surprised it sat back on its tail, causing a huge pileup as the other dragons caught up with it.

I grinned. The little guy was amazing. Skeeve ought to be proud of him. Later I planned to tell him all about Gleep's adventures, with some judicious editing. It bothered him to hear too much about Aahz. He still felt guilty for Hot Stuff being without his magik, as if it was his fault that the moronic Imp assassins hit Skeeve's old master before he restored Aahz's powers. Skeeve also blamed himself for not catching and understanding all the words of the antimagik spell; the counterspell had to be exact, or it would make matters worse. Aahz would never get his powers back, and he might have some other problem. Skeeve wanted to make sure that would never happen.

Glory was in the straightaway now, with the drawbridge directly ahead of her. Out in the open for good, she wove from side to side. Now and then she threw a handful of brimstone out wide. The dragons on her tail couldn't resist the noxious little pellets, diving for them and crunching them up with gusto. They got in each others' way, squabbled over the titbits, and, suddenly, fell into pits that Glory had dug days before to delay them. She wasn't going to get caught, not if she could help it.

The 'hippuses started falling over dragon tails and flipping into the pits, too. From twenty, only fourteen hunters still remained in the chase. Ooops, ouch. I winced. Make that eleven, as three of them stumbled into a net that dropped out of the trees. Glory had leaped over the tripwire as she passed, but the 'hippuses had gone right through it, setting off the trap.

A shower of love-doe powder claimed four more, as the hunters suddenly had to fend off the advances of a herd of amorous deer-elk stags who bounded out of the woods, looking for the wonderful females they smelled. The number dropped again, as two riders were suddenly thrown out of their saddle ridges and onto the ground ahead of their 'hippuses. Their mounts, unable to move, bellowed for help. The remaining five leaped over the sward of stickum turf and pounded forward after the remaining dragons. The furry, skinny-butt female shrieked as she and another rider were lifted straight out of their saddles by huge birds of prey. They would be able to fight their way free, but they were effectively out of the contest for the time being. Glory had left all these surprises for last. That's my girl, I thought with pride.

Behind Gloriannamarjolie, only three hunters remained: the Samiram, the Deveel called Alf, and Prince Bosheer. They were all looking desperate, grim, and tired. I crossed my fingers. Glory didn't have far to run. She was going to win.

The woods thickened ahead of me. Fireball protested as I led him off the main path, making him pick his way through the undergrowth. I didn't want to interrupt the exchange, but I wanted to make sure no one else interrupted

it, either. The king and his litter clanked along. Navigating
behind him by sound, I paid attention to the rhythmic jingling, creaking, clattering, and clop-clop-clopping. Suddenly, the noise came to a halt.

"Have you got the chest?" a female voice demanded.
The representative from COW was a woman. They occupied about half the council seats. The current president
was a Gnome named Helvita.

"Of course!" the king's deep voice rolled out. I pulled
Fireball to a silent halt. I slid out of the saddle and tiptoed
forward, trying to see the exchange. Henryarthurjon and
his challenger were in a stand of woods too deep to let in
much light. Perfect place for a little daylight robbery, I
thought. I saw the silhouette nod.

"Hand it over, then. Hurry up! We haven't got much
time."

"Patience, patience, good dame," the king said. More
clinking and clunking as he untied the bindings holding the
chest in place on its litter. "My goodness, you're a strong
little thing, aren't you? Oh, I say! Take it easy, wench!"

"Shut up," the figure hissed. "We have to make this
look good. Hold still!"

"Ah, I see. Mmm. Mmmph!"

All was going according to the plan. I gave the COW
representative a few minutes to finish her work and leave
with the chest. A short implosion of air told me she'd used
a D-hopper to depart. I shoved through the trees. King
Henryarthurjon stood tied up like a bundle of sticks inside
a circle of his own spears stuck point down in the ground,
his hands tied behind his back and a gag in his mouth. I
loosened the gag.

"Yell," I said. "I'll get help."

"Aid! Aid to the king!" bellowed Henryarthurjon. "What ho! Aid to the king!"

"Aid for the king!" I shouted. I ran to Fireball and spurred him down the hill and into the midst of the hunt. "Help the king! He's up there! He needs help!"

"The king? What happened to the king!" Everyone not directly in the running went to the rescue, including most of the disappointed hunters. I was feeling kind of smug, being in on the facts. I tipped the king a wink as we untied him and helped him back onto his stallion.

"That was a little bit of a too-convincing robbery, what ho?" he told me in an undertone. "You could have reminded your compatriot it was all a sham, eh?"

"My compatriot?" I asked. I admit my expression went blank.

"Yes, a scaly wench, a little taller than you, but otherwise could have been your sister. Do you have a sister?"

"Not in this neck of the woods," I said. I kept my face impassive, but my heart sank.

A Pervect. The image in my mind slid over one notch and clicked down. That's where I had seen a silhouette like it: in my own mirror every morning. I gritted my teeth. If the COW rep from Perv was here, the least she could have done was to tip me the wink.

"Nothing to do with me, majesty," I assured him sincerely, though inwardly I was smarting with humiliation. I was still in disgrace at home for having lost my magik—not because it had happened, but because it had been in such a stupid accident. The Pervect representative probably didn't want anything to do with me. "I'm here with Massha."

"Eh?" the king asked, puzzled. "Oh. Her governess. Ah. 'Course y'are. Welcome, too. Welcome. Ah, well, let's go back to the castle. Glory ought to be getting there pretty soon. C'mon, we're all of ten minutes' ride away."

A few steps away we heard, *"Mmrrph! Mllph! Lllp!"*

"I say," the king exclaimed. "Do you hear something?"

But with my more acute hearing I was way ahead of him. The sounds were coming from a copse of nut bushes not far away. I swung off Fireball and pushed into the undergrowth toward the sound. I noticed that the twigs were broken off during some kind of struggle.

Behind a tree I found a mousy little Djinn in blue robes with his wire-rimmed glasses hanging from one pointed blue ear. He was bound and gagged with snare-ropes, magikal bindings that never let go unless you knew the release word. Fortunately, they're commercially available in nearly every dimension, and few people ever bother to re-set the factory passwords.

"Undo," I commanded. The ropes collapsed from him like overcooked pasta.

"You!" the Djinn said, leveling a finger at me. I noticed it was shaking. It took guts for a little Djinn like that to threaten a Pervect. We had a reputation throughout the dimensions, and it was well-earned. "How dare you restrain a representative of the most august Council of Wizards . . . wait a moment, you're not the one who tied me up!"

"No. It was a female, right?" I asked, helping him out of the bushes.

He adjusted his spectacles and peered up at me, wonderingly. "Yes. How did you know?"

"Ask the king," I said, hoisting him up into the now-empty litter. "His royal majesty, King Henryarthurjon of Brakespear."

"Temolo, of the Council of Wizards," the Djinn said, extending a hand, which was swallowed up by the king's huge paw. He straightened his spectacles. "Dear me, there seems to have been a terrible mistake."

The three remaining riders were in a line directly behind Glory. We five judges flew directly over them, making sure that no funny stuff would happen in the last few minutes of the race. For the first time, I saw Glory slow down slightly. In spite of her excellent condition, she was getting tired. She'd been running all day, a hard feat even for a Brakespearan.

The hunters were alone. The last three big dragons had been clotheslined by an almost invisible wire stretched from the top of one huge, ancient oak on one side of the castle to another. The trees bowed slightly as three adult dragons rammed into the wire, then sprang up taut. The dragons were flung backward, and lay in a heap wondering what had happened to them. Gleep sat down on the ground in front of him to chew mud out of his nails. Nunzio emerged from the crowd of trainers and courtiers to help groom him. His work was done.

But mine wasn't yet. Glory hadn't reached the draw-bridge. She was panting with exhaustion. The 'hippuses drew closer, and closer, and closer. The Samiram reached out one long, scaly hand, almost grabbing hold of the running girl's long tail of blond hair.

Suddenly, I lost my grip on the Samiram's dragon-control device that I was holding. It fell out of my hands and landed on his head. He bellowed a curse. The 'hippus between his knees, sensing a change, slowed a little. The Samiram looked up at me, his tongue flicking furiously.

"Oops," I said, holding my hands up to my shoulders. "Sorry."

Glory and the other two were by now far ahead. A hundred yards. Eighty. Sixty. The castle courtiers were lined up on the battlements yelling encouragement to their princess. Forty. Twenty. She was going to make it. I was afraid to breathe.

Suddenly, Alf, the Deveel, threw a handful of powder into Bosheer's face.

"Ten points off!" Carisweather boomed. And, mysteriously (my fingers were crossed), the cloud of dust rolled back into Alf's face, never touching the Prince. Alf went into a coughing and sneezing fit, and fell off his 'hippus.

Ten yards to go. Five. Two. One. Glory's foot was almost on the planks of the drawbridge, when Bosheer's strong arm scooped her up and deposited her onto the withers of his steed.

"Got you, my lady!" he yelled.

The cheers of the courtiers faded away. Glory looked upset for a moment. Then she looked up into the face of her captor, and grinned.

"Congratulations, my lord," she breathed. The two of them exchanged glances that left the princess's cheeks even more pink than before. Bosheer's face turned red, and he smiled. *Zing!* I thought. The cheers redoubled.

We judges wheeled around the couple on the drawbridge, compared notes, then Carisweather floated a dozen yards up into the air to make an announcement.

"My lords and ladies! I have the honor to announce the winner of today's hunt: Prince Bosheer! And here comes his majesty to award him his most desirable prize!"

Over the last rise came the king, followed by Aahz,

followed by the 'hippuses carrying the litter with the chest on it. I blinked. The chest was not on it. Instead, it contained a bemused-looking Djinn, and nothing else. Aahz's face was grim. His eyes met mine. The chest had been stolen. In spite of all our precautions, we'd failed.

The king rode over, and though she didn't look in any hurry to get down, helped his daughter dismount from Bosheer's saddle. The king shook hands with the prince, then held up his hands for silence.

"We wish to give thanks to our servants and friends, and especially to our new friend Aahz, who came to our assistance a few moments ago," he said, indicating me with a hand. "I'm sorry to say that the prize we'd originally intended to grant this most gracious winner has been foully robbed from our person." Bosheer looked crestfallen. Henryarthurjon slapped him on the back. "We apologize most heartily to Prince Bosheer. It would seem that crime may touch even the highest in the land. But this brave and puissant man will not go without a reward. Instead, I shall give him from among my many treasures . . ."

Gloriannamarjolie pushed forward, her hand hooked through Bosheer's arm. ". . . his daughter's hand in marriage!"

"What?" asked her father, then noticed the solid grip Glory had on the Whelf. "Oh. Jolly good. Yes. My daughter's hand in marriage."

The crowd cheered. Glory and Bosheer looked radiantly happy.

Massha settled down near me where I stood at the edge of the crowd with my arms crossed. "Well, all's well that ends well, I guess. I saw sparks shooting between those two even before the race started. I knew he was Mr. Right."

"He's satisfied," I said, nodding at the prince. "He got something he liked better than a safe."

"But what happened to the safe?" she asked. "You were following the king. How'd someone manage to rob him with you so close?" I scowled. No one likes to fail, even if it was in a good cause. Her face softened. She felt sorry for me.

"I didn't see a thing," I said, impassively. "It had to have happened when he went into that thick clump of woods on the other side of the hill."

"Well, did you notice any footprints? Can you tell which way the thieves went?" she demanded.

"Massha," I said, with infinite patience. "I came here to do you a favor. I blew it. I apologize. You deserve better, but I'm done. No one is paying me to track down a missing treasure chest."

"Sorry, Big Guy," Massha said. "I'm actually happier the way things came out."

"Me, too," I agreed. Nunzio and Gleep came up to join us. He and I exchanged comradely nods. Gleep leaped up, aiming for my face with his tongue. I pushed him away. "Let's go in. I bet they're pouring a toast to the happy couple. I could use a drink."

"So could I, Hot Stuff," Massha said, tucking her hand into my arm. "So could I."

M.Y.T.H. INC. PROCEEDS

By Jody Lynn Nye

The Klahd with the pinstriped suit coat stretched tight over his massive shoulders accepted the cup of tea offered to him by Bunny. Guido declined cream or sugar, as his habit, which I knew well, dictated. His cousin, Nunzio, not quite so muscular but more affable, accepted both. The fact that both were of a mind to take tea in the sitting room of our renovated inn when they were clearly rushed by other concerns told me how deep those concerns were. I settled myself at their feet to eavesdrop openly upon the proceedings.

"Much obliged," Guido said, taking a deep draught—less, I believed, to assuage thirst than to get the courtesies out of the way. He was never one for a cup of tea where coffee or ale were also on the menu, and he knew both were to hand. Bunny, who knew his mores, seemed to be using his acceptance of the ritual as a test to find out how desperate the Mob enforcers were to obtain the help of my pet. Bunny was nearly as protective as I of Skeeve's studies. The ruffled white pinafore that the red-haired female wore over her tight, green dress was a concession to her attempt to play hostess as well as guardian, but it did not conceal her voluptuous figure any more successfully than her mannered hospitality hid her annoyance and worry. Guido turned to the lanky, blond-haired male reclining in the chair to his right.

"Like I was sayin', Skeeve . . ."

"Cookie?" Bunny asked, handing around a plate of tiny, pink-sugared dainties. Guido obediently reached for one.

In my long study of the lesser species, the ability to juggle a container of hot liquid, a plate of delicate comestibles, and a difficult conversation was the mark of a being with its wits about it. Guido passed the test. Nunzio went him one better. When the plate came to him, he selected two of the sweet biscuits, one for himself, and one that he held out on his palm for me. In deference to my pet's affection for this creature, as well as my taste for the sweets, I scooped the cookie off the hand with my tongue. Nunzio reached out to ruffle my ears.

"Attaboy," he said, in his high-pitched tenor. "What a good dragon!"

"Thank you for your consideration," I attempted to say, but my immature vocal chords emitted only a sound: "Gleep!"

"You shouldn't be spoiling his appetite," Bunny said, reproachfully.

"Nunzio couldn't spoil that dragon's appetite if he fed him the whole plate and his right arm," Guido said. "Miss Bunny, we respectfully request that you relax. We are not here to ask the Boss to set foot out of his self-imposed exile. All we want is his advice."

Bunny eyed him with the suspicion of one who had heard such assurances before.

"Promise?"

"Cross my heart and hope to die," Guido said, suiting his motions to the former part of his pledge, no mean feat while holding a delicate porcelain cup in one's fingers. "If I take the Boss farther than a trot outside to walk the dragon, then you may spit me with the rotisserie fork you have so thoughtfully concealed behind the door."

"Well, all right," she said, subsiding.

"Good," Guido said. "Then, perhaps you will sit down and pour yourself a cup of your most excellent tea, and listen to us."

Bunny sank into the chair at the end of the low table with a just audible sigh of relief.

I was reassured, too. Guido, for all that he was a Klahd, had a nearly dragonish sense of honor, not to be sneered at considering many of the others with whom he associated on a regular basis; I do not include the days spent in the company of my pet, naturally. Skeeve had good instincts regarding the qualities of those whom he called his friends. Klahds, like many pets, function almost entirely on instinct. We of higher species can only hope that they will evolve in the next million years or so until they have a greater grasp of reason and logic. But superior as he was to his fellows, Skeeve was still inclined to turn away from his own interests and assist his friends, no matter how pressing the need for his own work. In a being as short-lived as a Klahd, I objected to him wasting that precious time.

"In any case," Guido went on, "there's nothin' we're concealin' from you. You can listen in to our whole tale of woe. In fact, we would be grateful if you had any input that would help us to deal with the problem in which we find ourselves. You have good insights, and we would be mugs not to take advantage of that."

"Nothing is wrong with Uncle Bruce, is it?" Bunny asked, suddenly concerned. Her avuncular relative was the employer of the two males. He went by the sobriquet "Fairy Godfather," which suited his dress and manner of speaking, but anyone who forgot the second part of his title while possibly finding the first part risible was likely to be reminded of his manners in a forcible fashion. Apart from not enjoying his cologne, which made me sneeze, I found Don Bruce more dragonish in character, and therefore more suited to my company, than most, if not all, of his subordinates.

"The Don is fine," Guido assured her. "I would pass along to you his kindest affections, but he does not know we are here at the moment. He is expectin' us to handle this problem ourselves, which we should, except that it seems to involve magik of a higher order than we are accustomed to dealin' with on our own. Hence, our risk of your displeasure."

"You remember King Petherwick, maybe?" Nunzio inquired.

"Sure, I do," Skeeve said, wrinkling his forehead thoughtfully. "He was one of the kings that Queen Hemlock more or less evicted when she expanded Possiltum's borders."

"To the detriment of the old reigning houses," Nunzio confirmed. "Including that of Shoalmirk, Petherwick's old realm. Yet, it is not to be denied that the current situation is more livable than under the previous management. Hemlock is holding it together pretty good, with the help of Massha and J.R. Grimble. The people is less revolting than before."

"Where's Petherwick now?" Skeeve asked. "I know Hemlock exiled the former rulers who wouldn't submit to her overlordship, if that's the right word. He didn't want to take a demotion to duke."

"Well, would you?" asked Guido. "When you're used to runnin' the whole show, it's tough when they build a layer of bureaucracy over your head. Especially when your family's been in charge since the species started walkin' upright. Petherwick's in the Bazaar, as it happens. He's gone into retail, in a big way. He bought an insurance policy from the Mob to protect his 'realm,' as he calls it, but it is no more than a big emporium featuring cheap household goods manufactured by those thousands of flunkies who did not want to be left behind to languish under Hemlock's reign. He calls it 'King-Mart.' He's doin' pretty good business, as it turns out. Deveels like a bargain. Petherwick's markups are less than theirs, as a rule, and he don't care if buyers resell his goods, so plenty of dealers take advantage of the sales. In any case, it don't work out for the secondary market so good. Once the shoppers figured out where the merchandise was comin' from, they went back to the source. Petherwick's makin' money hand over royal fist."

"So, what's the problem?"

"He's bein' robbed. It looks like some kind of big magikal beast is to blame, but it's one that the Shutterbug security system ain't picked up in their wing images. We've looked at dozens of frames, yet in the morning, there's big-time damage to the facilities, and a significant portion of the take is missing from the Treasury, as the old guy calls it. Here. I brought some of them wit' me."

Guido laid out a handful of small, square parchments upon which had been limned scenes of a huge room lit only by night-torches. I peered closely at the images, until Skeeve shoved my head out of the way.

"The biggest concern is the deaths and injuries," Guido continued. "A couple of the night guards, former knights, experienced men, have been killed by this beast, whatever it is. Bite marks on the bodies show somethin' very large and with sharp teeth took a vital piece out of them. Trouble is, this does not fall strictly under the purview of our policy. We are supposed to deal with matters of security, theft and minor nuisances. But he's callin' it minor, and we have to deal with it, or have him badmouth us around town."

At this, I admit my ears perked up. It sounded as if one of my countrymen, another dragon, had invaded the Bazaar.

If one had indeed infiltrated this King-Mart and was already eating the locals, the possibility might arise that if Guido and Nunzio failed, Skeeve himself might be called in to dispose of it, putting himself into grave danger the likes of which he might not be able to extricate himself from. I knew that if I went with them to reason with my countryman or woman, I might be able to persuade it to leave and find more fruitful pastures elsewhere. Besides, I was not above a spot of altruistic behavior myself. Logic dictated that I must accompany them. Therefore, I must first persuade my pet and his friends of that notion.

I offered my most winning facial expression, all wide eyes and open mouth to approximate the "smile" that Klahds wore to show that they were happy. I wound myself around the legs of Guido and Nunzio, and even, I am ashamed to admit, laid my head in Nunzio's lap so he could scratch my ears.

"Gee," Skeeve said, puzzled, "he's never done that before."

"That's because he likes me," the Mob enforcer said, flattered. "Right, little guy?"

I allowed him to scratch both ears thoroughly, as well as the sides of my jaw and my scruff . . . very well, I must admit that he was a man who knew his way around a dragon's skull. But I followed Skeeve out of the room when he went to bring up wine for his guests. Now that the formalities had been observed, it was time to let loose. I brought my head up under Skeeve's arm as he was filling a pitcher from one of the many kegs in the cellar.

"I . . . go with."

"You really want to?" Skeeve asked, scratching the spot between my ears. I concentrated momentarily upon the pleasant sensation that afforded me. Nunzio was good at caressing, but Skeeve was far better.

"Yes. Curious."

"Okay," he said. "As long as you're sure you'll be all right."

"Of course I will be all right," I tried to say. "I am strong and quick, my senses are keener than your weakling Klahdish organs are, and I am capable of knowing when it is wise to withdraw from a perilous situation. I shall also take care to safeguard the lives of your two pets, since you prize their welfare."

Alas, all that came out was "Gleep!"

"How can you call dat a *pest control* problem?" Guido asked, as we all surveyed the stone pillar with the bite mark taken out of it that stood a few yards away from

Petherwick's grand, padded throne. A broad bite mark, I
observed, sniffing it closely. At least forty centimeters
wide, and ten at its deepest point, denoting large and unusually powerful jaws, I concluded.

I took a full survey of my surroundings as the pets
holding on to my leash spoke heatedly with King Petherwick of King-Mart. What might in other circumstances
have been a warehouse with cashbox desks like most of
the other bigger emporia in the Bazaar had been turned
into a combination throne room and general store. Situ-
ated in the center just behind the checkout desks, where
shoppers had to pass him on the way inside, the exiled
Klahdish king held court. Attendants of both genders, attired in the brown and teal livery of their lost realm, clustered on both sides of the grand seat. About them on tall
standards hung pennants of the king's coat of arms, and
tapestries picked out in silk threads depicting valiant bat-
tles between fierce and handsomely attired opponents, or
fantastic gardens containing plants that could never exist,
most of them lacking such necessary parts as sepals, or
indeed stems. Such impracticality hinted at a lack of fore-
sight by the makers of the tapestries, which did not surprise me. Klahds were, as a rule, incapable of making
plans beyond a certain elementary complexity. All around
this small audience chamber, the room was lined with
banks of shelves, hanging racks for clothing, and stacks
of crates, cartons, and boxes of every size arranged in
aisles, through which hundreds of shoppers from a hundred dimensions were pushing wheeled baskets and
wearing the bemused looks of the up-to-date hunter-
gatherer. No doubt the brush with royalty was one of the
attractions of shopping at King-Mart. I fell back to sniffing

the area, seeking in vain for a familiar scent that I had expected to find here. No dragon save myself had ever set foot in this space. I was relieved, but left with the puzzle of what had. A jerking of my collar brought me back to the argument going on over my head.

"This mystery beast is pestering my people," Petherwick said, indignantly. "Therefore, I expect you to handle it." A large, fleshy Klahd with a florid face and triple-layered bags under his eyes, slumped in his throne. As we watched, a couple of Imp females entered, and curtsied to the throne before picking up wicker baskets from the stack at the head of the first aisle. Petherwick acknowledged them with a curt nod of the head. "To death, in two cases already! I do not see how is this stuffed toy of yours is supposed to help," he added, looking down at me with disdain. I opened my eyes as widely as I could, to simulate gentle innocence. "He'll just make matters worse!"

"He's not a toy," Nunzio said gently. "He's young, but he's a real dragon."

Petherwick looked alarmed. "You can't trust a dragon!"

"Gleep ain't like other dragons," Guido said, his thick black eyebrows drawn down over a brow that just missed being Neanderthal in nature. "He don't wreck things. He's house-trained. And he's smart."

"Your employer assured me that if I agreed to his contract, internal security in my capital would never be a problem. We would be protected from annoyances, as your employer put it."

"This isn't a typical example of a security problem," Nunzio pointed out, with some justice. "Don Bruce meant problems with other people. You say that this is pest control. That makes it your problem."

"This is not *just* pest control! I am sure it is sabotage! Someone is attempting to put me out of business. That makes it a security issue. Some of my best men have died! I have lost large sums in gold at least once a week for the last three weeks! And if I start telling other people that Don Bruce had failed to solve a problem that occurred on his watch, that he showed no flexibility in dealing with problems," King Petherwick said, a sly light shining in his porcine eyes, "then your other contractees might want to stop doing business with you."

"That," Guido sighed lustily, "is why we are here. The Don is willing to give you one 'gimme' on the basis that you've been a good customer, always payin' up on the dot when the premiums are due. He has noticed this. And you have to admit that we have cleaned up all the other situations that have come around. But you have pushed this contract to limits that the Don did not anticipate."

The king planted an indignant hand on his overfed chest.

"Do I not have the right to go into business, to support myself and my dependants, now that that harridan has taken over my ancient bailiwick? May I not open a store?"

"Yeah, but no one ever said you were gonna open *fourteen* of 'em," Guido said, in frustration.

"Five more opening next month," one of the courtiers standing by the throne remarked.

"Lord Dalhailey," Petherwick said, by way of cursory introduction. "My Minister of Marketing, just newly returned from a buying trip. I believe you two have not met before?" The Klahd dipped his head slightly, noblesse oblige. Guido tipped him a casual salute with two fingers off the brim of his fedora hat.

"Pleased to meetcha. Look, there's gonna be some renegotiatin' come the expiration of this current contract," he said, turning back to the king. "I just want to warn you what is in the Don's mind."

"There will *be* no renegotiation if this is not solved, because I will refuse to renew your service contract if you don't help me," Petherwick said, majestically. "We have so far successfully explained to shocked shoppers that the dead or dismembered bodies they have come upon unawares as being part of Slay Days, a period of deep discounts symbolized by models of fierce beasts being dispatched by knights and wizards." He gestured to a pair of displays that flanked his throne room. Cardboard cutouts of reptiles snarled at bay as Klahds in silver mail pierced them with swords or spears.

"I thought you said that these were armored knights that they were finding," Nunzio said.

Petherwick shrugged. "The dragon doesn't always lose, my friend. But my customers have been most understanding, and we have responded with generosity if they do not overreact. If they find a dead body in the aisle, they are entitled to a twenty percent discount off one item that day."

"Thirty percent, if the item comes from that aisle," Lord Dalhailey added. "We call it our 'Blue Blood Special.' I added that clause myself. As a service to the consumer, of course. We don't want them thinking that we are bloodthirsty vultures interested only in the bottom line."

"Even if you *are* bloodthirsty vultures interested in the bottom line," Guido said.

Dalhailey looked as indignant as Petherwick had. "Sir, I resent your implication! We have mouths to feed, thousands of them. Almost a third of the population of Shoalmirk followed his majesty into exile." Here he bowed toward Petherwick, who waved a hand in acknowledgment. "You have no idea how difficult it has been to keep them convinced that this move to Deva is in their best interests."

"But the chief concern is the depletion of the treasury. This beast is managing not only to attack my people, but to rob us of our legitimate proceeds," Petherwick said, dragging the enforcers' minds back to what I believe was his main point all along. "We have been holding a one-week special on luxury dry goods that has proved surprisingly profitable. The proceeds from all the stores are brought in and amassed here in our flagship location. I do not wish to lose any of the gold we have earned from those sales. Do you think that two of you and this . . . this lizard can succeed before we are robbed again?"

"That would be our intention," Guido said, carefully keeping his tone level.

I felt it incumbent upon me to make a comment at this stage.

"Gleep!"

Everyone turned to look at me. King Petherwick sneered.

"Not too impressive, is he? I thought your employer would send the wizard he's got working for him. Sneeze, I think he said the name is?"

"Skeeve," Nunzio said, restraining Guido with a palm to the chest. "He's on vacation. This is his dragon."

"Hardly a substitute." Petherwick waved an imperious hand. "Well, get on with it. The sooner you find what happened to my gold, the sooner we can talk about the next contract."

"I knew it," Guido exploded the moment we were out of earshot of the retail monarch. "I knew this mook would be trouble. When we was signin' up prospects, once I heard he was from Klah and checked him out a little with Big Julie, I said skip this place. But no, the Don says he's gotta have a hundred percent subscription in the area. This guy calls us in for all kinds of petty stuff that are none of our Business, and I sez this with a capital B, as you can tell."

"Are you questioning our boss?" Nunzio asked, with a lifted eyebrow that was the sole skepticism he showed his much larger cousin.

"Not officially, no," Guido sighed. "The Don tells us to do somethin' and we do it. I just don't think this penny-ante loser is worth our time."

"The Don says he is, so he is. Our allegiance is to our boss, not to King Petherwick. I agree he's not much of a king, though he's turnin' into some kind of hot-shot retailer."

"Still, there are elements of rank deception involved here. How many times we been called out to one or another of his establishments for what has turned out to be one kind of false alarm or another, just to prove that he has the Don Bruce Protection Plan workin' overtime for him? I have lost what parts of my girlish laughter I still retained in trottin' over to here or one of the other many stores. It has caused us to bring in other associate members of the Mob to look after those other places, and with no additional recompense to absorb that expense. And you heard his marketing guy. Five more to come! The guy is a filch."

Nunzio shook his head. "But here I am worried about the loss of life. Somethin' that can take that big a bite out of a solid stone pillar is a danger to the public. We gotta take it out."

"I agree, too," I exclaimed, but as usual, my comment came out "Gleep!"

Guido reached over and roughly touseled my ears. "You said it, fella," he told me with a grin.

As I continued to sniff around the great hall of merchandise I caught a scent that was unfamiliar to me—unfamiliar and dangerous. It caused a frisson to race down the scales along my back. We dragons are not easily frightened. Nor was I now, not until I had the facts of the matter in sum before me. It appeared, therefore, that my sensation of fearfulness was caused by the scent itself. I judged that it contained a pheromone that, unlike the mating chemicals that caused attraction, provoked a feeling of fear and dread. I found I was curious, but I would proceed with caution. I dropped lower until my belly was virtually sweeping the spotless black-and-white tiles of the floor.

The two Mob enforcers noticed the change in my stance, and followed my lead in applying caution. Both of them drew from inside their coats the miniature crossbows that they carried. Deveel shoppers plying the aisles for soap flakes might have been taken aback had they encountered the two Klahds on the street, but within King-Mart, where marketing was an element of the shopping experience, such behavior was accepted as playacting. That would explain why the presence of bodies had aroused neither fear nor a visit from the Merchants' Association.

Guido had been correct in his assessment of the source of the former king's wealth. The huge hall, seemingly a tent on the outside, was built of wood. I smelled enchantment in its seams; that would serve to keep out intruders. Yet, according to accounts, something had penetrated the interior and had managed to conceal itself while committing several sallies against pelf and personnel alike.

Hair wash, board games, garden implements, handbags ... there seemed no end to the types of goods that the former Shoalmirkers could produce. A sheaf of rakes with wooden handles leaned drunkenly in a tall crate that was studded with small boxes containing paper envelopes of flower seeds. Sacks of food lay beside shelves of toys; racks of garments ranged back out of sight in the right-hand third of the store. I thought the colors were vulgar, but as I had noted with regard to my pet, there is no accounting for taste.

A middle-aged Klahd with the pot-belly of prosperity wearing the king's livery came striding toward us. He wore a determined smile, and maneuvered past the weapons to shake the two males' hands.

"Mr. Guido and Mr. Nunzio!" he said. "Finding everything you want?"

"Not exactly," Guido said, wryly. "I believe we are lookin' for somethin' in a large-jawed monster with a taste for gold and ambuscade. You got one of those?"

The Klahd's smile became somewhat pained. "You jest, sirs, but it is not a matter for amusement. As Chancellor of the Exchequer, it is *my* men who are taking the brunt of these nighttime raids."

"You will excuse, I hope, the effort at levity," Guido said smoothly. "We take all our visits seriously, Lord Howadzer. Maybe you can tell us what's changed since we was here last in your flagship location?"

Howadzer thought for a minute. "Not much. A few changes in personnel, perhaps. His majesty commanded that we rotate the staff so that everyone has a chance to take part in every job. He likes to see a variety of servants at each of the stores when he holds court. It is meant to make employees more flexible, but we are getting a number of complaints. You cannot make a craftsman into a salesman, nor a seamstress into a security guard, no matter how easy it seems to interchange one peasant for another. After all, we have to pay them now."

"You hadda pay them before," Guido pointed out.

"Not as much as we do today," Howadzer said, obviously aggrieved. "They have been speaking with the neighbors." The ultimate word was accompanied by a visible shudder. "Brr."

"Don't like Deveels?" Nunzio asked.

Howadzer frowned at him. "Well, you are from our world, too, aren't you?"

"Yeah, we're all Klahds."

"Please! I don't like that word! It was imposed upon us by people not like us, who do not live in our world! I am not happy about living in exile, especially in a place like this. I am only willing to put up with it if prosperity follows, but if I may say so in confidence, it is too long in coming for my taste."

"No, I can see where that would be a problem," Nunzio said, with a commendable degree of tact.

"There must be better places than this," Howadzer said.

"You could leave," Guido suggested.

The chancellor looked at him disdainfully. "And go where? With what? His majesty pays but poor wages compared with going concerns in the Bazaar. Besides," he sighed, "I remain loyal to my fellow Klahds, if you must call us that. At least we do not have horns and tails, or green skin. Or consort with strange monsters." He eyed

me nervously. I sidled up and deliberately slurped his
hand with my tongue.

From his reaction, you would have thought that I had
cut off the limb with a dull knife. Howadzer grabbed a
stack of embroidered tea towels off a shelf and swabbed
himself vigorously until he had taken off not only the of-
fending saliva, but the first layer of skin underneath as
well.

I automatically decided that I did not care for this person, and it seemed that Guido and Nunzio shared my
distaste. Howadzer realized he had lost his audience's
sympathy. He gave them a worried smile.

"Let me show you the scene of the crime," he said.

We wended our way nearly to the rear of the showroom.
As at the front of the store, Petherwick had commanded to
be built a facility that must have been very much like the
facility that he had left behind in Shoalmirk.

"Behold the Treasury," Howadzer said, with a flourish
of his flabby hand.

It was very impressive. Guido and Nunzio had seen it
before, since they had made many visits to King-Mart, so
they surveyed it with experienced eyes. I, on the other
hand, had a good look.

Like many castle strong-rooms, the King-Mart Treasury had been created in the shape of a round tower, this
one two stories high, bringing it within a few feet of the
lofty ceiling. Instead of cage bars or heavy stones, the
walls were constructed of clear crystalline blocks, giving
the customers a slightly distorted view of the interior. We
approached from the left side of the small building. Two
guards in chainmail coifs over their tabards and holding
polearms stood stiffly at the door, and two more flanked
glittering heaps of treasure inside the crystal structure.

I walked all the way around it, sniffing. The heady smell was present, though only near the entrance. There was no other way inside.

"We have four men on duty at all times," Howadzer said. "On the nights when we were attacked, the guards told us that they heard loud noises coming from the aisles nearby. The men who survived said that they never saw the monster coming, and none of them can give us a description."

"That's convenient," Guido said.

"What?"

"I mean, that's terrible," Guido corrected himself. "Petherwick said you had another robbery just last night?"

"King Petherwick to you, if you do not mind," Howadzer said, haughtily. "Whether or not he retains his kingdom, he is royal to his marrow. "Yes, we did. I blame all this magik! Here is your puzzle. A strong-room that has never been breached, yet gold is stolen and men are dead. We seek a monster that goes abroad when no one can see it, yet leaves behind horrendous damage and dead bodies, and steals gold without breaking into the vault."

"This stinks of inside job," Guido said, looking the Chancellor square in the eye. "You gotta know that is what springs to the eye on first examination. Gold doesn't walk away by itself. Someone who knows the works here is involved."

Howadzer snorted. "You would say that. But talk is cheap. Gold is money. Earn yours."

With that as his exit line, the Chancellor of the Exchequer, Shoalmirk in exile, turned on his heel and strode away.

"He is right about the value of money," Nunzio said.

"But people, no matter of what stripe or shape, will do very strange things for money. In my experience, few creatures without pockets see much use in gold.

"Excepting dragons, of course," he added, reaching into his pocket for a strip of jerky for me. I accepted it, and forewent my usual slurp in gratitude for his recognition of my species' affection for the imperishable and noble metal.

Dragons and gold have been inseparable in legend for millenia, but no one has ever asked us why we accumulate hoards of it in our own as well as other dimensions. We do not prize it for its purchasing value, since we do not buy that which we need. No, gold occupies a much simpler stratum in our culture. When dragonlets hatch out from their eggs, our mothers care for us while our fathers seek prey to feed us. During our earliest days, we can only consume soft meat, such as eggs and flesh pre-chewed for us by our doting parents (Yes, in spite of their fearsome reputation, dragons are as devoted to their offspring as any other intelligent being.) Soon, though, our baby teeth grow in. To hone them sharp enough to pierce skin, bone, and armor, we need substances to teethe upon that are resistive yet not hard enough to break juvenile dentition. Our mothers seek out and obtain soft metal for us to chew. Most minerals available are either toxic, like lead, or are prone to rust or corrosion, such as copper and steel. Therefore, the metal of choice is gold. A clutch of active youngsters can go through a large quantity until they are large enough to leave the nest. Even afterward, the sight or smell of the metal brings us back to times when we were happy and protected, so we amass a hoard of treasure to keep that feeling alive. We prize gold because it reminds us of Mother.

I sniffed through the bars of the door, to the discomfiture of the guards both inside and outside the vault. I could tell that the day's takings had come from a multitude of dimensions. The pile of gold gleamed invitingly. I am afraid that the avid gleam in my eyes made the Klahds on duty very nervous. Quite a quantity of it smelled of dragon, meaning that at one time it had come from a hoard possessed by one of my kind. Since dragons never *give* away any of their amassed wealth, I only hoped that it had been obtained by stealth that did not result in harm or death to its possessor. To put it mildly, I would take against that. Still, the strange scent was not that of a dragon. It seemed that it should be familiar to me, but I just could not place it.

"Sirs, sirs!" A squeaky chorus of voices came from above. I looked up to see a small flight of Shutterbugs sail out of the air and land on the colorful display of storybooks beside the Treasury.

"There you are," Guido said, greeting the black and silver insects. These were denizens of Nikkonia. Their especial talent was the ability to capture an image on the sensitive film that lined their wings. A trained magician could transfer these images to larger pieces of parchment. "How come you didn't report in when I got here, Koda?"

Koda, the largest of the Shutterbugs, rubbed at his nose with the tip of his foreleg. "That Klahd is distrustful of us, sirs. He swats at us."

"Yeah, he's a regular xenophobe," Guido said. "I already caught that. Anything new to report?"

Koda turned to his number. They each spread out one wing, and small scales sifted down onto the bookshelf. "Nothing of much helpfulness, good sirs. The sight lines are not good, and the light levels are low. On the night of the last attack, we saw nothing at all, though we have taken many images, as you see. We wish to please Don Bruce!"

"You're good employees," Nunzio said, soothingly, to the agitated Shutterbug. "Just keep on doing the good work you've been doing." He and Guido picked up the small, translucent cells and held them up to the light. "I don't get it. What kind of monster have you ever heard of that can't be seen or smelled or heard, but can crunch up a stone pillar?"

"I dunno," Guido said. "One thing I learned, once we started workin' with the Boss, and here I am not speakin' of Don Bruce, is that there's way more out there than either of us will ever find out in our lifetimes. This, though, is not one of those things. We need to figure this out, and pronto!"

I turned back for one more scent of gold, but I felt a tug at my leash.

"C'mon, Gleep, boy," Nunzio said. "We will stake out this place tonight. In the meantime, I know a little place that does wyvern parmigiana like Mama used to make."

At precisely the evening hour of nine, gargoyle mouths attached to pillars and sconces around the vast shop all emitted the following announcement at once.

"Attention, please, guests of his royal majesty, King Petherwick. Thy visit, alas, draws to a close. Within five minutes the doors will be locked, and for security's sake, thou must be on the other side of it. Pray carry the goods thee wishes to purchase to any of our willing servants at the desks near the front, and they will count up thy expenditure for today. We wish to tender to thee our most sincere thanks that thou have visited King-Mart, and prithee have a nice day."

Guido put down the ceramic Kobold-shaped nightlight that he had been examining at the head of aisle 2.

"Anything, Gleep?" he asked.

The two enforcers, knowing the keenness of my sense of smell, had instructed me to sniff the inside and outside of the Treasury, and to compare the scents I found there with those of any of the customers. Nunzio's assessment was that the criminal would be unable to resist returning to the scene of the crime.

"Especially with all that nice gold piling up," he said.

"Too temptin'," Guido agreed. "How about it, little fellah?"

"Gleep," I said, ruefully.

I had just finished escaping for the eighth time from a family of Deveels who had been shopping for a birthday present for their daughter, a four-year-old future diva who screamed out her displeasure at anything offered to her by her increasingly desperate parents. She had decided upon first entering the store and spotting me that I would be the ideal present, and nothing she had been shown in the interim, a very long forty-five minutes, had dissuaded her. At the moment, she was hanging over her father's shoulder, crying and pointing at me, as he paid for an expensive doll and a lace-trimmed dress. I was forced to assume the Deveels' innocence on two counts. First, that they bore no scent that I could associate with the ravaged Treasury, and second, that the parents, unless they were geniuses at dissimulation and advanced multitasking, could not possibly have been "staking out the joint," as Guido put it, while they were trying to control their brood. I examined once again the area surrounding the Treasury and the aisles leading up to it. Nothing seemed out of place. I was perplexed.

The little Deveel and her family were at last ushered out and the door locked behind them by exhausted-looking guards. A couple of young women with brass cones on poles snuffed out three out of every four sconces. A team of sweepers in cross-gartered trews and floppy leather shoes swabbed the floor and emptied all of the wastepaper baskets. A matched team of four men in mail and tabards marched in formation around the Chancellor of the Exchequer as he gathered up the day's take from each of the sales desks and shut them into a small strongbox. Within half an hour, an armed team of guards arrived, escorting a wagon with a locked chest upon it, the proceeds from the other thirteen King-Marts spread out across the Bazaar. Howadzer counted up the proceeds and escorted it to the cage at the rear of the store.

We followed. In the gloom, the Treasury stood out like a beacon. The crystal walls had their own sconces, unextinguished, which caused the whole thing to glow brightly. The gold inside glittered in the flickering torchlight.

The lead escort came to the barred door of the Treasury and stamped his left foot twice.

"Who goes there?" asked the first guard.

"Me, Willis the Cobbler."

"No, you're not a cobbler tonight," Howadzer said, impatiently. "You are a guard!" He shook his head. "Try again."

The sentry at the door of the Treasury scratched his head. "Er, all right. Who goes there?"

This time the erstwhile cobbler rose to the occasion.

"Willis the Guard! And some friends. Marit, from the sheep farm, only he's a guard tonight, too. Braddock from the Fishermen's Guild, and Corrie the Woodworker. He's my neighbor, and a dab hand with a chisel, let me tell you." At an exasperated "ahem!" from Howadzer, he added, "They're guards, too."

"Well, pass, Willis, Marit, and you other two, and you, my lord," added the sentry. "He sort of forgot to mention you, but he'll get it next time, won't you, Willis?"

"Sure, sure. Sorry, my lord."

"Not one of 'em was ever in uniform, or I'll eat my hat," Nunzio whispered to his cousin.

"Your hat is safe," Guido whispered back. "While you were runnin' a check through the aisles a little while ago, I was readin' the employee roster, such as it is. To tell you the truth, it consists mostly of a list of names, professions, and villages, plus some comments penciled in on the side. Not real systematic, and it don't take into account strengths and weaknesses, not like what we keep in the Mob. These are all what you might call the little people who make everything possible."

We watched as the newcomers replaced the daytime guards, who stamped their left feet in unison, and marched away. The four night guards took up their posts as Howadzer upended the little chest and spilled coins on top of the pile already there.

"Wouldn't it make more sense to leave the money in the boxes?" Guido asked the chancellor.

"His majesty likes the public to see the amassing of King-Mart profits," Howadzer said, with a grimace. "I think it is a risk, especially under the circumstances."

He took his leave.

"We'll be right over there," Guido said. "Just go about your business like we wasn't here."

We withdrew to a point that Guido had identified as an

excellent coign of vantage inside a tent in a display of camping gear several yards distant. We had a good view of the entrance to the lighted tower. The guards were notably nervous, knowing that they would be under constant scrutiny. They fidgeted and glanced at one another, whispering. Guido put up with this for fifteen minutes or so, then he stormed out of the tent, and lowered his face until it was nearly touching theirs.

"Awright, you mugs," he barked. "Tenn-HUTT! Eyes forward! Backs straight! No talking' in the ranks. I don't want to hear another peep outta you guys unless it's to tell me that the monster's eatin' your leg. You got me?"

"Yes, my lord!" they chorused.

"I ain't your lord," Guido snarled. "I work for a livin'! Now, pay attention! You're guardin' the king's gold!"

He stomped back to the tent.

The guards became stalwart, silent, and upright. If they slewed their eyes sideways at one another now and again, Guido pretended not to notice.

Up in the rafters, my keen hearing detected the rustle of the Shutterbugs' wings as they flew about taking images.

Hours passed. Dinner was long past, and my stomach emitted rumblings audible in the silence of the aisles. At each emission, Guido and Nunzio removed themselves to the extreme other end of the tent. At the sound, the guards shifted from foot to foot, but they kept their eyes forward, and their right hands on sword hilt or spear haft. If they had been responsible for the theft of gold, they would not repeat their pilfering tonight, not with the eyes of the enforcers upon them. I was more curious to see the beast that had left the scent on the aisle floor and on the pillar of the king's audience chamber.

In the darkest hour, I heard the hiss of feet on the tiles.

I sprang up and shot out of the tent. Guido and Nunzio barely had time to don their hats and follow me.

WHAM!

By the time they caught up with me, I was standing on the intruder's chest, glaring into his face. Guido held a torch aloft and looked down into the perpetrator's face.

"Lord Howadzer! Gleep, let him have some air."

I realized my mistake and hastily vacated the chancellor's ribcage.

"Gleep!" I said, and licked his face by way of apology.

"Pthah!" he said, wiping his visage vigorously. "I was only coming in to see if everything was all right! Is this how you run a security check, by jumping on your employers?"

"When they come upon us unawares in the middle of the night, we do," Guido said, replacing his miniature crossbow in his inside breast pocket. "Gleep did exactly what I would have expected him to do. You didn't announce yourself, and I would have heard footsteps louder than a tiptoe myself."

"I still don't like it," the chancellor said. With a disdainful look at me, he turned on his heel and marched away. His retreating footsteps were twice as loud as the approaching ones. Nunzio and Guido looked thoughtful.

"I do not like that guy," Nunzio said. "He is just too self-righteous for his own good."

No further intrusions marked our night of surveillance.

In the morning, the blare of trumpets heralded the arrival of King Petherwick. With heralds and pages trotting ahead of him, his majesty made a visit to the Treasury.

He was accompanied by Lord Dalhailey and a handful of attendants.

"We are most pleased to see that no one was hurt overnight," he said. "And my gold is safe!"

He patted the pile of coins. With a *clang*, it shifted and collapsed in on itself. It was hollow! Petherwick let out a wail.

"My gold! The monster must have come up through the floor and stolen it!" He rounded upon the enforcers. "You were supposed to prevent this! I want reimbursement for every coin that went missing! Lord Howadzer will make up a reckoning. Your organization will make me restitution, as per our agreement."

"That remains to be seen," Nunzio said. "Naturally, we hope to recover your gold."

The Chancellor of the Exchequer looked harried, but the Minister of Marketing looked secretly pleased. I remarked upon the expression. Perhaps it was a sign of a rivalry between the two lordlings.

"We were supposed to keep an eye out for a monster that was causing loss of life," Guido said. "The Shutterbugs saw nothing. We saw nothing."

But I smelled something. That elusive scent touched my nostrils, and I went on alert. Determined to track it to its source, I dragged Nunzio behind me on my leash.

Sniff, sniff, sniff, sniff!

The enforcer's voice behind me was encouraging. "Find anything, boy? Whatcha got there, eh?"

Guido and the chancellor followed in our wake as I raced up the aisle. A memory was stirring. I couldn't really place my claw upon it, but I know I had smelled it before. But in a moment I should see the source, and my mystery would be solved!

Just before the display of cleaning products, the scent terminated without a clue as to whence it had come. I looked around forlornly.

"What's the matter, boy?" Nunzio asked, dropping to a crouch beside me.

"I lost the scent," I said. My woeful admission came out as "Gleep!"

Howadzer turned up his fleshy nose.

"Hmph! His majesty told you that cuddly-looking dragon would be of no use."

"So, tell me about the guys who were killed," Guido said, loitering about on ale break with a few of the Treasury guards.

"Like us, they worked for my lord chancellor," said a neatly turned out Klahd with a dark mustache. "Each of them went out to respond to noises we heard in the aisles, and didn't come back."

"Both of them were on nights when we had guys from Marketing with us, wasn't it?" asked a ginger-haired fellow.

"That's right," the mustachioed male said. "They went out, too, but they weren't hurt, or even killed."

"Interestin'," Guido said. "I'll have to keep an eye on the marketin' department."

Two more nights passed, uneventfully except for worrying withdrawals of gold from under our noses. I myself lay upon the threshold of the Treasury to forestall the arrival of the monster. My presence did little to instill confidence in the hearts of the guards, since they seemed to find me more of a threat than the invisible menace that had killed two of their fellows.

Guido's words about the marketing department had aroused my interest. As a result, any time new personnel came on shift, I inspected them and the weapons they bore closely. None of them bore the scent of Klahdish blood. None of these men were involved. The second night, four Klahds whom I did not recognize from previous visits took up their stations. Guido, Nunzio, and I made ourselves comfortable on woven lounge chairs from the outdoor furniture department. Nothing seemed to be happening. I was disappointed that our vigilance was failing to pay dividends in intelligence.

In the early hours toward dawn, voices at a distance from us in the dimly lit store broke the silence. Guido and Nunzio rose as if to check out the disturbance, but I recognized the voices. They were Lord Howadzer and Lord Dalhailey. I made a point of cocking my head, then stretching luxuriously and settling down again upon my rattan couch.

"Guess it's nothing' to worry about," Nunzio said, sitting down again. "Ugh! We have to speak to King Petherwick about real, live pest control." He stamped his shiny shoes down on the tiles.

"What's the matter?" Guido asked.

"Bug ran right over my foot!" He continued to step, but his quarry eluded him. "Fast little monster!" CRUNCH! "There." He pointed triumphantly. "Got it."

I caught the scent and scooted forward to slurp up the squashed body. 'Never miss an opportunity to try a new taste sensation' is my motto. I swallowed the morsel, and stopped, jaws agape.

"You okay, little buddy?" Nunzio asked.

I turned to lick his face in delight. Light had dawned!

I realized I should not have been inspecting only the customers, but the merchandise! One of the rakes smelled of Klahdish blood. It had been washed, but that was not enough to remove the scent for one with such as sensitive a sense of smell as mine.

I hearkened back upon my earliest dragonlet memories. The flavor of the titbit had reminded me of a lesson my mother had taught me and my siblings when I was but fresh out of the egg. She had brought some of these creatures back to our nest to teach us that there was a beast that was feared even by dragons for its insidiousness.

Goldbugs!

Goldbugs are the scourge of dragons, because they eat gold. They do, in fact, consume and digest it. They crave even tiny, minuscule morsels of the precious metal, and can winkle it out of even the tightest confines, destroying anything that might keep them from their favorite comestible. I realized in a flash of enlightenment that would explain the "bite mark" that had been taken out of the pillar. If someone who had handled gold, such as the Chancellor of the Exchequer, had touched the wall, it would have left a trace that was irresistible to the little pests. They would have swarmed up to the handprint, invisible to all but them, and chewed the stone until they had every atom of gold safe in their bellies.

They left a mark that played well into the grasp of the thief or thieves, who were able to spread rumors of a monster on the loose, and so distract attention from the series of burglaries that had been committed directly under the nose of the employees and lords of King-Mart! Since the bugs had been intercepted before they had walked very far, that spoke of a mortal agent, one of above-animal intelligence. Since all the robberies took place at night, the culprit could not be a customer. It had to be one of the staff. Guido was quite correct when he stated that he believed this to be an inside job. Somehow an employee, or more than one, had brought it to bear upon King-Mart and commit depredations against same for the purposes of theft.

But whom?

I was so excited at my discovery that I went in search of more of the insects. Entirely absent in the light of day, they abounded at this hour. I scented hundreds of them on the floor, scurrying away from me. I could not run them down without accidentally running them over. I swallowed a few by accident.

"What is it, boy?" Nunzio asked. I sucked up the nearest bug and spat it into the hand of the Mob enforcer.

"A bug?" Guido asked.

Nunzio's eyes lit up. I thought that his knowledge as a naturalist would not let him, or me, down. "Not an ordinary bug, cousin," he said. "It's the key to the whole conspiracy. Good boy, Gleep!"

He rumpled my head.

"Gleep," I exclaimed in relief.

"Since the two of you understand one another so well," Guido said, dryly, "perhaps you will let a poor ignorant Klahd in on your secret knowledge."

"Well, Guido, it is like this."

What followed was a learned discourse upon the biology and habits of the Goldbug. Nunzio had studied far more about *Genus Arthropoda Aureliphagus* than I ever dreamed he could absorb. Guido listened carefully, his eyes narrowing more and more as his cousin expounded.

"That explains it all," he said. "Now all we have to do is work out a means of exposin' the culprit. Now that we know what we're lookin' for, it should be a piece of cake."

We huddled for the rest of the night to work out our plan.

King Petherwick was extremely displeased that more of the gold had been abstracted from the Treasury, and none of the Klahds could explain it to him.

"I swear, your majesty," the leader of the knight-shift said fervently, when the king and his entourage inspected the Treasury the next morning, "nothing got past us, yet gold is gone again. We all swear we had nothing to do with it. You may search us. You will find no gold secreted about our persons. We will take a test of loyalty to you. The monster must have cast a spell upon us, and robbed us unaware."

Petherwick turned to my associates. "I take it that no spell was cast upon *you*. So, where is this monster?"

"We haven't found any evidence of a monster," Guido said. "At least, not a demon kind of monster, like you're thinking."

"What do you mean?" the king asked, aghast. "Of course, there must be something. The gold is gone! Men are dead!"

"Well, if a monster exists," Guido said smoothly, "then it never left the Treasury, because we've been watchin' it every minute. So, if it was here, it must still *be* here."

"But, where?"

I could not ask for a better cue. As the guards shifted and looked around nervously for a hidden monster, I crouched and began growling.

"Do you see it, boy?" Nunzio asked. He let go of my leash. The guards gasped and stepped backward.

I gathered my haunches and sprang upward, onto the roof of the Treasury, and clamped my jaws—half-open. I let out an eldritch wail from the depths of my chest, simulating the sound of another monster. My head twisted to the left, as if my prey was struggling, then I fell backward, flailing my claws.

"Gleeeeeep!" I wailed. I landed with a deafening jangle in the heap of money. The gold cushioned my fall. I was up in a moment, at bay, my eyes turned upward toward the an unseen enemy. The guards backed out of the small room in fear. I continued to do battle with my invisible foe.

It was a terrible battle, though the Klahds, and the customers looking astonished over their shoulders, only saw the half of it. I tore at the air, batting as my opponent appeared to fasten its teeth in my stubby right wing. I rolled painfully on one side and rabbit-kicked. The grimace on my face showed what efforts I was putting out as my third kick dislodged my foe and sent him sailing across the round room, where he must have landed near the wall. I flung myself onto the spot I had chosen, and turned over and over, gnashing and clawing, and occasionally letting out a yelp to indicate I had been bitten or clawed myself.

I had to congratulate myself on a masterful performance. When at last I "bested" my foe, I stood atop the heap of gold. I took an invisible mouthful and shook it vigorously, let it drop, then turned my back on the "corpse." With my rear foot, I raked a few clawsful of gold over the body to show my disdain, then trotted obediently to Nunzio to have my leash reattached.

"What a good dragon!" the enforcer said, reaching into his pocket for some dried earthworms. I slurped down my treat.

"Gleep!" I acknowledged with pride.

The rest of the onlookers were silent in awe.

"There you go, your majesty," Guido said, waving a huge palm. "Gleep took care of your monster for you. It's dead. You won't have to worry about it stealing from you anymore. You're gonna have to move the body, but that should be no big deal."

"But . . . but there is no body," Lord Dalhailey said. Then he realized his mistake. "I mean, I can't see anything. I'll have to get a closer look." He started toward the pile of gold. I slithered quickly to cut him off and sniffed him closely, from the toes up. I ended up peering into his face. He blanched. Klahds have said time and again that they do not like my breath, which if I may say, is rather sweet for a dragon. I did not like his smell, which reeked of Goldbug. He was the master of the metal-eating insects!

I growled.

Guido and Nunzio caught on in a trice (I told you that they were bright for Klahds), and surrounded him, two crossbows pointing at the daunted lordling's ribcage.

"So, there's no monster, huh? Just exactly how do you know that?"

Cornered, Dalhailey babbled.

"I mean, I don't see one, and though I've never heard of an invisible monster, I'm sure that maybe they exist in some dimension, but what is it doing here?" Terrified, he turned to Petherwick. "Help, my liege!"

"You see," Nunzio said, "he was using Goldbugs to steal the money right out from underneath your noses. They can't get far on their own, so he must bring them in on nights when there's a lot of gold in the Treasury. He knows when you've had a successful promotion; it's his job."

"Traitor!" Petherwick spat.

"So that's what you were doing in the store last night!"

Howadzer boomed. "You were spying out the Treasury, planning to steal more of our hard-earned receipts!" He turned to the Treasury guards. "Seize him!"

The guards hesitated. Howadzer's face turned crimson with fury.

"What are you waiting for?"

"They're all in on it," Guido said. "Those bugs are kind of hard to see in the dark, but this tower is very well lit. You couldn't miss a swarm of the size that can eat a pile of gold in a single night. I bet that he started turning them to his side a long time ago. It don't pay good to be a guard, and you're risking your life for someone else's coins, right? A few more coins here and there would help make life much more comfortable. Wouldn't it?"

"Kill them," Dalhailey gritted through his teeth.

The guards turned toward us. Guido and Nunzio swung the points of their crossbows to cover the quintet. I showed my teeth. It was clear that though we were outnumbered, we were not outmatched. The guards' hands dropped from their hilts.

"All right," Guido said. "Are you gonna surrender, or am I gonna have to call someone for a cleanup on aisle 3?"

The customers of King-Mart applauded.

"Great show," said a Deveel with a goatee. "That's why I shop here."

"Turns out," Guido said, after a satisfying pull at a big mug of ale brought to him by Bunny upon our return from Deva, "that Dalhailey was settin' up to finance his escape from King Petherwick's service. He bought a few of Lord Howadzer's men to get them to go along with his plot.

Usually it was the same guys night after night, until
Petherwick got the idea to teach everybody all the jobs.
When a newcomer wouldn't go along with the scheme,
well, by morning he was in no shape to tell anyone about
it. About the whole Treasury guard staff was in on it.
Howadzer never knew. You think he was unhappy *before*.
I think eventually Petherwick's gonna have to pension
him off and ask Hemlock if he can go live in his old
home town, he's so homesick. But Dalhailey's in big-time
trouble."

"And we were able to work it out all because of your
little pal here," Nunzio said, patting me on the head.

"Gleep!" I exclaimed, thanking him for recognizing
my contribution.

"Yeah, he kept circling the old boy and sniffing, until
Dalhailey finally confessed how he did it, by bringing in
a whole swarm of Goldbugs.

Skeeve sat forward, his face alight with interest.
"Goldbugs! I've never heard of them."

"I figured maybe not," Guido said, producing a crystal
vial. "So I brought you a few."

"King Petherwick was right all along that the problem
was pest control," Nunzio said. "He just didn't know that
it was his own minister who had infested the store with
them. He kept the ones he was using for the night in a box,
and let them loose within sniffing-range of the Treasury.
Later, he held out a lure to get them back to the box. If we
caught him walking around in the dark, well, he was just
looking out for the king's interests, or figuring out a new
display that would advertise the merchandise. It was the
perfect cover."

Skeeve examined the container. "Matt black, so you
can't see them in the dark even if they're moving."

"Yeah, I don't blame the Shutterbugs for missin' 'em, or us, either. But Gleep spotted 'em. He brought 'em to us, but if Nunzio hadn't known what they were, we might have missed the significance, since Gleep couldn't explain to us."

"Gleep!" I said. My pet and I exchanged knowing gazes.

Skeeve poured a few of the bugs out onto his palm. "They really eat gold?"

Nunzio grinned. "They sure do. Then, if you wait long enough, they excrete it, too. It's a slow way to make a fortune, but Dalhailey was plenty patient, and he had lots of bugs."

I snaked out my tongue and scooped a couple of the bugs off Skeeve's palm.

"Hey!" Skeeve said. "Those are my specimens!"

CRUNCH! CRUNCH! CRUNCH!

"But we got the confession outta Dalhailey too late. The bugs was already gone from the hiding place. Dalhailey wailed that one of his confederates musta gotten away with 'em. Petherwick filed a claim with Don Bruce to make his losses good. The Don wants shut of this guy so bad that he sent over a messenger with a strong box and a quit claim. We're rid of King-Mart, but the Don is out the money. We'll never get it back."

I felt the sensations of regurgitation beginning that I knew that small number of Goldbugs would trigger, on top of the vast number I had already eaten. I crouched at Guido's feet.

HUCK! HUCK! HUCK!

"No, Gleep!" Bunny commanded. "Not on the rug!"

Obedient to her wishes, I moved a few inches to the left. In a moment, I heaved up my prize at Guido's feet.

A steaming mass of molten gold the size of a prize pumpkin shimmered on the floor. I sat back on my haunches with a fragrant sigh.

"Guess we know what happened to the Goldbugs," Skeeve said, with a smile.

"Gleep," I said.

"I take back anything I ever thought about this dragon of yours, Skeeve," Guido said, patting me. "He's smart."

Skeeve and I exchanged a secret wink. I settled down on the carpet with my head on his foot.

MYTHING IN DREAMLAND

By Robert Asprin and Jody Lynn Nye

The dark green roof of the forest stretched out endlessly in every direction. To most, it would look like an idyllic paradise. To me, it was a major problem.

I gazed out over the massed pine trees, wondering what kind of wilderness we'd gotten stuck in. A few bare crests, like the one I was sitting on, protruded above the treeline, but they were miles away. None of it looked familiar, but no reason why it should. There were thousands of dimensions in existence, and I'd only been to a few.

At the very least, it was an embarassment. Here I was, considered publicly to be a hotshot magician, the great Skeeve, utterly lost because I'd tripped and fallen through a magic mirror.

I went through my belt pouch for the D-hopper. I was sure it was there somewhere. I wasn't alone, of course. Behind me, my partner and teacher Aahz paced up and down impatiently.

"I told you not to touch anything in Bezel's shop," the Pervect snarled. When a native of the dimension called Perv snarls, other species blanch. The expression shows off a mouthful of four-inch razor-honed fangs set in a scaly green face that even dragons considered terrifying. I was used to it, and besides, I was pretty much to blame for his bad mood.

"Who'd have thought anybody could fall through a looking glass?" I tried to defend myself, but my partner wasn't listening.

"If you had paid attention to a single thing I've said over the last however many years it's been . . ." Aahz held up a scaly palm in my direction. "No, don't tell me. I don't want to know. Garkin, at least, should have warned you."

"I know," I said. "It's my fault."

"It's just basic common sense when it comes to magik. Don't eat anything that says "Eat me." Don't drink anything that says "Drink me." And don't touch Klahdforsaken magik mirrors with barriers around them that say "Don't touch! . . . What did you say?" Aahz spun around on his heel.

"I said I know it's my fault. I was just trying to keep Gleep from eating the frame," I explained, sheepishly.

"Gleep!" the dragon beside me added brightly.

"So why didn't you tie him up before we went in?" Aahz said.

"I did tie him up!" I protested. "You know I did. You saw me knot the leash around a post." But we could both make an educated guess as to what had happened.

My dragon was not allowed in most reputable places, or what passed for reputable at the Bazaar at Deva, the largest trading area anywhere in the multitude of dimensions. It often happened that unscrupulous Deveel shop proprietors ridded themselves of unwanted merchandise at a profit, by arranging for accidents to occur. Such as having a convenient fire during which time the owners have an unshakeable alibi. Such as leaving the door ajar while they just run next door to borrow a cup of sugar. Such as loosening the tether on a baby dragon whose reputation for clumsiness was almost as impressive as its masters' reputation for magical skill and deep pockets. Said dragon would go charging after its beloved owner. Merchandise would start to hit the tent floor as soon as it entered. More goods, not even close to being in range of said rampaging dragon, would shatter into pieces. Outraged shopkeeper would appear demanding reimbursement at rates inflated four or five times their true worth. Unlucky customer would be forced to shell out or risk expulsion (or worse) from the Bazaar. All genuine valuables would have been removed from the shop ahead of time, of course.

"Maybe one of Bezel's rivals let him loose," I suggested hopefully, not liking my skill at tying knots to be called into question.

"What were you doing looking at that mirror anyhow?"

I felt a little silly admitting the truth, but it had been my curiosity that had gotten us stranded out here. "Massha told me about it. She said this was a really great item. It shows the looker his fondest dream. . . . Naturally, I wanted to see if it was anything we could use in our business. You know, to scope out our clients, find out what it is they really want . . ."

"And what did you see?" Aahz asked quickly.

"Only my own dreams," I said, wondering why Aahz was so touchy. "Daydreams, really. Me, surrounded by our friends, rich, happy, with a beautiful girl . . ." Although the mirror had been a little sketchy about the actual physical details I remembered vivid impressions of pulchritude and sex appeal.

A slow smile spread over Aahz's scaly features. "You know those dream girls, partner. They never turn out like you hope they will."

· I frowned. "Yes, but if it's your own dream, wouldn't she be exactly what you want? How about yours? What did you see?"

"Nothing," Aahz said flatly. "I didn't look."

"But you did," I insisted, grabbing on to a fleeting memory of Aahz with an astonished expression on his face. "What did you see?"

"Forget it, apprentice! It was a big fake. Bezel probably had a self-delusion spell put on the mirror to spur someone stupid like you into buying it. When you got home you'd have seen nothing reflected in it but Bezel's fantasy of a genuine sucker."

"No, I'm sure the mirror was real," I said thoughtfully. I knew what I'd daydreamed over the years, but those wishes had been piecemeal, little things now and again. I'd never had such a coherent and complete vision of my fantasies. "Come on, Aahz, what did you see?"

"None of your business!"

But I wasn't going to be put off that easily.

"C'mon. I told you mine," I wheedled. Aahz's wishes were bound to be interesting. He had seen dozens of dimensions, and been around a lot more than I had. "You probably have some sophisticated plan about an empire with you at the top of the heap. Hundreds of people begging for your services. Wine! Women! Song!"

"Shut up!" Aahz commanded. But by now, my curiosity was an unignorable itch.

"There's no one around here for miles," I said, and it was the truth. "Nobody could get up here in hearing range. They'd have to build a bridge to that next peak, and it's miles away. There's no one here but us. I'm your best friend, right?"

"I doubt that!"

"Hey!" I exclaimed, hurt.

Aahz relented, looking around. "Sorry. You didn't deserve that, even if you did make a boneheaded move by touching that mirror. Well, since it's just us. . . . Yeah, I saw something. That's why I think it's a delusion spell. I saw things the way they used to be, me doing magik? Big magik? Impressing the heck out of thousands? No, millions! I got respect. I miss that."

I was astonished. "You have respect. We respect you. And people in the Bazaar, they definitely respect you. The Great Aahz! You're feared in a hundred dimensions. You know that."

"It's not like in the old days," Aahz insisted, his gaze fixed on the distance, and I knew he wasn't seeing the endless trees. "Time was we'd never have been stuck up here on a bare mountaintop like two cats on a refrigerator . . ."

I opened my mouth to ask what a refrigerator was, then decided I didn't want to interrupt the flow. Aahz seldom opened up his private thoughts to me. If he felt like he wanted to unload, I considered it a privilege to listen.

"I mean, it ain't nothing showy, but time was I could have just flicked my wrist, and a bridge would've appeared, like that!"

He flicked his wrist.

I gawked. A suspension bridge stretched out from the peak on which we were standing all the way to the next mountain. It was made completely out of playing cards, from its high arches down the cables to the spans and pylons that disappeared down into the trees. We stared at each other and gulped.

"That wasn't there before," I ventured. But Aahz was no longer looking at the bridge or at me. He was staring at his finger as if it had gone off, which in a sense it had.

"After all these years," he said softly. "It's impossible." He raised his head, feeling around for force lines. I did the same.

The place was full of them. I don't mean full, I mean *full*. Running through the ground like powerful subterranean rivers, and overhead like highly charged rainbows, lines of force were everywhere. Whatever dimension we'd stepped into was chockablock with magik. Aahz threw back his head and laughed. A pretty little yellow songbird flew overhead, twittering. He pointed a finger at it. The bird, now the size of a mature dragon, emitted a basso profundo chirp. It looked surprised.

It had nothing on me. For years I had thought only my late magik teacher Garkin could have removed the spell that robbed Aahz of his abilities. I didn't know a dimension existed where the laws of magik as I had learned them didn't apply. It seems I was wrong.

Aahz took off running toward the bridge.

"Hey, Skeeve, watch this!" he shouted. His hands darted out. Thick, fragrant snow began to fall, melting into a perfumed mist before it touched me. Rainbows darted through the sky. Rivers of jewels sprang up, rolling between hills of gold. I tripped over one and ended up in a pool of rubies.

"Aahz, wait!" I cried, galloping after him as fast as I could. Gleep lolloped along with me, but we couldn't catch him. As soon as Aahz's foot hit the bridge, it began to shrink away from the mountainside, carrying him with it. He was so excited he didn't notice. Once when I hadn't really been listening he had told me about contract bridge. This must be what he meant. This bridge was contracting before my eyes.

"Aahz! Come back!" I called. There was nothing I could do. Gleep and I would have to jump for it. I grabbed his collar, and we leaped into space.

I was pushing with every lick of magik in my body, but we missed the end of the bridge by a hand's length. A card peeled itself up off the rear of the span. It was a joker. The motley figure put its thumbs in its ears and stuck out its tongue at me, just before the bridge receded out of sight. I didn't have time to be offended by its audacity, since I was too busy falling.

"Gleeeeeeeep!" my dragon wailed, as he thudded onto the steep slope beside me. "Gle-ee-ee-eep!"

"Gr-ra-ab so-ome-thi-ing," I stuttered, as we rolled helplessly down the hill. Where had all those force lines gone? I should have been able to anchor myself to the earth with a bolt of magik. We tumbled a good long way until my pet, showing the resourcefulness I knew was in him, snaked his long neck around a passing tree stump, and his tail around my leg. We jerked to an abrupt halt. I hung upside down with my head resting on a shallow ledge that overlooked a deep ravine. We'd only just missed falling into it. As soon as I caught my breath, I crawled up the slope to praise Gleep. He shot out his long tongue and affectionately planted a line of slime across my face. I didn't flinch as I usually did. I figured he deserved to lick me if he wanted to. He'd saved both of us.

I studied my surroundings. If there was a middle to

nowhere, I had unerringly managed to locate it. The remote scraps of blue visible through the forest roof were all that was left of the sky. Once my heart had slowed from its frantic "That's it, we're all going to die now" pounding to its normal, "Well, maybe not yet" pace I realized that the ledge we almost fell off was wide enough to walk on. I had no idea where it led, but sitting there wasn't going to help me find Aahz or the jokers who had carried him off.

"You lost, friend?" a male voice asked.

I jumped up, looking around for its source. I could see nothing but underbrush around me. Out of reflex I threw a disguise spell on me and Gleep, covering my strawberry-blond hair with slicked-back black and throwing my normally round and innocent-looking blue eyes into slanted, sinister pits. Gleep became a gigantic red dragon, flames licking out from underneath every scale.

"No! I'm just . . . getting my bearings."

A clump of trees stood up and turned around. I couldn't help but stare. On the other side of the mobile copse was the form of a man.

"Well, you sure look lost to me," said the man, squinting at me in a friendly fashion. He was dressed in a fringed jacket and trousers, with a striped fur cap perched on his head and matching boots on his feet. His skin was as rough as bark, and his small, dark eyes peered at me out of crevices. Hair and eyebrows alike were twiglike thickets. The eyebrows climbed high on his craggy forehead. "Say, that's pretty good illusion-making, friend! You an artist?"

"Huh?" I goggled, taken aback. How could he have spotted it so readily? "No. I'm a master magician. I am . . . the Great Skeeve."

The man stuck out a huge hand and clenched my fingers. I withdrew them and counted them carefully to make sure none had broken off in his solid grip. "Pleased to meet you. Name's Alder. I'm a backwoodsman. I live around these parts. I only ask because illusion's a major art form around here. You're pretty good."

"Thanks," I said dejectedly. An illusion was no good if it was obvious. I let it drop. "I only use it because I don't look very impressive in person."

Alder tutted and waved a hand. "It don't matter what you look like. It's only your personality anybody pays attention to. Things change around here so often." He lifted his old face, sniffed, and squinted one eye. He raised a crooked finger. "Like now, for example."

Alder was right. While I watched, his leathery skin smoothed out a little and grew paler. Instead of resembling a gnarled old oak he looked like a silver-haired birch instead. I was alarmed to discover the transformation was happening to me, too. Some force curled around my legs, winding its way up my body. The sensation wasn't unpleasant, but I couldn't escape from it. I didn't struggle, but something was happening to my body, my face.

"Gleep!" exclaimed my dragon. I glanced over at him. Instead of a blue dragon with vestigal wings, a large, brown fluffy dog sat looking at me with huge blue eyes. Once I got past the shock I realized the transformation really rather suited him. I pulled a knife out of my pocket and looked at my reflection in the shiny blade. The face looking back at me was tawny skinned with topaz-yellow eyes like a snake and a crest of bright red hair. I shuddered.

"What if I don't like the changes?" I asked Alder.

Meditatively he peeled a strip of bark off the back of one arm and began to shred it between his fingers. "Well, there are those who can't do anything about it, but I'm betting you can, friend. Seeing as how you have a lot of influence."

"Who with?" I demanded. "What's the name of this dimension? I've never been here before."

"It ain't a dimension. This is the Dreamland. It's common to all people in all dimensions. Every mind in the Waking World comes here, every time they go to sleep. You don't recognize it consciously, but you already know how to behave here. It's instinctive for you. You're bending dreamstuff, exerting influence, just as if you lived here all the time. You must have pretty vivid dreams."

"This is a dream? But it all seems so real."

"It don't mean it ain't real, sonny," Alder whistled through his teeth. "Look, there's rules. The smarter you are, the more focused, the better you get on in this world. Lots of people are subject to the whims of others, particularly of the Sleepers themselves, but the better you know your own mind, the more control over your own destiny you've got. Me, I know what I like and what I don't. I like it out in the wilderness. Whenever the space I'm in turns into a city, I just move on until I find me a space where there ain't no people. Pretty soon it quiets down and I have things my own way again. Now, if I didn't know what I wanted, I'd be stuck in a big Frustration dream all the time."

"I just had a Frustration Dream," I said, staring off in the general direction in which Aahz had disappeared. "How is it that if I have so much power here I couldn't catch up with my friend?"

"He's gone off on a toot," Alder said, knowingly. "It happens a lot to you Waking Worlders. You get here and you go a little crazy. He got a taste of what he wants, and he's gone after more of it."

"He doesn't need anything," I insisted. "He's got everything back at home." But I paused.

"There's got to be something," Alder smiled. "Everyone wants one thing they can't get at home. So what does your friend want?"

That was easy, Aahz had told me himself. "Respect."

Alder shook his head. "Respect, eh? Well, I don't have a lot of respect for someone who abandons his partner like he did."

I leaped immediately to Aahz's defense. "He didn't abandon me on purpose."

"You call a fifty-mile bridge an accident?"

I tried to explain. "He was excited. I mean, who wouldn't be? He had his powers back. It was like ... magik."

"Been without influence a long time, has he?" Alder asked, with squint-eyed sympathy.

"Well, not exactly. He's very powerful where we come from," I insisted, wondering why I was unburdening myself to a strange old coot in the wilderness, but it was either that or talk to myself. "But he hasn't been able to do magik in years. Not since my old mentor, er, put a curse on him. But I guess that doesn't apply here."

"It wouldn't," Alder assured me, grinning. "Your friend seems to have a strong personality, and that's what matters. So we're likely to find your friend in a place he'd get what he wanted. Come on. We'll find him."

"Thanks," I said dubiously. "I'm sure I'll be able to find him. I know him pretty well. Thanks."

"Don't you want me to come along?"

I didn't want him to know how helpless I felt. Aahz and I had been in worse situations than this. Besides, I had Gleep, my trusty ... dog ... with me. "No, thanks,"

I said, brightly. "I'm such a powerful wizard I don't really need your help."

"Okay, friend, whatever you want," Alder said. He stood up and turned around. Suddenly, I was alone, completely surrounded by trees. I couldn't even see the sky.

"Hey!" I yelled. I sought about vainly. Not only couldn't I see the backwoodsman, but I'd lost sight of the cliffside path, the hillside, and even what remained of the sky. I gave in. "Well, maybe I need a little help," I admitted sheepishly. A clearing appeared around me, and Alder stood beside me with a big grin on his face. "Come on, then, youngster. We've got a trail to pick up."

Alder talked all the way through the woods. Normally the hum of sound would have helped me to focus my mind on the problem at hand, but I just could not concentrate. I'm happiest in the middle of a town, not out in the wilderness. Back when I was an apprentice magician and an opportunistic but largely unsuccessful thief, the bigger the population into which I could disappear after grabbing the valuables out of someone's bedroom, the better to escape detection. Alder's rural accent reminded me of my parents' farm that I had run away from to work for Garkin. I hated it. I forced myself to remember he was a nice guy who was helping us find Aahz.

"Now, looky-look here," he said, glancing down as we came to a place where six or seven paths crossed in a knot of confusion. I couldn't tell which one Aahz and his moving bridge had taken, but I was about to bolt down the nearest turning, just out of sheer frustration. "Isn't this the most interesting thing? . . . What's the matter?" he asked, noticing the dumb suffering on my face. "I'm talking too much, am I?"

"Sorry," I said, hiding my expression too late. "I'm

worrying about my partner. He was so excited about getting his powers back that he didn't notice he was getting carried away—literally. I'm concerned that when he notices he's going to try to come back and find me."

"If what you say is true it's going to take him a little time to get used to wielding influence again," Alder said. I started to correct him, but if this was the way the locals referred to magik, I wouldn't argue. "Right now we're on the trail of that bridge. Something that big doesn't pass through without leaving its marks, and it didn't. He lifted a handful of chocolate-colored pebbles from the convergence, and went on lecturing me.

"Now, this here trail mix is a clear blind. Those jokers must have strewn it to try and confuse us, but I'm too old a hand for that. I'm guessing that bridge is on its way to the capital, but I'd rather trust following the signs than my guesses. We have to hurry to see them before the winds of change blow through and mess up the tracks. I don't have enough strength myself to keep them back."

"Can I help?" I asked. "I'm pretty good at ma— I mean influence. And if my partner packs a kick here, I should, too."

Alder's branchlike eyebrows rose. "Maybe you could, at that. Let's give it a try!"

Let's just say I wasn't an unqualified success to start. Dreamish influence behaved like magik in that one concentrated hard picturing what one wanted to achieve, used the force lines to shape it, then hoped the committee running the place let one's plans pass. Like any committee they made some changes, the eventual result resembling, but not being completely like my original intention, but close enough. Over the several days it took us to walk out of the forest, I attained a certain amount of mastery over my surroundings, but never enough to pop us to the capital city of Celestia or locate Aahz. I did learn to tell when the winds of change were coming through. They felt like the gentle alteration that had hit me and Gleep the first day, but far stronger. They were difficult to resist, and I had to protect the entire path we were following. This I did by picturing it, even the parts we couldn't see, as a long rope stretched out in front of us. It could have knots in it, but we didn't want it breaking off unexpectedly. I might never find Aahz if we lost this trail. I did other little tasks around the campground, just to learn the skill of doing two things at once. Alder was a great help. He was a gentler teacher than either Garkin or Aahz. For someone who had little influence of his own, he sure knew how to bring out the best in other magicians.

"Control's the most important thing," he said, as I struggled to contain a thicket fire I had started by accident when I tried to make a campfire one night. "Consider yourself at a distance from the action, and think smaller. What you can do with just a suggestion is more than most people can with their best whole efforts. Pull back and concentrate on getting the job done. A little effort sometimes pays off better than a whole parade with a brass band."

I chuckled. "You sound like Aahz."

"What?" Alder shouted.

"I said . . ." but my words were drowned out by deafening noise. The trees around us were suddenly thrust apart by hordes of men in colorful uniforms. I shouldn't say "horde," though they were dressed in red, black, and gold, because they marched in orderly ranks, shoving me and Alder a dozen yards apart. Each of them carried a musical instrument from which blared music the likes of which I hadn't heard since halftime at the Big Game on the world of Jahk.

I picked myself up off the ground. "What," I asked as soon as my hearing returned, "was that?"

"That was a nuisance," Alder said, getting to his feet and brushing confetti off his clothes.

"No kidding," I agreed, "but what was it?"

"A nuisance," Alder repeated. "That's what it's called. It's one of the perils of the Dreamland. Oh, they're not really dangerous. They're mostly harmless, but they waste your time. They're a big pain in the sitter. Sometimes I think the Sleepers send them to get us to let go of ourselves so they can change us the way they want. Other people just plain attract them, especially those they most irk."

I frowned. "I don't want to run into any more of them myself," I said. "They could slow us down finding Aahz."

Alder pointed a finger directly at my nose. "That's exactly what they might do. Stick with me, friend, and I'll see you around the worst of them, or I won't call myself the finest backwoodsman in the Dreamland."

Using the virtually infinite reservoir of power available to me, I concentrated on keeping the trail intact so that Alder could find it. I found that the less influence I used, the fewer nuisances troubled us. So long as I kept my power consumption low, we had pretty easy going. It would have been a pleasant journey if I hadn't been concerned.

It was taking so long to locate Aahz that I began to

worry about him. What if the contracted bridge had trapped him somewhere? What if he had the same problems I did with influence? He might have trouble finding enough food, or even enough air! He wasn't as fortunate as I had been, to locate a friendly native guide like Alder. Visions of Aahz in dire straits began to haunt my dreams, and drew my attention away from admiring the handsome, though sometimes bizarre, landscape. Gleep, knowing my moods, tried to cheer me up by romping along and cutting foolish capers, but I could tell that even he was worried.

One day Alder stopped short in the middle of a huge forest glade, causing me and Gleep to pile up against the trees growing out of his back.

"Ow!" I said, rubbing my bruises.

"Gleep!" declared my dragon.

"We're here," Alder said. He plucked a handful of grass from the ground and held it out to me. It didn't look any different from the grass we'd been trudging over for the last three days. "We're in Celestia."

"Are you sure?" I demanded.

"Sure as the sun coming up in the morning, sonny," Alder said.

"All this forest in the midst of the capital city?"

"This is the Dreamland. Things change a lot. Why not a capital made of trees?"

I glanced around. I had to admit the trees themselves were more magnificent than I'd seen anywhere else, and more densely placed. The paths were regular in shape, meeting at square intersections. Elegant, slender trees with light coming out of the top must be the streetlights. Alder was right: it looked like a city, but all made of trees!

"Now, this is my kind of place," Alder said, pleased,

rubbing his hands together. "Can't wait to see the palace. I bet the whole thing's one big tree house."

Within a few hundred paces he pointed it out to me. What a structure! At least a thousand paces long, it was put together out of boards and balanced like a top on the single stem of one enormous oak tree. The vast door was accessible only by way of a rope ladder hung from the gate. A crudely-painted sign on the door was readable from the path: "Klubhse. Everywun welcm. The King." In spite of its rough-hewn appearance there was still something regal about it.

"No matter what shape it takes, it's still a palace," Alder said. "You ought to meet the king. Nice guy, they tell me. He'd like to know an influential man like you. Your friend has to be close by. I can feel it."

A powerful gale of changes prickled at the edge of my magikal sense. I fought with all my might to hold it back as Alder knelt and sniffed at the path.

"This way," he said, not troubling to rise. Unable to help himself, he became an enormous, rangy, blood-red dog that kept its nose to the path. Overjoyed to have a new friend, Gleep romped around Alder, then helped him follow the tracks. The scent led them directly to two vast tree trunks in the middle of a very crowded copse. Alder rose to his feet, transforming back into a man as he did.

"We're here," he said.

"But these are a couple of trees!" I exclaimed. Then I began to examine them more closely. The bark, though arrayed in long vertical folds, was smooth, almost as smooth as cloth. Then I spotted the roots peeking out from the ground. They were green. Scaly green. Like Aahz's feet. I looked up.

"Yup," said Alder with satisfaction. "We've found your buddy, all right."

A vast statue of Aahz scratched the sky. Standing with hands on its hips, the statue had a huge smile that beamed out over the landscape, Aahz's array of knife-sharp teeth looking more terrifying than ever in twenty-times scale. I was so surprised I let go of the control I was holding over the winds of change. A whirlwind, more a state of mind than an actual wind, came rushing through. Trees melted away, leaving a smooth black road under my feet. White pathways appeared on each side of the pavement. People rushing back and forth on foot and in vehicles. Across the way the palace was now undisputedly a white marble building of exquisite beauty. But the statue of Aahz remained, looming over the landscape, grinning. I realized to my surprise that it was an office building. The eyes were windows.

With Alder's help I located a door in the leg and entered. People bustled busily around, unlike the rest of the Dreamland where I had seen mostly Klahds, here there were also Deveels, Imps, Gremlins, and others, burdened down with file folders and boxes or worried expressions. Just as I had thought, given infinite resources Aahz would have a sophisticated setup with half of everybody working for him, and the other half bringing him problems to solve. And as for riches, the walls were polished mahogany and ivory, inlaid with gold and precious stones. Not flashy— definitely stylish and screaming very loudly of money. I'd always wondered what Aahz could do with infinite resources, and now I was seeing it. A small cubicle at one end of the foot corridor swept me up all the way to the floor marked "Headquarters."

A shapely woman who could have been Tananda's twin

with pink skin sat at a curved wooden desk near the cubicle door. She spoke into a curved, black stick poking out of her ear. She poked buttons as buzzers sounded. "Aahz Unlimited. May I help you? I'm sorry. Can you hold? Aahz Unlimited. May I help you? I'm sorry. Can you hold?"

I gazed into the room, at the fanciest office suite I could imagine. I knew Aahz was a snazzy dresser, but I never realized what good taste he had in furniture. Every item was meant to impress. The beautifully paneled walls were full of framed letters and testimonials, and every object looked as though it cost a very quiet fortune. All kinds of people hurried back and forth among the small rooms. I found a woman in a trim suit-dress who looked like she knew what she was doing and asked to see Aahz.

"Ah, yes, Mr. Skeeve," she said, peering at me over her pince-nez eyeglasses. "You are expected."

"Gleep?" added my dragon, interrogatively.

"Yes, Mr. Gleep," the woman smiled. "You, too."

"Partner!" Aahz called as I entered. He swung his feet off the black marble-topped desk and came to slap me on the back. "Glad to see you're okay. No one I sent out has been able to locate you."

"I had a guide . . . ," I said, looking around for Alder. He must have turned his back and blended in with the paneling. I brought my attention back to Aahz. After all the worrying I had done over the last many days I was relieved to see that Aahz seemed to be in the very best of health and spirits. "I was worried about you, too."

"Sorry about that," Aahz said, looking concerned and a little sheepish. "I figured it was no good for both of us to wander blindly around a new dimension searching for one another. I decided to sit tight and wait for you to find me. I made it as easy as I possibly could. I knew once you spotted the building you'd find me. How do you like it?"

"It's great," I said firmly. "A good resemblance. Almost uncanny. It doesn't . . . put people off, does it?" I asked, thinking of the seven-foot fangs.

"No," Aahz said, puzzled. "Why should it?"

"Oh, Mr. Aahz!"

A small thin man hurried into the office with the efficient-looking woman behind him with a clipboard. "Please, Mr. Aahz, you have to help me," the man said. "I'm being stalked by nightmares."

Aahz threw himself into the big chair behind the desk and gestured me to sit down. The little man poured out a pathetic story of being haunted by the most horrible monsters that came to him at night.

"I'm so terrified I haven't been able to sleep for weeks. I heard about your marvelous talent for getting rid of problems, I thought . . ."

"What?" Aahz roared, sitting up and showing his teeth. "I've never heard such bunkum in my life," Aahz said, his voice filling the room. The little man looked apprehensive. "Pal, you've got to come to me when you really need me, not for something minor like this."

"What? What?" the little man sputtered.

"Miss Teddybear," Aahz gestured to the efficient woman, who hustled closer. "Get this guy set up with Fazil the Mirrormaster. Have him surround this guy's bed with reflectors that reflect out. That'll scotch the nightmares. If they see themselves the way you've been seeing them they'll scare the heck out of themselves. You'll never see them again. Guaranteed. And I'll only take a . . . thirty percent commission on the job. Got that?"

"Of course, Mr. Aahz." The efficient woman bowed herself out.

"Oh, thank you, Mr. Aahz!" the little man said. "I'm sorry. You're just like everyone said. You are absolutely amazing! Thank you, thank you!"

Aahz grinned, showing an acre or so of sharp teeth. "You're welcome. Stop by the receptionist's desk on the way out. She'll give you the bill."

The little man scurried out, still spouting thanks. As soon as the door closed another testimonial popped into existence on the already crowded wall. Aahz threw himself back into his chair and lit a cigar.

"This is the life, eh, partner?"

"What was that about?" I asked, outraged. "The guy was frightened out of his life. You gave him a solution without leaving your office. You could have gone to see what was really going on. He could have someone stalking him, someone with a contract out on him . . ."

Aahz waved the cigar and smoke wove itself into a complicated knot. "Psychology, partner, I keep telling you! Let him worry that he's wasting my time. He'll spread the word, so only people with real troubles will come looking for me. In the meantime, Fazil's an operative of mine. He'll check out the scene. If the guy just has some closet monsters that are getting above themselves, the mirrors will do the trick. If it's something worse, Fazil will take care of it." He pounded a hand down on a brown box on the desktop. "Miss Teddybear, would you send in some refreshments?" Aahz gestured at the wall. "Your invisible friend can have some, too. I owe him for getting you here safely."

"It's nothing, friend," the backwoodsman said. He had been disguised as a section of ornamental veneer. He turned around and waddled over to shake hands. "You've made yourself right at home here."

"You bet I have," Aahz said, looking around him with satisfaction. "I've been busy nonstop since I got here, making connections and doing jobs for people."

The efficient aide returned pushing a tray of dishes. She set before Gleep a bowl of something that looked disgusting but was evidently what every dragon wishes he was served every day. My pet lolloped over and began to slurp his way through the wriggling contents. My stomach lurched, but it was soon soothed by the fantastic food that Aahz's assistant served me.

"This is absolutely terrific," I said. "With all the information you've gathered, have you figured out a way to get us back to Deva?"

Aahz shook his head.

"I'm not going back."

"We'll tell everyone about this place, and . . . What?" I stopped short to stare at him. "What do you mean you're not going back?"

"For what?" Aahz asked, sneering. "So I can be the magik-free Pervert again?"

"You've always been Pervect without them," I said, hopefully trying to raise his spirits with a bad joke.

It didn't work. Aahz's expression was grim. "You don't have a clue how humiliating it is when I can't do the smallest thing. I relied on those abilities for centuries. It's been like having my arm cut off to be without them. I don't blame Garkin. I'd have done the same thing to him for a joke. It was just my bad luck that Isstvan's assassin happened to have picked that day to put in the hit. But now I've found a place I can do everything I used to."

"Except D-hop," I pointed out, slyly, I hoped. "You're stuck in one dimension for good."

"So what?" Aahz demanded. "Most people live out their whole lives in one dimension."

"Or hang out with your old buddies."

Aahz made a sour face. "They know me the way I was before I went through the mirror. Powerless." He straightened his back. "I won't miss 'em."

I could tell he was lying. I pushed. "You won't? What about Tanda and Chumley? And Massha? What about the other people who'll miss you? Like me?"

"You can visit me in here," Aahz said. "Get the mirror from Bezel, and don't let anyone else know you've got it."

"You'll get bored."

"Maybe. Maybe not. I've got a long time to get over being powerless. I can't do anything out there without magikal devices or help from apprentices. I'm tired of having people feel sorry for me. Here no one pities me. They respect what I can do."

"But you don't belong here. This is the world of dreams."

"*My* dream, as you pointed out, apprentice!"

"Partner," I said stiffly. "Unless you're breaking up the partnership."

Aahz looked a little hurt for the moment. "This can be a new branch office," he suggested. "You can run the one on Deva. You already do, for all practical purposes."

"Well, sure, we can do that, but you won't get much outside business," I said. "Only customers with access to Bezel's mirror will ever come looking for you, and you already said not to let anyone know we've got it."

"I can stand it," Aahz assured me. "I'm pretty busy already. I'm important here. I like it. The king and I—we're buddies." Aahz grinned, tipping me a wink. "He said

I was an asset to the community. I solve a few little problems for him now and then." The efficient aide leaned in the door. " 'Scuse me, partner." He picked up a curved horn made of metal and held it to his ear. "Hey, your majesty! How's it going?"

If there was ever a Frustration dream, I was living it. For every reason I presented as to why Aahz should return to Deva, Aahz had a counter-argument. I didn't believe for a moment he didn't care about the people he would be leaving behind, but I did understand how he felt about having his powers restored to him. He'd get over the novelty in time.

Or would he? He'd been a powerful magician for centuries before Garkin's unluckily timed gag. Would I be able to stand the thought of losing my talents twice? He did seem so happy here. He was talking with the local royalty like an old friend. Could I pull him away from that? But I had to. This was wrong.

"I'd better leave, sonny," Alder said, standing up. "This sounds like an argument between friends."

"No, don't go," I pleaded, following him out into the hallway. "This isn't the Aahz I know. I have got to get him through the portal again, but I don't know how to find it."

Alder cocked his shaggy head at me. "If he's half the investigator he seems to be, he already knows where it is, friend. The problem you're going to have is not getting him to the water, but making him drink. Right now, things are too cushy for him. He's got no reason to leave."

I felt as though a light had come on. "You mean, he hasn't had enough nuisances?"

Alder's rough-skinned face creased a million times in a sly grin. "I think that's just what I do mean, youngster. Best of luck to you." He turned his back and vanished.

"Thanks!" I called out. Using every bit of influence that was in me, I sent roots down into the deepest wells of magikal force I could find, spreading them out all over the Dreamland. I didn't try to dampen Aahz's light. I brightened it. I made every scale on the building gleam with power, both actual and perceived. Anyone with a problem to solve would know that this was the guy to come to. Aahz would be inundated with cases, important, unimportant, and trivially banal. There would be people looking for lost keychains. There'd be little girls with kittens up trees. There'd be old ladies coming to Aahz to help them find the eye of a needle they were trying to thread. Most important, unless I had missed something on my journey here, with that much influence flying around, every nuisance in the kingdom would converge on the building. If there was one thing my partner hated, and had lectured me on over and over again, it was wasting time. If I couldn't persuade Aahz to leave the Dreamland, maybe nuisances could.

My gigantic injection of magik took effect almost immediately While I watched, things started to go wrong with the running of Aahz Unlimited. The files the efficient employees were carrying to and fro grew so top-heavy that they collapsed on the floor, growing into haystacks of paper. Some of the employees got buried in the mass. Others ran for shovels to get them out, and ended up tangled with dozens of other people who came in to help. Framed letters began to pop off the wall, falling to the floor in a crash of glass.

Then the entire building seemed to sway slightly to the right.

"What's going on here?" I could hear Aahz bellow. He emerged from his office, and clutched the door frame as

the building took a mighty lurch to the left. I grabbed for
the nearest support, which happened to be Gleep. He had
become a giant green bird with a striped head and a flat
beak and curved talons, which he drove deep into the
wooden parquet floor. "Why is everything swaying?"

Miss Teddybear flew to the eye-windows and looked
down.

"Sir, giant beavers are eating the leg of the building!"

"What?" Aahz ran to join her, with Gleep and me in
close pursuit. We stared down out of the huge yellow oval.

Sure enough, enormous brown-black creatures with
flat tails and huge square front teeth were gnawing away
at the left leg of Aahz Unlimited. As each support in the
pylon snapped, the building teetered further.

Aahz leaned out of the window. "*SCRAM!*" he shouted.
The attackers ignored him.

"Everyone get down there and stop them!" Aahz commanded. Miss Teddybear hurried away, following the
flood of employees into the moving-box chamber.

As Aahz and I watched, his people poured out of the
building. They climbed the leg, clinging to it in an effort
to keep the monsters from burrowing any further. The
beavers turned, and swatted them off with flips of their
flat tails. Wailing, the employees whirled out of sight like
playing cards on the wind. The monsters went on chew-
ing. I felt bad about the people, though Alder has assured
me that Dreamlanders were not easily hurt or killed.

"Call for reinforcements!" Aahz bellowed. I stared in
amazement as white circles whirled out of the air, plaster-
ing themselves all over the leg, but the beavers chewed
right through them. In no time they'd whittled the leg down
to a green stick. The building was going to fall. Aahz's empire was crumbling before our eyes. Gleep seized each of

us in one mighty claw and flew with us to the elevator. The floor split under us as we crowded into the small cabinet.

The ride down seemed to take forever and ever. Aahz paced up and back in irritation, dying to get out there and do something to stop the destruction. I could tell he was trying to focus his magik on driving the monsters away and keeping his newfounded empire intact. I concentrated all my magik on keeping us from getting hurt. The forces I had stirred up scared me. I didn't know if I'd get us killed trying to bring Aahz home.

"Come on," he snarled, leaping out of the chamber as it ground to a stop. "We've got to hurry."

It was too late. Just as we emerged from the front door, the enormous Aahz-shaped structure wobbled back and forth, and crashed to lie flat in the park. I gulped. One second sooner, and we'd have been inside when it fell. Aahz stared at the wreckage in dismay.

"Oh, well," I said, trying to look innocent. "Easy come, easy go."

"Yeah," Aahz said, with a heavy sigh. "It was just a dream. There's always more where that came from."

A boy in a tight-fitting uniform with a pillbox hat strapped to his head came rushing up. He handed Aahz a small package the size of his hand. Aahz gave the boy a coin and tore open the paper. Inside was a small mirror. I recognized the frame. "It's the portal back to Deva," I said in surprise. "You were looking for it after all."

"This was supposed to be for you," Aahz mumbled, not meeting my eyes. "If you had wanted to use it. If you had wanted to stay, I wouldn't be upset about it."

The change of tense made me hopeful. "But now you want to go back?" I asked encouragingly.

"I don't need to be bashed over the head with it," Aahz said, then looked at the fallen building, which was already beginning to be overgrown with vines. "But I almost was. I can take a hint. Come on." He took hold of the edges of the mirror. With a grunt of effort, he stretched the frame until the mirror was big enough for all of us.

Through it, instead of the reflection of our dreams, I could see Massha, my apprentice, my bodyguards Nunzio and Guido, and Tananda, our friends all surrounding the hapless Bezel. The Deveel, scared pale pink instead of his usual deep red, held his hands up to his shoulders, and his face was the picture of denial. Terrified denial. He might not be guilty for setting us off on this little adventure after all.

Aahz grinned, fearsomely.

"C'mon. Let's let him off the hook." He took a deep breath and stepped through the mirror.

"Hey, what's all this?" Aahz asked, very casually. "You trying to raise the roof?" He lifted a hand. In the Dreamland the gesture would have sent the tent flying. In this case, it was merely a dramatic flourish. Aahz looked disappointed for less than a second before recovering his composure. I experienced the loss he must have felt, and I was upset on his behalf, but relieved to have gotten him home. He didn't belong in the world of dreams. Some day we'd find a way to undo Garkin's spell.

"Aahz!" Tananda squealed, throwing herself into his arms. "You've been gone for days! We were worried about you."

"You, too, Big-Timer," Massha said, putting a meaty arm around me and squeezing just as hard. The embrace was a lot more thorough coming from her.

"Thanks," I gasped out.

"Gleep!" my pet exclaimed, wiggling through behind

us. The trip through the mirror restored him to dragon-shape. In his joy he slimed all of us, including the trembling Bezel, who was being prevented from decamping by the firm grip Nunzio had on the back of his neck.

"Honest, I swear, Aahz," Bezel stammered. "It wasn't my fault. I didn't do anything."

"Altabarak across the way let the dragon loose, Boss," Guido said, peering at me from under his fedora brim.

"Okay, Bezel," I said, nodding to my bodyguard. If he was positive I was positive. "I believe you. No hard feelings. Ready to go get a drink, partner?" I said. "Everyone want to join me for a strawberry milkshake?"

"Now you're talking," Aahz said, rubbing his hands together. "A guy can have too much dream food." Bezel tottered after us toward the door flap.

"I don't suppose, honored persons," the Deveel said hopefully, the pale pink coloring slightly as he dared to bring business back to usual, "that you would like to purchase the mirror. Seeing as you have already used it once?"

"What?" I demanded, turning on my heel.

"They ought to get a discount," Massha said.

"Throw him through it," Guido advised. Bezel paled to shell-pink and almost passed out.

"Smash the mirror," Aahz barked, showing every tooth. Then he paused. "No. On second thought, buy it. A guy can dream a little, can't he?"

He stalked out of the tent. My friends looked puzzled. I smiled at Bezel and reached for my belt pouch.

MYTH-MATCHED

By Jody Lynn Nye

Premier Number One Daughter Renimbi of the Reigning House of Eyarll whirled around her personal chamber and came to a halt facing Tananda, who was sitting cross-legged on a cushion at the end of the huge bed.

"I can't marry Cordu of Vol Grun," she concluded, crystal-blue eyes flashing in her gold-scaled face. "So I want you to kill him."

The Trollop opened her big hazel eyes wider than they had been.

"Isn't that a little drastic?" she asked.

Renimbi whirled away again, too agitated to sit down.

"No more drastic than my father concluding a wedding contract with someone who is already married!"

"Unless I am forgetting my history of the dimension of Nob," Tananda said, watching her gyrate, "having more than one spouse is permitted in Vol Grun."

"But not in Eyarll." Renimbi tossed her head. "One

spouse. I refuse to do anything that will call my uniqueness into question. My father is desperate to join our nations and secure the safety of our western border, but that isn't good enough. I want to be the only woman in the life of the man whom I marry. I am, after all, a duchess of Eyarll. Will you take the contract, or won't you?"

Tananda sat thoughtful for a moment. The rules of the Assassins' Guild were pretty strict. If she took the contract and didn't complete it for any other reason than her own death, then two new assassins would be dispatched from the Guildhall, one to finish off the original target, and one to take care of her. There would be nowhere to hide, not here, not in the Bazaar at Deva, one of her favorite haunts, or at home on Trollia. This was one of the many reasons why she wasn't taking so many jobs lately off the employment board, and she was noticing similar discomfort among her fellow members. The reasons for disposal were getting more frivolous. Personally, Tananda blamed the crystal ether network. Watching the shows that came in on crystal ball made you think that life-threatening problems were easily solved in no more than forty minutes, and that no one really minded if you knocked off an inconvenient business rival. Or would-be spouse. She much preferred it if her client was in mortal danger, not just piqued. Not that she hadn't taken commissions like that in the past. Maybe she was just getting older.

"I want to make a few modifications to the standard boilerplate contract," Tananda said, unrolling a parchment from her belt pouch. "You won't mind, will you?"

"Oh, anything!" Renimbi said, throwing her hands into the air dramatically. "As long as when you're finished I never have to see Cordu again."

Tananda smiled. "Then, please, sign here."

Vol Grun's castle was a day's ride by camel, half a day by horse, or a few seconds if one used magik to blink one out of the dimension at one point and reenter it at another. Tananda had been there before, on Cordu's majority day, in fact. Her big brother, Chumley, had been at university with him. Cordu flirted with her, as he had with every female under the age of fifty who was present. He seemed to be a nice man. Tananda intended to observe him for a while. Whether or not she'd have to bump him off she left open to question. The contract in her pouch had no time limit on it, though arguably it was assumed she would have to complete it before Cordu and Renimbi got married. Still, Renimbi had signed it in such a hurry she didn't have time to review the alterations Tanda had made to its clauses.

Such as the one giving discretion to the operator on whether to execute.

Vol Grun had been at peace a long while. Tananda made a quick survey of the grounds immediately adjacent to the castle to make sure that the one sentry at the gate was the only guard on duty—except for signs of a commando hiding in the bushes somewhere inside the circle of the moat. It was no problem for her to avoid both of them. She didn't even have to use a lick of magik.

Instead, she used that to help her hang on to the steep stone wall as she climbed it. If she remembered correctly, Cordu's personal suite was in the center of the northeastern tower. If she had guessed wrong, she could disguise herself as a chambermaid.

The heavy blocks of stone afforded her many easy handholds. Tananda swung herself up onto the head of a gargoyle.

"Sorry," she said, as she realized she had been hanging from its tongue.

"No problem," the stone creature said. "Nice day, ain't it?"

"A little cool for spring," Tananda said, and struck an appealing pose. "You wouldn't mind not telling anyone you saw me, would you?"

"No problem," the gargoyle repeated, cracking a granite grin. "No one ever asks me anything anyway."

She patted him on his crested head before making a leap to the next step, the roof of a buttressed turret. Just two jumps away was a window frame, with the glass window just a hair ajar. Once she reached that, she could climb inside and find a good hiding place to observe her subject.

A careful stretch, and Tananda clung to the underside of the window frame. She levered herself up to peer inside. She saw a flight of the spiral staircase, but no living beings. She listened intently. The castle was bespelled against intruders, but since the window was slightly open, she could work a filament of magikal force through to lift the latch.

It swung open silently. Tananda was grateful to the cleaners who had oiled the hinges. And dusted, she observed, grasping hold of the upper window frame to swing herself in. It was clean as a whistle.

She nearly let one out in surprise.

A vast, hairy hand clamped upon her wrist and dragged her inside.

Tananda broke free with a dirty twist she had learned from a street-fighting master, and used a tickle of magik to land safely on the stairs. By the time her feet touched down, she had daggers in both hands, but the bulky defender was on guard, too. He let out a growl.

She feinted at the figure with one knife then started to lunge to the left.

Her opponent countered both her moves. He leaped back to avoid the knife, then closing with her inside the arc of her second dagger. Tananda retreated and riposted. He countered. Her right-hand dagger went flying. She and the defender ended up tangled in one another's arms, grappling for the remaining knife. The big, hairy hand felt its way down her arm to her back and up to her face. It stopped, as if in surprise.

"Little Sister!" a big, hearty voice boomed.

"Big Brother!" Tananda cried, recognizing both the voice and the scent of the fur.

The siblings stopped wrestling. Tananda squeezed her Troll brother until the air was knocked out of him then looked up at him. "What are you doing here?"

Chumley patted his chest, trying to get his breath back.

"I presume, my dear sister, that I am engaged in a counterpoint to what you intend to do here. Or do I fail to recognize the knot in the scarf around your neck?"

Tananda sighed and sat down on the step. "No, you're right. I've been hired to assassinate your friend."

His big furry brow lowered. The usually even-tempered Troll looked angry.

"Why? Why take the contract? Cordu is an old friend of mine, if not of yours."

She noticed a torch on the wall and lit it with a lick of magik force.

"Read the contract before you get upset, Brother," Tananda said, handing it over.

The brow lifted at clause three. "And she signed it?"

"She didn't even read it through. But it'll hold up before the Guildmaster, and that's all I care about. Mums would get so upset if the Guild punishers came looking for me. She might get blood on that new Djinni carpet she just had put in."

Chumley shivered. Their mother was a force to be reckoned with.

"So, what are you going to do?"

"Well," Tananda said. "I would say at this point, what are *we* going to do? He's your friend."

"Come and talk with him, Little Sister," Chumley said, wrapping her in a fond fraternal arm. "I think you will find what he has to say most interesting."

"I was a fool," Cordu said, pacing up and back in his own bedchamber. This room, Tananda noted with an eye toward interior decorating, was much more a male's idea of a cozy hideaway. The heads of animals stared glassily at her. Three very large, red-scaled hunting beasts lay asleep in front of a crackling fire. A suit of armor stood beside the doorway, holding a tray containing a square, cut-crystal whiskey decanter and a clutch of glasses. Cordu, rather a good-looking male of the Nobish type, poured out beverages for each of them. He held up his own glass in salute. Tananda surreptitiously used a thread of magik to test her own whiskey for poison. Chumley noticed her movement.

"Tsk tsk," he said.

"Sorry," she said. "I'm on duty."

"I understand," Cordu sighed. "I am glad that you are willing to talk to me. Rennie won't."

Chumley poured himself another glass of whiskey. "Casting my mind backward, Cordu, I seem to recall that you and Renimbi cared for one another."

"We do—I mean, did. We have been best friends all our lives. That is why I thought she would understand—the mistake I made. I had no idea that she would go so far in her displeasure as to hire an assassin. Truthfully, it's not entirely my fault. Her father and I . . . well, it is all a misunderstanding. I know he has always wanted to join our two realms. Perhaps you know that they were one country, three hundred years ago."

Tananda and Chumley shook their heads.

"My studies of your history are more of the first and last," Chumley said. "The ancient origins of your people, and most recent, social studies, if you like. So many dimensions, so little time."

Cordu found a map in the bookshelf that sat underneath the arched window and unrolled it to show them.

"The arrangement makes sense, for our mutual prosperity and defense. This part of the continent is one big river valley, best defended at its mountain passes on the circumference. My father and I had discussed it with our ministers and found it to be workable, so I went to the Tue-Khan with a diplomatic proposal. We would write a treaty that left our realms each under separate thrones, but as one with an open border to allow easy movement. I stressed that our peoples were of one blood, as close as kin could be. He got the idea into his head that I must marry Renimbi to seal the arrangement. And, well, there was a lot to drink. And, well . . . I didn't really read the document that he shoved underneath my nose early the next morning."

"Why would the Tue-Khan even do such a thing?" Tananda asked.

"It's his dream. He had told us ever since we were children that he hoped we would marry. My father, too, wished that Renimbi and I would marry. He found every opportunity to throw us together, even leaving us alone in romantic settings." Cordu's cheeks deepened in color to bronze. "For our parents' sake we tried. But we never really hit it off as lovers, and our relationship has only gotten worse over the last few years. It was with genuine regret that we decided it could never be. My father came to terms with our incompatibility. That is when I married Larica. Rennie and I agreed we would stay best friends. I still love her dearly, but not romantically."

"But after the, er, meeting with her father, you did press your suit to Renimbi?"

"Well, yes, I did. What with the document and all, I believed I had no choice. Larica is not happy about it, but she understands the customs of our culture. At first I thought that it could work."

"But Renimbi soon disabused you of that notion," Chumley said.

Cordu looked sheepish.

"Well, yes. She sent back all of my presents in pieces, except the horse. My page told me that she threatened him with a sword, too."

"Sounds serious," Tananda said, grinning.

"But the upshot is that her father and I signed a compact. I am as good as married to Renimbi already. We don't even need the priests to solemnize the union. That is why she wants me dead. She has more or less become my second wife."

Tananda shook her head. "Worse than I thought. Renimbi doesn't know it's already happened. She thinks she can forestall it by having you killed."

He sighed. "I was a fool."

"You certainly were. But why can't you simply have

the document vacated? Doesn't the Tue-Khan want his daughter to be happy?"

"I am afraid he has gotten what he always wanted, and he has convinced himself that we will eventually settle down and go along with it," Cordu said sadly. "I have tried to ask him to void the marriage contract, but he won't. As long as it exists, Rennie and I are husband and wife. Hence," he said, sighing, "your arrival."

Tananda looked at Chumley. "How did you get involved?"

"Oh, Cordu sent a message out to all of his old mates from school. What? We used to be on the skeet-shooting club together. Birkley, from Cent, is up on the roof. He's got a spear he uses as a focus for his wizardry."

Tananda fluttered her eyelashes. "I've always had a thing for Centaurs," she purred. "Especially ones with magikal spears. Anyone else?"

"Krans, from Imper, is hanging around outside, watching for intruders. He's deadly with a crossbow. I don't think any of us anticipated the method of your arrival, except for Chumley, who insisted on being in my chamber with me. And he was right to do so. If it had not been you, a friend, I might be dead already had Chumley not been here."

"Do you think that she will send another deadly envoy?" Chumley asked.

"No, and no other Guild assassin would take the contract as long as I am in the picture," Tananda said. "That's not to say she won't send an amateur."

"No, she won't do that," Cordu said. "Rennie always goes for the best. She thinks it's only her due, as a daughter of the Tue-Khan of Eyarll."

"Good," Tananda said. "That gives us a chance to

brainstorm. If I'm the only femme fatale you're waiting for, then why don't we get your friends in? I always think better in the presence of a lot of good-looking men." She flirted her eyelashes at Cordu.

"Spare me, my lady," he said, laughing. "I'm already in trouble with two women. I don't need a third."

The Centaur and the Imp had plenty of suggestions.

"Flood her with other suitors," Birkley said. "She'll forget about you."

"One thing you have to know about Rennie," Cordu said, "she is always faithful to promises. The other thing you must know is that she never forgets a grudge. No."

"Bribe her father," the Imp said. "You've got a lot of money."

"Money can't buy him off," Cordu said. "Nothing will buy him from this notion."

Chumley looked thoughtful. "What if your lady wife made an appeal to him? She wasn't planning to be supplanted."

"She is not supplanted. No matter what the rank of each successive spouse we might take, the first gains precedence. My mother had two husbands. The second one was a prince of Jongling, but my father was a butcher from Karpuling. Rennie loses rank. I know that will make her angrier when she knows."

The men turned to Tananda.

She shook her head. "Sorry, Cordu," she said. "I've thought it over, and you're going to have to die."

The Nob rose to his feet in alarm.

"What? Call for my guards! Call for my wizard!"

"Forget them," Tananda said, toying with her whiskey glass. "If I meant it, you'd be dead already. Big Brother knows that."

Chumley gawked. "Little Sister!"

She smiled at him. "I mean it, Big Brother. Let's get going. I can explain it all on the way."

"Way?" Cordu echoed. "Where are we going?"

"Eyarll. We've got a marriage to annul."

The heralds honked out a note on their yard-long trumpets.

"Lord Cordu, heir of Vol Gr—!"

Before they could finish announcing the new arrivals to the assembly in the throne room, Chumley stepped forward and shoved them aside.

"Sorry," he called as they went flying. He cocked his head to Cordu, who stepped into the room and stood framed in the doorway with his hands on his hips. After a deliberate three-count, he strode in. His entourage, led by Chumley, crowded in after him.

Behind them came the small figure of Larica, draped in sea-blue silk with a wreath around her head, and her ladies-in-waiting. The expression on her little round face clearly said that she did not like what was going on.

The Tue-Khan, a bulky Nob with a large nose, stood up from his damask-cushioned throne. Cordu swaggered up to him.

"Where's my bride?" Cordu demanded.

The Tue-Khan looked taken aback.

"She's not present at the moment, er, son," he said. "We weren't expecting you yet!"

"Well, why not?" Cordu bellowed, his voice making the amethyst chandeliers ring among the ceiling rafters. "Shouldn't take you that long to get her ready. You're her father—command her!"

The Tue-Khan assumed an indulgent smile.

"Come now, son, you've known her all her life. She's not that easy to command."

"Well, she's going to have to learn how to take orders! Things are about to change! Get her down here! I said," he repeated, thrusting his face into the Tue-Khan's, who cowered back in his throne, "get her down here NOW!"

Chumley could have applauded. Cordu always had been the pride of the Footlight Society at university. Such a mild personality as his had to be disguised in an aggressive role. It was an absolute inspiration on Little Sister's part to come up with this scenario. It seemed to be working very well. He tipped a wink in the direction of the rafters, hoping she could see him from her vantage point.

"You've changed so much, Cordu," the Tue-Khana, Renimbi's mother said, shaking her head. "I don't like it. You must not be too rough on Rennie. She's entitled to the courtesies as a duchess and daughter of the Tue-Khan."

"Yes, courtesies," Cordu said. He whispered desperately over his shoulder to Krans. "Line!"

"I want her to meet . . ." the Imp prompted.

"Ah, yes," Cordu said, recovering his aplomb. "I want her to meet my other wife, Larica. She's going to be Rennie's superior from now on. I'd like to see Rennie curtsy to her."

The Eyarllian courtiers gasped in unison.

The Tue-Khan clicked his tongue. "Son, dynastic marriages take time to arrange. We have to send for a priest, and call for guests, arrange gifts, draw up paperwork . . ."

"The document I signed is as good as a marriage, isn't it?" Cordu asked.

"Er, yes . . ."

Cordu spread out his hands.

"Then she is already my bride. I expect you to present her to me so we can get on with the honeymoon!"

The Tue-Khana looked horrified. "Decent people don't speak of such things in public, Cordu!"

"Who said I was a decent person? After that, I intend to make some changes around here."

"What changes, my son?" the Tue-Khan asked, frowning. "I am sure Renimbi will enjoy discussing them with you, for the day when you and she rule over our joined lands."

"In Vol Grun, the man becomes head of the household," Cordu said. "She will obey my will. But why wait? We signed a contract to join our lands. That means that what is yours is mine. So, I am moving in here, giving myself a little pied-à-terre that I can drop in on when I feel like it."

"Er . . . that wasn't exactly what I intended in the wording of our agreement, son."

Cordu looked shocked. "It wasn't? I thought you wanted one land, under one rule."

"In a way, over time . . ."

"Why wait?" Cordu rubbed his hands together and looked around. "For a start, I think this place is too full of decorator trash. I think we'll start to get rid of some of it right now."

He signed to the others. Chumley studied the room to see what could be removed or brought down without causing permanent damage. A hundred gilt-edged chairs stood arrayed on each side of the aisle leading to the throne, places for visiting nobles to sit. Only one was occupied. That left ninety-nine to play with.

"Roarrr!"

He charged the neat rows. A dozen chairs went flying into the others, knocking them flying. Courtiers raced to get out of the way of furniture. A few cowered behind the Tue-Khan's throne. Chumley picked out a chair that already showed signs of decrepitude and tore the legs asunder as easily as parting a wishbone.

CRACK!

"Cheap!" he declared.

"No!" the Tue-Khana cried. "Dear, make him stop!"

"Guards!" the Tue-Khan shouted. "Seize him!

A coterie of armored men lowered their spears and charged at him.

With one hand Chumley picked up a chair, drew it to his chest. He took three careful steps, and bowled the golden chair across the room. It spun over the floor. The guards windmilled their arms as they tried to get out of the way, but the chair caught four of them right in the knees. They fell, scattering. Two of the guards kept coming.

"Need spare," Chumley announced, reaching for another chair. "Seven-ten, not easy!" He rolled the chair at the two guards, but they dove for opposite walls. The chair smashed into the wall. "Darn!"

"Those are for people awaiting audience," the Tue-Khan said, agog.

"Oh, you don't need those," Cordu said. "I have something better. Bring it in!"

The *chef du protocol* who led Cordu's entourage raised a hand, and the huge double doors were flung open. Though they were two spear-lengths wide from lintel to lintel, it was still barely enough room for the huge Nobish beasts of burden, who were led in by a couple of ostlers. A dozen Vol Grun guards sprang to help untie the enormous parcels strapped to their backs. These were a pair of twelve-foot padded sofas that resembled giant cockroaches that had been upholstered in green and gold brocade, with piping around every fat, overstuffed cushion and a wealth of tassels at each end. They were arranged to flank a triangular end table possessed of a stunning orange-varnished finish, and overlooked by a skinny brass standard lamp with a marabou-fringed shade in brilliant pink. Tananda had spotted this furniture arrangement as they had passed a flea market on the way out of Vol Grun's capital city. The owner, who had inherited it from his rich aunt, had been on his way to deposit it in the dump. They were so ugly that the moths wouldn't touch them. She had bargained with him, and for less than a gold piece, the duke's party found itself in possession of an experiment in extreme distaste. Cordu's men placed the four pieces facing the throne, about five yards away, and lit the lamp.

"I thought you would be pleased," Cordu said, flinging himself full length upon the left-hand sofa. "I knew that my moving in here would probably strain the facilities, so I brought my own seats. Like them?"

The Tue-Khana looked as though she might faint, but the Tue-Khan smiled weakly.

"They . . . will take a little getting used to."

Clearly he was not yet outraged enough to take action. Chumley signaled to Krans to start the next onslaught.

The grinning Imp made a beeline for the king's personal wine rack, under the guard of a butler and sommelier. The two Nobs tried in vain to protect it from him, but he levitated them out of his way.

"Hey, Cordu!" he shouted, holding up a bottle. "Chateau Punding '04. What do you think of this swill?"

"Only the '03 was any good," Cordu replied. "Pour it out!"

"Right-o!" The Imp sent the bottle sailing into the air. The cork seemed to pop, and a cascade of purple liquid glugged down onto the priceless hand-knotted carpet. The two servants ran to intercept it and stop the flow. Krans made the bottle dance around the room just out of their reach. When the last dregs had poured out, he let it drop and chose another.

"How about this one?"

Cordu waved a dismissive hand.

"Vinegar! Get rid of it!"

"His Excellency's favorite!" the butler cried, racing to stop him. Krans lofted up out of his reach. The butler jumped for him, his belly jiggling.

"Aha!" Krans cried, drawing a ceramic jug to him with a wisp of magik. "Finiffian brandy!"

"I'll take some of that," Cordu said. Krans threw him a priceless balloon glass. Cordu caught it just before it hit the ground. The sommelier fainted dead away.

Birkley the Centaur, a good-looking male with a long blond mane and beard, galloped around the room, picking up women and heaving them onto his back.

"May I have this one, Cordu?" he asked. "Or perhaps this one?"

"Take them all!" the heir called back. The ladies screamed and beat at him, but he grabbed their wrists, laughing.

Instead of ordering them rescued, the Tue-Khan stood gawking. Chumley thought he ought to cause a little more havoc. He started toward the wall full of tapestries, roaring.

"I do not like your color scheme!" he bellowed. He yanked the colorful hangings down. They fell on his head. He tore his way out through a seam, and lurched out of

them, toward a wall full of gleaming glass vases and sculp-
tures. The Tue-Khana followed him, pleading.

"Not my granny's crystal, please!"

At the last moment, Chumley veered off, and headed
toward a suit of armor on a stand. He kicked and tore at it
until the pieces were scattered all over the costly rug.

"Not fit me!" he shouted. "Discriminatory against
Trolls!"

"What is all this?"

Chumley tossed aside the helmet at the sound of the
outraged voice. At last, Renimbi had appeared.

Premier Number One Daughter stood in the archway,
a look of absolute horror on her face. Horror changed to
fury as she scanned the room and spotted Cordu on the
ugly couch, drinking. Larica stood by him, head proudly
erect, with an expression on her face that boded ill for her
husband once the two of them would be alone.

She turned to her father. "What is he doing here?"

"Moving in, it would seem," the Tue-Khan said.

"And you let him!"

"I don't seem to have had a choice, my dear. He . . . he
brought all of his friends. And some furniture."

"It's horrible," Renimbi said. "Like something from a
fun fair. And look what else he is doing! They're tearing
up the entire room!"

"High spirits, child. Be a good hostess. We are going
to be kin from now on."

"No, we're not," Renimbi said. "I told you I didn't
want to marry him. I won't. You can't make me!"

The Tue-Khan actually dropped his gaze and shuffled
his toe on the marble floor. "I'm afraid that you already
have, child."

"What?"

The Tue-Khan produced a paper from the inside of his over-robe. "The clauses written in here . . . the lawyers, you know . . . insisted I include a consideration to make the contract valid . . . and I have always wanted to see the two of you together. I was sure you'd be happy, my dear."

"You tied me to him? And you didn't *tell* me?"

At last the Tue-Khan was beginning to look more angry than doubtful. "I didn't know he had become such a . . . lout!"

"Tear up the contract!" Renimbi demanded.

The Tue-Khan hastily stuck the parchment roll back into his robe. "Child, my dream has always been to unite our lands. It is already accomplished. We are now one great country. Surely you can put up with one another, say on state occasions, and perhaps to give us a grandchild or two? For your dear old father?" He held out his hands to her.

"No! Never!"

"What a great idea, Rennie!" Cordu called from his reclining position. "We can give him grandchildren. We can start today." He patted the couch. "This is comfy."

Renimbi's cheeks turned ochre with fury, but she didn't move. Chumley walked over and tucked her under his arm. She beat and kicked at him as he carried her to Cordu's couch. The prince edged out of reach when Chumley plopped her down. She didn't notice. She sprang up and raced back to the steps of the throne.

"You tied me to him! Now I am stuck with your choice! I hate you! I hate him!"

"My darling, I have only the best intentions for you in my heart!" The Tue-Khan said. Cordu finished his brandy and tossed the priceless glass over his shoulder.

CRASH!

It burst into shards on the floor. The Tue-Khan winced.

"Rennie, I'm glad you showed up," Cordu said. He stood up, swaying. Chumley admired his acting technique. Cordu wasn't drunk at all. Most of the priceless brandy had been poured down between the cushions. He hoped Cordu could get through his entire speech without fumbling. This was the one he had been the most nervous about on the trip there. "I thought your father had a great idea. I mean, how else could I conquer a whole country with the stroke of a pen? From childhood, we've been good friends. I want . . . hic! . . . I want you to meet Larica. She's my wife, too. You're gonna be good friends. She said she's got some great ideas about how the two of you are going to get along. She wants to change your wardrobe, and teach you needlework. My personal chamber back home needs a whole new tapestry, and you haven't been doing anything useful over the last few years, so this will be a nice change for you."

"Urrrrrgggh!" Renimbi shrieked, wringing her hands in anger. "I wish you were dead!"

"Bingo, what?" Chumley said to himself. "Couldn't have scripted it better myself."

"Rennie!" Cordu said reproachfully. "How could you say such a thing? I'm sho—"

THUNK!

His words were cut off suddenly, because a crossbow bolt buried itself in the center of his chest.

"Gack!" Cordu exclaimed. He clutched the feathered end of the arrow. Larica let out a terrified cry. Cordu staggered to the left. He goggled at the Tue-Khan, whose expression of horror matched his own. He grasped at the air with his free hand then staggered back to the right. He held up a hand as though he was about to make a statement, but his knees collapsed under him. As the assembly in the throne room watched in horror, Cordu toppled over. His eyes sagged closed. Renimbi ran to kneel beside him. She took his wrist, feeling for a pulse.

"Cordy? Cordy? Speak to me!"

"One side. I examine," Chumley said, kneeling beside the prone Cordu. Both women clutched each other. The Troll shook his head with magnificent gravity.

"Dead."

"Dead?" Renimbi said.

Tananda descended magnificently from the ceiling, foot in a loop of rope. The crossbow was slung at her back.

"As ordered, Duchess," she said. "I think I've earned my fee."

"But I didn't really want him *dead*," Renimbi wailed. "He's my best friend."

"Did you want him as a husband?" Tananda asked, surprised. "He has been acting like such a jerk."

Renimbi wrung her hands.

"I know, but that's just the way he is . . . I mean, was. Oh, how could I have been so *stupid*?"

The Tue-Khan came down from his throne and stood over the body of his momentary son-in-law. Shaking his head, he took the document out of the pocket in his robe. Sorrowfully, he tore it into strips and let the pieces fall down onto the body.

"This agreement becomes null and void on the death of one of the couple," he said. "I should never have let my ambition get in the way of my good sense. I am so very sorry, daughter. Your oldest friend, dead, and all because of me." He turned and pointed a finger at Tananda. "Seize her!"

"You really can't arrest me," Tananda said, as burly

Nobs crowded in on her from all sides. "My contract was properly registered with the Assassins' Guild."

One of them fastened manacles around her wrists, and bent to loop lengths of chain around her ankles. She winked outrageously at him.

"You know, I don't usually go in for this kind of thing, but I'll try anything once."

The Nob turned away, nervously. Chumley almost laughed out loud.

"You are very bold for a wench who is about to suffer torture and death," the Tue-Khan rumbled. "You . . . you Trollop!"

"Why, you noticed!" Tananda said, flirting her eyelashes at him. Chumley surreptitiously yanked the arrow out of Cordu's chest.

"You will die most painfully!" the Tue-Khan roared.

"Oh, I don't think so," Tananda said. Her wrist chains jangled as she raised a hand to pat a yawn. "It's not on my schedule, you know."

Renimbi and Larica hung on each others' shoulders, weeping. The Tue-Khan and Tue-Khana came to wrap their arms sympathetically around them.

"Oh, this is all my fault!" Renimbi said. "He was my best friend. I didn't really want him to have him killed. I just didn't see any other way out of my father's contract."

"Well, it worked, didn't it?" Cordu asked.

Renimbi spun, gasping.

"Cordy!"

"Rennie!"

"Cordy!"

"Larrie!"

The three of them enjoyed a group hug, then Renimibi's parents made it five.

"But you were dead!" Renimbi exclaimed.

"Not really," Tananda said. "The arrow's just a party gag I picked up in Deva. The person you plunge it into falls into a magical coma until you pull it out again. It doesn't even leave a mark." She pulled one from the quiver at her belt and stabbed it into the arm of the guard beside her. His eyes rolled up in his head, and he collapsed on the floor. "See?"

"So your behavior was all an act?" the Tue-Khan said. His face darkened.

"Of course, sire," Chumley said. "They could not be free of your machinations unless you destroyed the compact. You wouldn't do that unless Cordu was dead, or was so reprehensible in nature that you would not countenance him as a son-in-law any longer. We decided to make doubly certain."

"I didn't know he was such a good actor," Renimbi said, giving him a pinch on the cheek.

"He was a star," Tananda said, with a grin, "and you were his cross lover. It all played out just as we hoped. I knew you didn't really want him to die, but you were a classic mismatch."

"Cordu is alive, so the contract is in force again!" the Tue-Khan said. He reached to gather up the torn pieces of parchment.

Tananda pointed a finger.

"Don't do that," she said.

The fragment in the Tue-Khan's fingers blazed up.

"OW!" He dropped it. The ashes fluttered away. "I'll have it rewritten," he howled.

"Don't bother," Cordu said. "I wouldn't sign it again. Rennie and I will be good joint rulers, with our respective spouses by our sides. I hope she finds someone who loves her as much as Larica loves me, to put up with my hi-jinks." He hugged both of the young women, and they kept their arms around him. "Who knows, perhaps our offspring will like one another enough to marry. It's been over three centuries. Why hurry?"

"I think I will write a drama based upon this for the re-union of our university Footlights Club." Chumley put a hand to his hairy chest and declaimed. " 'Never was there a tale of such a row, than that of Rennie and her mis-matched beau.' "

"It'll be a great hit," Tananda said, hugging her Big Brother's arm. "I love a tragedy with a happy ending."

MYTH-TRAINED

By Robert Asprin

I focused on the candle's flame. Forcing myself to remain relaxed, I reached out and gently wrapped my mind around it.

The flame didn't flicker. If anything, it seemed to steady and grow. Moving slowly, I extended a finger, pointing casually at the object of my attention. Then, as I released a quick burst of mental energy, I made a small flicking motion with my hand to speed the spell along it's way. There was a tiny burst of power, and the flame flared and went out. Neat!

I leaned back in my chair and treated myself to a bit of smug self-congratulation.

"Have you got a minute, Skeeve?"

I glanced toward the doorway. It was my curvaceous assistant. At least, the theory was that she was my assistant. Since she tagged along when I retired from M.Y.T.H. Inc., however, she had taken over not only running the household and the business side of things, but also my life in general. Some assistant.

"Bunny!" I said with a smile. "Just the person I wanted to see. Com'on in. There's something I want to show you."

With a casual wave of my hand, I relit the candle.

"So?" Bunny said, unimpressed. "I've seen you light a candle before. If I remember right, it was one of the first spells you learned."

"Not that," I said. "Watch this!"

I wrapped my mind around the flame, pointed my finger, and released the spell again.

The candle exploded, scattering droplets of hot wax across the table and onto the wall behind it.

"I see," Bunny said, drily. "You've learned a new way to make a mess. Some day you'll learn a spell that helps with cleaning up. Then I'll be impressed."

"That's not how it's supposed to work," I protested. "I did it perfectly just before you came in."

"What is it, anyway?" she said.

"Oh, it's a new spell that was in my latest correspondence lesson for the Magikal Institute of Perv," I said. "It's a magikal way to extinguish a flame. It didn't seem very difficult, so I've been puttering around with it as a break when I'm working on the other lessons."

"A magikal way to extinguish a flame," she repeated slowly. "Is it really a vast improvement on simply blowing the candle out?"

"It's an exercise," I said, defensively. "Besides, if I get good enough at it . . . I don't know, maybe I could put out a whole burning building."

"Hmpf," she said, and I realized I was losing an argument when we weren't even arguing.

"Anyway, what was it you wanted?"

It's an old ploy. When in doubt or in trouble, change the subject. Sometimes it works.

"I just wanted to say that I think you should take a look at Buttercup."

"Buttercup? What's he done now?"

Buttercup was a war unicorn I sort of inherited early in my career. While he isn't as inclined to get into mischief or break things as Gleep, my dragon, that still leaves him a lot of room for minor disasters.

"Nothing I know of," Bunny said. "He just doesn't seem as perky as he usually is. I'm wondering if he's coming down with something."

"Maybe he's just getting old." I realized that I know even less about the longevity of unicorns than I did about their ailments. "I'll take a look at him."

We were currently based in what used to be an old inn. Actually, I had a bit of my history tied up in the inn even before my current relocation. When I first teamed with Aahz, this very inn was the headquarters for our adversary of the moment, one Isstvan. After successfully vanquishing him and sending him off to roam the dimensions, Aahz and I used it as our own base until our subsequent move to Possiltum, and eventually to the Bazaar at Deva. It seemed only natural to return to it when I retired and was looking for a quiet place to pursue my studies.

Buttercup shared the stable area of the inn with Gleep, though more often or not they only used it to sleep. The rest of the time they roamed the grounds, playing with each other and getting into the aforementioned mischief. To say the least, this insured that our neighbors and folks from the nearby village gave the place a wide berth as a general rule.

I wasn't wild about running him down if they were out terrorizing the countryside, as they were both fleeter of foot and in better condition than I was. Fortunately he was in residence when I reached the stables.

"Hey, Buttercup! How's it going?"

The unicorn raised his head and glanced at me, then let it sag once more. Bunny was right. Buttercup did seem very droopy, not at all his normal manner. What was more, his coat seemed dull and dry.

"Are you okay, fella? What's wrong?"

That inquiry didn't even earn me a second glance.

Normally, I'd be at a loss for what to do. This time around, however, I had an idea. Glancing out the stable door to be sure Bunny wasn't within hearing, I turned to Gleep who was watching the proceedings with interest.

"Gleep? Do you know what's wrong with Buttercup?"

I had discovered that my dragon could actually talk, though only in halting sentences. At his request, I had withheld that particular bit of information from my colleagues.

Gleep craned his neck to look out the door himself, then brought his head close to mine.

"Buttercup . . . sad," he said.

My pet's breath was foul enough that it usually drove me back a step or two. My concern was such, however, that I held my ground.

"Sad?" I said. "About what?"

Gleep seemed to struggle to find the words.

"You . . . not . . . use . . . him."

"Not use him?" I echoed, trying to understand. "You mean he wants me to play with him more?"

The dragon moved his head slowly from side to side in ponderous negation. "No. Not . . . play. You . . . not . . . use . . . him . . . to . . . fight."

Slowly it began to sink in what the problem was.

Buttercup had been working with a demon hunter when we first met. The hunter, Quigley, had moved on to a career in magik, leaving the unicorn with me. While there had been many and varied adventures since then, I had never called on Buttercup to assist in any of them, preferring to deal with the problems by magical means. Well, magik combined with a fair amount of underhanded double talk. Whatever the reason, though, what was once a proud fighting animal had been reduced to the status of a house pet . . . and he didn't like it.

That seemed to be the problem. The trouble was, I had no idea what to do about it.

For a change, this lack of knowledge or a specific plan did not distress me. If nothing else, in my varied career prior to my retirement, I had amassed an impressive array of specialists, most of whom were usually all too happy to advise me in areas where my own experience was lacking. In this case, I thought I had a pretty good idea of who to turn to.

Big Julie had been commanding the largest army this dimension had ever seen when we first met. I can refer to its impressive size with some authority as, at the time, I was on the other side. Shortly thereafter, he had retired and was living in a villa near the Royal Palace of Possiltum. We had gotten to be pretty good friends, however, and he had helped me and my colleague out several times on an advisory basis. Not surprising, with his background, his advice was unswervingly helpful and insightful. As such, his was the first name that sprang to my mind to consult with regarding my current dilemma with Buttercup.

As always, he was happy to see me when I dropped in, and we immediately fell to reminiscing about old times like old war comrades . . . which we sort of were. The wine and lies flowed in roughly equal quantities, making for a very pleasant, relaxed conversation.

[Author's note: Yes, that was an abrupt shift of time and location. Short stories don't give you much space for lengthy travel sequences. Besides, if they can get away with it in *Star Wars*, why can't I?]

As he was refilling our goblets with yet another sample from his extensive wine cellar, he cocked an eye at me and winked.

"So! Enough small talk. What's the problem?"

"Problem?" I said, taken a bit aback. I had figured to ease into the subject slowly.

Big Julie leaned over and clapped me on the knee with his hand. "You're a good boy, Skeeve," he said. "I'm always glad when you take time to visit. Still, you're busy enough, so I figure you don't come all this way just to chit chat with an old soldier. To me, that means you've got some kind of a problem you think I might help you with."

A little irked a being found out so easily, I filled him in on my perception of the problem. For all his self-deprecating comments about being an "old soldier," as I mentioned before, Big Julie had the finest mind regarding things military that this dimension had ever seen.

"A war unicorn, eh?" he said, raising his eyebrows.

"Don't see many of those anymore. Still, you could be right. Do you know much about war unicorns?"

"Practically nothing," I admitted easily. "I sort of inherited this one."

"Well, you can forget about that poetic stuff with unicorns and virgins," the retired general said. "Unicorns are fighters, bred specifically for their ferocity and loyalty. They're particularly popular in certain circles because they're all but immune to magik."

"Really? I didn't know that."

"I don't think I've ever heard of one retiring, though," Julie continued. "Usually they die in combat. Once they're trained, it's pretty much all they know. I've had men in my command like that. Been soldiers all their lives and can't imagine being civilians."

I nodded my head thoughtfully. I had thought my problem with Buttercup to be fairly unique. I had never really stopped to think about what soldiers do once they leave the service.

"A lot of the boys go into police work or some other kind of security in the private sector. If you look at it close, though, that's just another form of wearing a uniform and being ready for a fight if the situation calls for it. That's why that plan you came up with to use some of the boys for tax collectors was such a good idea. It took care of our problem of what to do with our excess personnel once Queen Hemlock put her expansion policy on hold. It let us give them an option of a new assignment instead of just cutting them loose after a lifetime of service."

It seemed I had done something intelligent for a change, though I'll admit that at the time I had not been aware of the full ramifications of my action.

"So how does that help me figure out what to do with Buttercup," I said, frowning.

"Well, it seems to me you need to find Buttercup some action, even if it's just a dummied-up training exercise," Big Julie said. "Between the two of us we should be able to come up with something."

"A training exercise?"

"Sure. We do it all the time in the service. Schedule a war game to keep the troops on their toes." He dropped his voice to a conspirator level. "We don't ever admit it, but sometimes we even deliberately position our forces a bit too close to an opposing force . . . like over their border accidentally on purpose. Of course, they respond, and by the time things are sorted out and apologies have been made, the boys have had a little action to clear away the cobwebs. We could rig something like that for your unicorn."

I got up and did the honors of refilling our goblets. I didn't really want more wine, but it gave me a few minutes to mull over what Big Julie had said. Something about it wasn't sitting right with me.

"Actually, I don't think so," I said finally, shaking my head. "I appreciate the advice, Big Julie, and it's given me something to think about, but I think I'll try a different kind of solution."

"What do you have in mind?"

"Well, instead of hunting down or making up some kind of conflict to make Buttercup feel useful," I said, carefully, "I'm thinking what I need to do is spend some time retraining him."

Big Julie cocked his head. "Retraining him to do what?"

"I don't really know just yet." I sighed. "As you were talking, though, it occurred to me how sad it was that all

Buttercup knows how to do is to fight. More specifically, that, in his opinion, his only value is as a fighter. Instead of trying to re-enforce that problem, I think I want to spend the effort to try to change his self-image."

The general stared at me for several moments.

"I've never asked you, Skeeve," he said at last. "Why did you retire?"

"Me?" I said, caught off guard by the subject change. "I wanted to spend more time studying magik. I'm supposed to be this hot shot magician, but I really can't do all that much. Why?"

Julie made a derisive noise. "Like the world needs more magicians," he said. "As I understand it, there's barely enough work for the ones we already have."

That stung a little.

"Now I know you military types don't think much of magik or magicians, Big Julie," I said a bit stiffly, "but it's what I do."

"Uh-huh," he said. "Like fighting is what Buttercup does."

"How's that again?" I frowned.

"You should listen to yourself, Skeeve." the general said, shaking his head. "You're saying that your only value to anyone is as a magik user. You still think that even though you admit that you don't really know all that much. Do you really think that's why you old team gave you their respect and followed your lead? You think I ended up running the army because I'm a rough, tough, invincible fighter?"

That really gave me pause for thought. I had never really considered it, but looking at his frail body, even allowing for age, it was doubtful that Big Julie could go toe to toe with any of the heavyweights I knew like Guido or Hugh Badaxe.

He leaned toward me.

"No, Skeeve. What you did just now, thinking through what's best for other people . . . in this case, your unicorn . . . that's a rare talent. To me, that's more valuable than any new magik tricks you might pick up. The world needs more of that kind of thinking."

Someone, sometime, might have said something nicer than that to me, but if so, it didn't spring readily to mind.

"So what is it exactly that you're suggesting that I do? Come out of retirement?"

"Exactly?" He smiled and winked at me. "I haven't got a clue. You're the thinker. So think about it. Maybe while you're working on Buttercup's self-image you can do a little tinkering with your own."